PENGUIN BOOKS

Every Three Hours

Chris Mooney is the internationally bestselling author of the Darby McCormick thrillers. His third novel, *Remembering Sarah*, was nominated for an Edgar for Best Novel by the Mystery Writers of America. His books have been translated into more than twenty languages. He teaches writing courses at Harvard and the Harvard Extension School, and lives in Boston, Massachusetts, with his wife and son.

Books by Chris Mooney

THE DARBY MCCORMICK THRILLERS

The Missing

The Secret Friend

The Dead Room

The Soul Collectors

Fear the Dark

Every Three Hours

OTHER WORKS

Deviant Ways

World Without End

Remembering Sarah

The Killing House

Every Three Hours

CHRIS MOONEY

PENGUIN BOOKS

PENGUIN BOOKS

UK | USA | Canada | Ireland | Australia
India | New Zealand | South Africa

Penguin Books is part of the Penguin Random House group of companies
whose addresses can be found at global.penguinrandomhouse.com

First published 2016
001

Set in 12.5/14.75 pt Garamond MT Std
Typeset by Jouve (UK), Milton Keynes
Printed in Great Britain by Clays Ltd, St Ives plc

A CIP catalogue record for this book is available from the British Library

ISBN: 978-1-405-92243-2

For Ron and Barbara Gondek

It's so odd, how I don't feel scared right now, not even nervous. All those months spent rehearsing, going through every conceivable scenario, and now, as I watch the taxi turn the corner, knowing the moment is upon me, I don't feel scared or nervous or have the urge to walk away or have any reservations.

It feels right, what I'm about to do.

I know it's right.

After I climb into the back of the cab, shivering from the cold, I lean close to the small window separating the driver from the back seat, my gloved hand gripping my throat, which is bundled in a scarf. The black hoodie is tied tightly around my head and my eyes are covered with sunglasses.

'One Schroder Plaza,' I rasp.

The driver looks like an old dockworker, someone who has spent too much time in the elements, his gaunt face cragged and peppered with deep grooves and, I'm guessing, all sorts of skin cancers. He leans his head closer and cocks an ear to me and says, 'Sorry, I didn't hear you?'

I make a practice show of how painful it is to talk. 'One Schroder Plaza,' I rasp. 'Boston Police Department.'

The driver nods, puts the car in gear.

'You getting over a bad cold? The flu?'

I nod eagerly and lean back in my seat, the back of the cab wonderfully warm. I don't take off my hat or gloves. I don't want him to see my face, to describe me later to the police and FBI.

'Bad flu season this year,' the driver says. 'My nephew, he's thirteen? Kid's a star athlete – basketball and football – works out like a fiend, eats real healthy, takes his vitamins and everything. He gets the flu and ends up in the hospital for a week, can you believe that?'

I stare out my side window, watching the early morning traffic under the grey sky –

'And today we're going to get hit with another snowstorm, and I'm saying to myself, "Mike, the hell are you living here for? They got cab drivers in Florida, ya know."'

The cab driver keeps talking. I drown out his voice, losing myself in my thoughts, about how we all lead two lives – the one we present to the world, and the one we live behind our eyes. This isn't a profound thought, I know. I'm sure some philosopher or hack songwriter already said something like that – and probably said it better, too – but I don't have the benefit of a college education, and I'm not all that well read. The one thing I know – that I'm sure of – is that at the end of the day we want to know the real person, the one he or she keeps hidden from everyone. The one where you find out that your next-door neighbour, Mr Vanilla, a man who volunteered at a suicide hotline and did animal rescue work, who never had a bad word to say about anyone and was shy and quiet and extremely nice, liked to prance about his house wearing clothes belonging to the dozens of women he'd killed and buried in his basement, or something. We want to know the real person – what made him that way, how he kept so secret for so long. We need to know the things we hide from everyone but ourselves, because that's where the real truth lies.

I

–00.45

'I don't want to do this,' Darby said.

Coop drank deeply from the cup of coffee he'd made quickly back in his hotel room. They were both staying at the Bunker Hill Inn right around the corner from Mass. General, and directly across the street from Beacon Hill, the place she had called home for ten years before deciding to sell everything off and live as sort of a vagabond forensic consultant. No home, all of her possessions whittled down into a four-by-six hardtop motorcycle suitcase that fit nicely on the back of her Triumph.

It was coming up on eight on Monday, the start of the work week, and they were sitting in the back of a cab, Darby wearing sunglasses even though the early morning sky was overcast. Last night's wedding reception had run into the early morning hours, and she'd had a little too much bourbon and too little sleep and she was paying for it this morning. She pinched her temples between her fingers and then rubbed the skin above her eyes, trying to massage away the hangover while she gazed out the window at the Boston streets packed bumper-to-bumper with traffic.

'You were the one who volunteered our services, not me,' Coop said.

He was right. Last night at the reception, Anna Lopez, a mutual friend and former coworker who was now the head of the city's Criminal Services Unit, had asked Darby if she and Coop would be willing to stop by BPD's main headquarters this morning, Monday, to consult on the murders of a pair of retired Boston homicide detectives from last year. Both men were victims of what appeared to be a home invasion. Both men were in their late sixties and lived alone – one a longtime divorcee, the other a widower. The killer tied both men to either a kitchen or dining room chair with duct tape and, after working them over with a heavy, blunt object for several hours, tied a plastic shopping bag around their heads, suffocating them.

That was all the information Darby had. The fine details of a double-homicide were not generally discussed during the reception and cocktail hour, even if the groom and half of the wedding guests were Boston cops and people from the crime lab.

'It's the right thing to do,' Coop said. 'I know you don't want to go back there – and I don't blame you – but we're talking about Lopez here. How many times did she cover your ass back when you were head of CSU?'

Too many to count, Darby thought.

'How many all-nighters did she pull? How many weekends did she give up for you?'

'You've made your point,' she said.

'And *you've* learned a valuable lesson, which is never,

ever make decisions or agree to anything while drinking. Really, you need to be more mature.' He grinned. His smile disappeared when he glanced out the front window and saw the dead-stop traffic. 'We should've taken the T. Would've been quicker – cheaper, too.'

He was right, of course. But when you had a hangover and less than five hours of sleep, a taxi was the only way to go.

She was glad for the hangover, though; it would create a good distraction from her feelings. She didn't want to go anywhere near the BPD. She had put that life behind her – and for good reason.

She thought she did okay last night at the reception.

'Let's walk,' Coop said.

'It's fifteen degrees out.'

'We're not that far away, and the fresh air will do us both some good.' Coop didn't wait for her answer; he handed the driver a twenty through the window and asked the guy to pull over.

Outside, Coop tossed his cup into a nearby city trashcan. Despite her foul mood, Darby couldn't help but marvel at how he not only didn't seem to age the way normal men did – he was in his mid-forties but could have easily passed for someone a decade younger – but also how he managed not to look even the slightest bit tired after late nights of drinking. Coop was like a Chanel suit: classically good-looking year-after-year, and never went out of style.

He pulled his phone out from his pocket and read the screen. 'They cancelled our flights,' he said.

'It's not even snowing yet.'

'Weathermen are saying the storm will be here this afternoon around two or so.' He stuffed his hands into the pockets of his long camel-hair overcoat and began to walk next to her, his head tilted into the wind. 'What sort of info did Lopez give you about these cases?'

'Just the basics. She say anything to you?'

'She told me she talked to you and asked that I tag along.'

'Why?'

'Because you need constant monitoring and supervision,' he replied playfully.

They turned right on to Ruggles, the corner taken up by a brick-façade apartment building. The kerbs here, like all the others, were crusted with small mounds of ice and snow, and the small city trees planted along the concrete sidewalks were stripped of their leaves, their fragile, gnarled limbs still strung with Christmas lights.

'It's weird being back here, back in the city,' he said. 'You miss it?'

'Nope.'

'Bullshit. You have to miss it a *little*. You grew up here. We both did.'

But she didn't miss it. *Too many ghosts*, she thought.

Her father had died when she was twelve – shot by a schizophrenic drug addict. Three years ago, she had discovered the real killer: cops inside the Boston Police Department – the so-called Blue Brotherhood. They had killed him and framed an innocent man, who later died in prison, to protect the head of Boston's Irish mob during the late seventies and early eighties, a man named Frank Sullivan who was in reality an undercover federal agent.

Ruggles ended at a streetlight. They turned right, on to Tremont. The main headquarters for the Boston Police Department, a squat and rectangular-shaped glass castle set on top of concrete, took up nearly six blocks. Darby felt her pulse quicken. She squeezed her hands into fists inside her jacket pockets as she watched the three flags set up in front of One Schroder Plaza snap like canvas sails in the wind. From behind the green tint of her Ray-Ban sunglasses, she stared at the flag holding the Boston Police crest and rode the greasy swell of her hangover, the building growing taller and wider, like it was coming to life, about to devour her.

2

–00.25

'You have a good time at the reception?' Coop asked.

Darby nodded. 'You?'

'Absolutely. Jimmy was fun, as always. Can't believe he's married, though. Last of our bachelor friends from BPD. How did it feel seeing your ex get married?'

'We only dated for six, maybe eight months.'

'He proposed to you, didn't he?'

'He was working up to it, I think.'

'You told me you were in love.'

'No, I told you he was in love with me.'

'So why'd you call it off?'

'He's a good guy, fun, but when it comes to relationships he's pretty much a spineless limp dick who's looking for someone to replace his mother.'

'Good thing he didn't ask you to make a toast last night.'

The sidewalk ended. The road in front of them turned into a porte-cochères-like area for taxis and other vehicles that needed to drop off people for the main entrance into One Schroder Plaza.

Coop held open the heavy glass door for her. As she stepped inside the warm lobby of brown-and-black speckled marble, her chest tightened and blood pounded in her ears like the roar of a crashing wave.

Her father, long since dead, spoke to her: *Never let the bastards grind you down.*

They killed you, she replied. *They killed you, and when I finally exposed the people who did it – exposed them and their laundry list of corruption dating all the way back before I was born – they shoved me out the door.*

'You haven't said anything about my date last night.'

'She was nice.'

'That's it? Nice?'

'I really liked her,' Darby replied as they walked, the pathway sectioned off by raised marble planters bursting with ferns. She knew he was trying to distract her, keep her out of her head and away from her thoughts, and she loved him for it. 'Not only could she count to ten without using her fingers, she knew all her A-B-C's.'

'That's a little harsh – and *she* has a name, you know. Nevaeh.'

The metal detector and X-ray machine, Darby noticed, had been upgraded since the last time she was here, and there were a lot more blue uniforms manning the checkpoint: a man and a woman to conduct pat-downs, three others standing behind the conveyor belt to open briefcases, backpacks and other packages. She had heard that BPD had beefed up their security after the Boston Marathon bombing.

'Did she tell you what it means? Her name?'

'Yeah,' Darby replied, snaking around the corner and then breaking off to her right, to the back of the visitors' line. 'It's "Heaven spelled backwards".'

'She has two million followers on Instagram.'

'No, her ass has two million followers.'

'Heaven-spelled-backwards is a fitness model.' Coop grinned from ear-to-ear. 'Did she tell you she was last year's runner-up for Brazil's Miss Bum Bum?'

'Repeatedly.' Darby unzipped her jacket. 'Well, she's certainly bright,' she said, removing her Class 3 gun-carrying permit from her inner pocket. 'You know Dan Carter?'

'Dr Dan the Foot Man.'

'She asked him what he did for a living. Dan tells her he's a podiatrist, and Heaven-spelled-backwards says, "Oh, I love children!"'

The Hispanic woman standing in front of Darby and thumb-keying on a BlackBerry stifled a laugh. She was young and curvy and dressed in a sharp suit, and she looked familiar – a lawyer, Darby believed, from the federal court.

'It was loud in there,' Coop said. 'Nevaeh probably thought he said paediatrician.'

Darby took off her sunglasses. 'Hmm, I don't think so.'

There was a holdup at the front of the line. A very pregnant woman who looked like she had a boulder taped to her stomach dropped her coat on the conveyor belt as she spoke to one of the guards, probably asking if she could have a pat-down instead of going through the metal detector. A lot of women still subscribed to the myth that metal detectors and the full-body scanners at airports gave off radiation that could harm their child. The man standing behind her, the one wearing a black rolled-up beanie drawn across his forehead and ears, swallowed back his impatience, his jaw muscles bunching. He reached for a backpack sitting on the conveyor belt, waiting to be examined by X-ray, and when his hand clutched the strap he decided to let go and wait. He didn't look happy about it.

'Dr Feet seemed like a real party,' Coop said. 'You two have a good time last night?'

'He's a nice guy,' Darby replied, still watching the aggravated man in the black beanie standing behind the pregnant woman, watching as he unzipped the black hoodie he wore underneath his stylish black wool overcoat. He wore a suit jacket underneath the hoodie, a scarf knotted around his neck.

Why would someone wear a hooded sweatshirt over a suit jacket?

'Did you and Dr Feet do the dance with no trousers?' Coop asked.

Darby turned to him. 'What're you, twelve?'

'Emotionally, yes. And the fact that you're deflecting means you and Dr Dan –'

'How about we talk about these mutant Barbie dolls you keep dating? Where do you find them? Do you hang outside eating disorder clinics?'

'Not only is that *not* true, it's hurtful. I'm just looking for love like everyone else.'

Darby rolled her eyes. 'What's the longest relationship you've ever had?'

'I dunno,' Coop said. 'Three, maybe four lap dances?'

The Hispanic woman shook her head, looked like she wanted to make a comment, maybe join in on the conversation. She turned slightly so she could get a look at Coop from the corner of her eye. Like most women, she liked what she saw and responded to it. Smiled radiantly.

The man wearing the black beanie removed a gun from underneath his overcoat.

Pointed it at the ceiling.

Fired.

3

– 00.15

Cops were trained to duck and seek cover the moment they saw a weapon or heard gunfire. Civilians ran. A handful might freeze for a second or two, but they always ended up running like frightened cattle and didn't think twice about pushing or shoving whoever was standing between them and their safety. Children, an old lady using a walker, a litter of puppies – it didn't matter. They would be knocked down and walked over and trampled because a shooting took on the exact same frenzy and chaos of a Black Friday sale at a Wal-Mart, only the most-sought-after item in this scenario was reaching the exit without getting shot and killed.

The first gunshot was still ringing in Darby's ears when she saw the gunman grip the pregnant woman in a chokehold and then push her past the metal detector, triggering its subtle but noticeable alarm – a brief trill followed by flashing orange lights.

Then the stampede started.

Darby dropped to the floor beside the conveyor belt, her hand already pulling the SIG from her shoulder holster. A pot-bellied man dressed in a cheap suit and looking like some ambulance-chasing lawyer seen on late-night commercials roughly pushed aside an older, heavy-set Hispanic woman with bleach-blonde hair bundled inside a puffer jacket. He didn't stop to help her – didn't so much as even pause. No one did.

A howling typhoon of denim and polyester legs stormed past Darby, towards the building's revolving front doors. The woman, now lying on her side, brought up her arms to try to protect her face from the boots and shoes kicking at her, and she screamed when someone dropped a steaming cup of coffee on her thighs. Darby scrambled to her feet and fought her way past the tide of bodies. As she grabbed the woman underneath the arms and lifted, from the corner of her eye she saw Coop inching his way along the side of the conveyor belt, heading for the metal detector so he could get a better tactical view.

Once the woman got to her feet, she brushed past Darby and was immediately swept inside the current of bodies. Darby clicked off the safety and inched forward to the main lobby, a long cavernous space maybe half the size of a football field, the walls, floor and ceiling lined with tile that magnified every sound. Underneath the handful of canister lights, she saw maybe a dozen or more cops, a mix of plainclothes and blue uniforms, all of them armed. Some were set in tactical positions behind the raised marble planters and columns. Handfuls were dragging civilians out the line of fire, and she saw a small group tucked inside the lobby for the elevators. Several cops were barking police codes into their chest radios, a few others were on their cell phones. No one appeared to have been shot. The floor was littered with abandoned briefcases and backpacks, spilled coffee cups and cans of soda and bags of food. She didn't see any blood.

A thread of relief swam underneath the hurricane of adrenaline pounding through her limbs. The gunman hadn't shot anyone – and he hadn't wandered in and started firing at random. He had waited in line and, it appeared, as far as she could tell, that he had fired all his shots into the ceiling, all of which suggested he wasn't some crazed gunman or terrorist looking to rack up a high body count. He wanted something – and he had taken a hostage.

The gunman stood behind the pregnant woman in the far northeast corner, near the end of the long podium of lacquered dark walnut that served as the front desk where, at any given time of day, three to five blue unis worked the phones and handled the check-in process for all visitors. There were three people behind it right now – all men, all of them white-haired and pale and looking like they had lived well beyond their expiration date – and they had their sidearms pointed at the balaclava-covered face nestled behind the woman's head. The black fabric was cut only to reveal the eyes.

The gunman pressed the muzzle of what looked like a Glock 40 with an extended mag against the woman's right temple. His arm didn't shake, and his eyes didn't jump around the room. Twenty, maybe thirty seconds had passed since the first gunshot, and during that time police had secured the two exits – the one behind Darby, the alcove holding the security checkpoint that led back to the main front doors; and, on the west side of the main lobby, a glass door secured by a keycard that led into the first-floor suite of offices for the Missing Persons Unit. Two cops there. Three cops behind the front desk and six, maybe seven, inside the small lobby for the elevators. A cop behind each of the six marble columns and a half dozen or so cops standing fifteen, maybe twenty feet away from the gunman. The man was boxed in and had twenty or so weapons pointed at him and he didn't shake and his eyes didn't move, just stared straight ahead at some fixed point in space, watching a movie only he could see. He seemed too calm, too still.

The same wasn't true of his hostage. Her legs kept giving out, the red-painted nails desperately clutching at the dark wool fabric of the coat arm wrapped firmly around her throat, her mouth opening and closing, trying to gulp in air as her frightened gaze darted across the sea of weapons and strange and angry faces, all of which seemed to be aimed directly at her.

No one had stepped up to take charge of the situation, and someone needed to. Darby holstered her weapon, about to speak when she saw a tall, doughy man with perfectly combed black hair and fake teeth as white as a toilet lower his Glock and step forward. Darby recognized him: Bob Murphy, a middling detective from Kenmore's D-3 district.

'Let's talk,' Murphy said in a booming voice. He holstered his weapon, and as he stepped over a puddle of coffee, Darby felt a collective and palpable relief sweep through the lobby. While every cop in here was justifiably afraid of saying or doing something that would cause the hostage situation to rapidly deteriorate, their real terror had to do with the security cameras posted throughout the lobby, recording their every movement, spoken word, and action (or lack thereof), all of which would be reviewed down the road, Monday-morning quarterback-style, by a taskforce or panel of bureaucratic career climbers and pencil-lickers that had never found themselves in the heat of combat. Cops now lived in a world where their best efforts were reviewed, criticized and often vilified. The world wasn't looking for heroes. It wanted scapegoats.

And now Detective Robert Murphy had stepped up to the plate, putting his career on the line. Whatever happened next, good, bad, or indifferent, would fall on him.

'My name's Bobby. You've got my attention, so talk. Tell me what you want.'

The gunman didn't speak. *Murphy's too intimidating*, Darby thought. *And he's not speaking the right way.* Rule one in hostage negotiation was to develop a rapport. You didn't bark out commands.

Murphy broke rule two – no yes or no questions – when he said, 'How about you let everyone out of here so you and I can talk? How's that sound?'

The gunman grabbed the woman in a chokehold.

'Easy,' Murphy said. 'No need to hurt anyone, okay? Nobody here is going to hurt you.'

Then, to the lobby: 'Everyone put your weapons away right now. Go on. Do it.'

Murphy turned and watched as people, some begrudgingly, holstered their weapons. Darby kept her attention on the gunman. His calmness set off alarms inside her, making her think, for some reason, of the stillness of a suicide bomber, a man who had already surrendered to dying.

The last weapon holstered, Murphy turned back to the gunman and said, 'Now everyone is gonna leave so you and me can talk.' Then, louder to the room: 'Everyone go ahead and leave, nice and slow out through the front doors.'

The gunman slid the Glock away from the woman's head.

Dug the muzzle into her swollen belly.

Murphy put up his hands near his shoulders, and Darby saw a slight bulge underneath his jacket, near the back waistband – the sort of bulge a handgun would make. Was Murphy packing a second piece?

'Everyone keep walking nice and slow,' Murphy said.

Darby zipped up her jacket to hide her sidearm. Murphy had the best of intentions, but he was out of his depth. Winging it. She had to diffuse the tension and try to gain some control. Now.

'They killed my father,' Darby called out.

The gunman's eyes darted around the crowded lobby to see who had spoken.

'He was a good man. Honest,' Darby said. 'That's what got him killed.'

Then she moved past a wall of cops and stepped into the gunman's line of sight.

'Detective Murphy can't help you, has no interest in helping you. No one in here does.'

On the periphery of her vision Darby could see more than one angry and reproachful gaze aimed at her. *Traitor*, their expressions said. *Bitch. Liar.*

Darby raised her hands to her shoulders and took a few steps forward. 'Whatever your agenda is, your grievance, I want to hear it. I don't answer to these people. I know how they think, how they operate. I'll listen to you and I'll help you any way I can.'

You don't belong here, their expressions said. *You're not one of us any more. You never were.*

'We can talk now, or we can talk privately,' Darby said. 'Which would you prefer?'

Silence. The lobby, packed with the sharp odours of gun smoke, the warm air crackling with police radios and ringing telephones, felt eerily still.

The gunman's blue eyes appraised her. They reminded her of Coop, his eyes: large and expressive and bordering on feminine, with the kind of thick lashes generally only seen on women.

He's too calm, Darby thought. Only someone who had mentally rehearsed this exact moment thousands of times and surrendered to whatever fate would hand him would appear this relaxed.

But what does he want?

The gunman turned his head slightly, towards his hostage, as though he wanted to whisper a secret. The pregnant woman closed her eyes, and her lips trembled when she said, 'He asks that you come closer.'

Smart, Darby thought, making her way around the items and puddles. *Real smart.* Using the hostage as his spokeswoman automatically engendered sympathy. It was simple biology and evolution: there wasn't a single person in here who could stand the thought of seeing a woman, let alone a pregnant one, get hurt. Using her as his mouthpiece forced everyone to take his threats and demands seriously.

That would change if Darby could convince him of her real plan: exchange the hostage for her. If that happened, with the exception of Coop, no one would shed a tear if she became collateral damage. *BPD will probably hold a parade*, she thought.

'Stop,' the hostage said, still gripping her captor's arm.

Darby, now standing less than ten feet away, got a good, close look at the pregnant woman. She appeared to be somewhere in her early to mid-thirties and had the kind of pale and freckled Irish skin that always burned and never tanned. Boston accent. Shoulder-length blonde hair that was tangled around part of her face and mouth. No make-up or rings on any of her fingers. Her clothing – sneakers and maternity jeans with a red top worn underneath a long and baggy grey hoodie with a ripped right-front pocket – were well-worn, thrift-store purchases or items donated to her by her girlfriends.

The hostage said, 'He asks that you please put your hands behind your head.'

Darby complied. For some reason, the woman triggered memories of her mother. After her father died *(no, murdered, he was murdered by people who once worked in this very building, his so-called brothers-in-blue)* they had lived on a shoestring budget. Sheila McCormick clipping coupons and only buying store-brand groceries and clothes from yard sales and department-store clearance racks – and only when it was completely and absolutely necessary.

The gunman trained his weapon on Darby.

'Get on your knees,' the hostage said.

4

— 00.10

Darby didn't move.

'Down on your knees, hands behind your head,' the hostage said, her voice trembling. 'He won't ask you again.'

Seeing the raw terror in the woman's eyes, how it was eating its way through her, quickly transforming her into a shell of a person who, if she survived this, would be for ever scarred and mistrusting and constantly frightened, made Darby want to lunge for the gunman.

'*Please*,' the woman nearly screamed. 'Do what he says . . .'

'You got it,' Darby replied. Her voice didn't tremble. She breathed deeply and slowly. 'What's your name?'

'Laura –'

The gunman tightened his chokehold, cutting off her words.

Locked back the Glock's hammer.

He won't kill me, Darby told herself as she dropped to one knee, then another. *Shoot me or anyone else and he'll lose all of his negotiation power. He's smart enough to know that.*

Was he? She had no way of knowing. For all she

knew, the gunman was mentally unstable and had some personal death wish. Maybe he was going to splatter her brains across the cold marble floor to demonstrate his power. Maybe he was going to make some proclamation and start firing wildly. Right now anything was possible because she knew next to nothing about the man and his intentions. Right now she was operating solely on gut instincts and experience, both of which told her he needed to voice some grievance before listing his demands. Right now all she could do was wait for him to speak. When he did, she would listen with trained empathy. Give him her full attention and build a rapport with him.

You're making a helluva lot of assumptions, an inner voice countered. *Let's hope to God you're right.*

The hostage let go of her captor's arm. The woman fought like hell to keep her legs from buckling, and her arms shook as she reached around, behind *her* back. Then her gaze cut sideways, to a civilian: an older black woman with grey dreadlocks and thick-rimmed eyeglasses who was sitting on the floor with her back resting up against the reception desk, her mouth working rapidly in silent prayer.

'You. Yes, you,' the hostage said. Darby could see the woman's fingers fumbling at the buttons of the man's overcoat but kept her attention focused on the gunman, studying him, trying to commit his every gesture and movement to memory. 'That cane lying on the floor, is it yours?'

'Yes, sir.'

A pause as the gunman spoke to the hostage.

'You're to remain seated,' the hostage said. 'Nod if you understand . . . good.'

Now the pregnant woman turned her attention to the centre of the room.

Then, louder: 'You, the woman with the white curly hair standing in the back. Please come forward.'

Over her left shoulder Darby saw a bull of a woman with a round face thread her way past a pair of armed blue uniforms: Caucasian, somewhere in her late fifties, stocky and thick, about five foot five inches. She had a slight overbite and wore a forest green L. L. Bean winter parka that had a hood lined with fur.

Another pause as the gunman spoke to his hostage.

'Face down on the floor, please,' the pregnant woman stammered. Then, with her left hand, she pulled back the lapel of the gunman's overcoat and held it open.

Darby had seen suicide vests in photographs and on the news, but never one up close. The gunman had fashioned his using an olive-coloured military tactical vest which, given its thickness, suggested it was not only bulletproof but held ceramic armour plating. She could only see the left side of the vest, but what she saw was enough: detonator cords running into five bricks of C-4 or some other plastic explosive tucked inside five tactical pockets.

A wave of terror washed through her before she could catch it. On the periphery of her vision she saw people inch back, fighting the urge to run. She wanted to join them. Bombs were nasty, hateful things, wildly unpredictable and wildly destructive. They ranged from crudely constructed devices using ordinary kitchen items like pressure cookers to the elegantly simple pipe bomb. Assuming the right side of the vest was a mirror image of the left meant the gunman had a total of ten blocks of plastic explosive strapped to his body – nowhere near enough to blow the building but more than enough to destroy the lobby and kill everyone in here – especially if he, like other suicide bombers, had packed the vest with ball bearings, screws, bolts, and other metal objects to serve as shrapnel.

The hostage spoke again: 'The three women are to stay. Everyone else, clear the lobby.'

While people filed out, Darby tried to study the gunman, who was still crouched behind the hostage, his body pressed up against the woman's back. He was about a good five inches taller than the hostage, putting his height around six feet. He wore polished black Oxford shoes and a black suit with a white shirt and a dark tie – funeral attire, she thought.

But it was the man's calm demeanor that worried her. It made her think of suicide bombers who had willingly and eagerly surrendered to the belief that their actions would grant them entrance into a paradise of unlimited pleasures.

Again the gunman whispered against the hostage's ear. Whatever he said caused the woman to break into tears. Then he released his grip on her throat and with his left hand he reached inside his jacket pocket and came back with a black, circular device that looked like a gasmask filter. He placed it against the black fabric covering his mouth and used the Velcro straps to attach it to his balaclava.

Not a filter; a voice-altering device. 'Remove your coats and place them on the floor,' he said, his voice taking on the robotic quality of a computer. 'All of you.'

They complied. The black woman, Darby saw, was having a difficult time. She saw the gunman glaring at her and said, 'I just had shoulder surgery. I can't take it off myself.'

But the gunman was no longer paying attention to her; his attention and weapon were now on the white-haired woman, who wore a hip holster strapped with a nine.

'You're a cop,' the gunman said. The voice-altering device didn't allow for inflection. Darby didn't know if the man was asking a question or making a statement. 'Are you a member of the Boston Police Department?'

The woman nodded. She wore a grey cable-knit sweater with jeans and boots.

'Active duty?'

Again she nodded.

'Where?'

'District Three,' she said. 'Fenway.'

'Homicide?'

'Yes.'

'Place your service weapon on the floor. Then lie down and push it over to me.'

Active duty, Darby thought. *Service weapon*. Cop speak.

She sensed he was fighting some internal conflict. Taking a cop as a hostage maybe wasn't part of his plan.

His attention swung back to Darby, at the nine tucked in her shoulder holster.

'I'm not a cop,' she said. 'I work in the private sector.'

'As what?'

'I'm a forensic consultant. My name is Darby McCormick. Tell me how I can help you.'

'Remove your handgun and slide it over to me.'

She did.

'Now rise,' he said.

5

– 00.04

'What was his name?' the gunman asked. 'Your father?'

'Thomas McCormick,' Darby said. 'Everyone called him Big Red, like the gum.'

'Big Red. I like that. Was he a detective?'

'No, a patrolman in Belham, where I grew up. It's a city –'

'I know where it is. Why was he killed?'

'Because he was a good man. Honest.'

The cold blue eyes from the balaclava squinted at her, as if trying to decipher some hidden meaning behind her words. The pregnant woman gripped the boulder that was her stomach with both hands as if trying to hold it up. She was clearly in pain.

'She needs a doctor,' Darby said to him. Then, to the woman: 'Laura, how far along are you?'

The woman gasped; the gunman had tightened his chokehold.

'You'll address me and only me,' he said to Darby.

'She's a liability. You should take me instead.' If he took her as his hostage, Darby could, with a few well-placed blows, have him on his knees, sobbing and begging to return to the safety of his mother's womb.

You don't know if he has a detonator, an inner voice added. *If he does and if he reaches it before you can subdue him, they'll be scraping what's left of you and everyone else in here with spatulas.*

'I don't think so,' the gunman said. 'You're a dangerous woman. In more ways than one, I suspect. On the conveyor belt you'll find a black backpack. Retrieve it for me. Please.'

The backpack weighed at least twenty pounds, the tight nylon fabric stretched to its limit.

'Bring the bag to me and place it on the floor,' the gunman said. 'Now open it.'

Darby squatted on her haunches, found the zipper and pulled. When she opened the mouth of the bag, a strong, chemical odour like bleach assaulted her. Inside, she saw two rolls of duct tape, plastic zip ties, and what looked like a portable and battery-operated router – what everyone called a mobile hotspot – sitting on top of a mountain of what she assumed was plastic explosive. It had the colour and texture of dough. She suspected the gunman had crafted the explosive himself, using some homemade recipe he'd found on the internet. Terrorists loved sharing their baking secrets.

'Remove the router and place it on the desk behind me. After you're done, come back to me so I can see your pretty face.'

Darby reached inside the bag and used a fingernail to scrape off a piece of the explosive. It was hard, like putty, and it remained trapped underneath her fingernail as she stood with the router in her hand. The gunman, she saw, had painted the areas on the router containing its make and model.

'My demand is simple and easy,' he said after she returned. 'I want to speak with Mayor Edward Briggs here, face-to-face, in the lobby. You will escort him and a cameraman and reporter to interview me live on TV. Once the interview is over, I'll release the hostages and surrender myself to you. It's that simple.'

'Edward Briggs is no longer the mayor. He retired last year.'

'Your watch,' the gunman said, ignoring her statement, 'does it have a timer function?'

'It does.'

'Good. Please set it for a three-hour countdown.'

Darby went to work, pressing the various plastic knobs on her cheap digital Casio with its scuffed-up face. She had worn it for years – the watch and the small gold crucifix under her shirt, the last gift her father had given her before he died. Over the years they felt like talismans that protected her from harm, even death.

'My timer is set,' Darby said.

'Thank you. Don't start it yet – I want you to give me your full attention, because this next part is critical. Do I have your full attention?'

'You do.'

'You will have exactly three hours to deliver the honorable Mayor Briggs, a reporter and cameraman into the lobby – you and only you. If they don't arrive within the three-hour timeframe, the first bomb will go off. Another bomb will go off every three hours until Briggs arrives. Do you understand?'

'I understand.'

'The suicide vest I'm wearing is connected to my heartbeat. If I die, the vest and the bombs I've planted in and around the city will go off. If members of the Boston Police or FBI or anyone else try to infiltrate the lobby, if I see a bomb robot deliver a throw-down phone, I will detonate one of the bombs, maybe even the one strapped to my chest. Do you understand?'

'I understand.'

'Please repeat back what I said.'

She did.

'I'm electing you as my spokesman – excuse me, my spokeswoman,' the gunman said. 'I will speak to you and only you. No one else is to enter the lobby.'

'You have two explosive devices in here. They're not going to allow anyone to enter.'

'The devices will be rendered safe once I see that Briggs has arrived.'

'And the other bombs you planted?'

'I'll give you their locations and the codes to disarm them.'

'How many are there?'

'Start your timer. Oh, and Darby? There will be no negotiation. Please remember that or there will be blood.'

6

00.00

The sample Darby had collected was still underneath her fingernail. Standing by the front doors and out of the gunman's line of sight, she quickly used the edge of a credit card tucked in her money clip to remove the white, putty-like substance. She pinched it between her cash and then slid her money clip back inside her pocket and moved outside.

Controlled chaos. Those two words immediately flashed into her mind when she saw what seemed like hundreds of cops scrambling across the front sidewalk and across Tremont Street, which was already in the process of being shut down and evacuated. Groups of blue uniforms manned the corners, busy redirecting traffic away from the station. The civilians who worked inside the building streamed from the fire exits, all of them being herded like spooked cattle across Tremont, to Mercy Park.

The first thing she had to do was nail down the panic – not just her own but everyone else's too. People were reading her face to see how to react. Panic acted in the same way as a contagious hot zone virus, infecting one person and then another with a deadly speed and efficiency. Instead of shutting down organs, it devoured common sense and all higher-level thinking – and nothing on earth created more panic and terror than knowing you were standing inside the blast radius of not one but two actual explosive devices, with every cell in your body telling you to run far and fast.

Darby slipped on her sunglasses to keep the wind out of her eyes as she darted to the nearest patrolman, a tall, square-jawed man who stood with the posture and confidence of a Marine. He pulled a bullhorn away from his mouth and looked down at her.

She had to yell over all the noise. 'My name is Darby McCormick. I was –'

'I know who you are. Tell me what's going on.'

'There are *two* improvised explosive devices inside the lobby – the vest he's wearing and another device inside a backpack. I need you to get on the horn and tell your people to widen the evacuation area. Have you seen Agent Jackson Cooper? About your height, looks like Tom Brady's twin brother?'

'Don't know who he is and, no, I haven't seen anyone like that.'

Coop had to be somewhere inside this bedlam, but where? If she called his phone, she wouldn't be able to hear him though all the noise and confusion.

Darby turned to the vehicles parked along the kerb. She moved to a truck, climbed onto the bed and then stood on the roof and looked around the sea of people, thinking about the other IEDs the gunman said he'd planted in the city. How many? And where?

She spotted Coop standing on the kerb at the end of the block, his cell gripped in his hand and his face impassive as he listened to the detective from the lobby, Murphy, screaming at him. Darby was too far away to hear what he was saying, and there was too much noise; but she saw spittle flying from the man's mouth, Murphy using his index finger like a dagger as he stabbed the air in front of Coop's face to make his point. A small crowd of Boston cops flanked him.

Darby jumped down from the truck roof and threaded her way through the fast-moving bodies, thinking about the former Boston mayor. She knew Edward Briggs only peripherally, but he seemed to have been fashioned from the same mould as former Massachusetts governor and former Republican presidential nominee Mitt Romney: perfect hair and white teeth, a 'gosh, golly and darn' man who smiled at the right times, didn't swear, and read flawlessly from a teleprompter. Like Romney, Briggs had the charisma and personality of a teleprompter. He seemed more Manchurian Candidate than an actual living, breathing human being. A robot that needed to be plugged into a wall outlet at night to be recharged.

She was taken out of her thoughts when she heard Murphy bark, 'You're not the ranking officer here.'

'I am until SAC Gelfand shows up,' Coop replied. 'And we're not going to argue jurisdiction, because we all know this is now federal. What's happening falls under ICS.'

ICS was yet another one of the Bureau's seemingly

endless stream of acronyms, this one for the Integrated Command System. Set up by the Feds in the wake of 9/11, the protocol created an immediate command hierarchy, along with an explicit list of detailed instructions to follow, in the event of a terrorist attack.

'That guy look like an Islamic terrorist to you?' Murphy spat. 'His skin was white.'

'White, black, brown, purple, we're still talking terrorism. The gunman is wearing a suicide vest. He could be a lone wolf, or he could be Boston's version of Timothy McVeigh.'

Murphy flinched a little at that. Prior to 9/11, Timothy McVeigh, an American Gulf War veteran and militia movement sympathizer, and his homegrown soldiers had orchestrated what was considered the single most significant act of domestic terrorism in US history: the bombing of the Alfred P. Murrah Federal Building in Oklahoma City. The chemical-fertilizer bomb he manufactured inside the van had killed 168 people and injured thousands.

But the real source of Murphy's anger, she knew, was her. Not only had she stepped in and undermined his authority in front of his peers, effectively emasculating him, she had prevented him from being the point man in dealing with the gunman.

When she appeared by his side, Murphy's expression turned apocalyptic. The heated and nearly bloodthirsty glares from his pack of supporters reminded her of the ending of the Shirley Jackson story *The Lottery*, where the townspeople, including its children, eagerly and excitedly grabbed rocks to stone the lottery winner, a woman, to death.

'*You've got some goddamn nerve,*' Murphy hissed.

Darby cut him off with her hand. 'You were going to get the woman killed – maybe even yourself –'

'Bullshit. I had everything under control until you opened those dick-sucking lips of yours with that crack about how neither I or anyone else –'

'It's called defusing the situation. I'll explain the rules of hostage negotiation to you later, Murphy. Right now we have to deal with the *bombs*.' Darby saw the surprise and fear bloom in his face and on the faces around her. Her gaze darted back to Coop. 'He brought a second one with him; it's in his backpack. I suggest evacuating the surrounding buildings and cordoning off a wider area to –'

'You're a civilian now, you don't have any authority here,' Murphy spat. 'Remove your ass or we'll do it for you.'

'Shut it down, Murphy. *Now*,' Coop said. 'Darby, you're with me.'

Coop walked away. She had started to follow when Murphy darted in front of her, his voice trembling with rage when he said, 'You think, what, you're gonna prove something here, get your old job back? Guess again. Nobody here would work with you.'

Darby tried to move around him. Again, Murphy darted in front of her, only this time he grabbed her roughly by the upper arm.

'You think you're so goddamn high and mighty, that

you're better and smarter than the rest of us – so fucking *righteous*.' He pointed a finger in her face and she could feel the fingers of his other hand sinking into the meat of her triceps. 'Your old man was the exact same way. *That's* what got him killed.'

Darby straightened, her jaw set. They were standing so close together, she could see the tiny blood vessels like red worms in his heated, watery eyes.

Over the course of her professional life, she had trained herself to cut her feelings the way an electrician snipped a wire – but not when it came to her anger. She felt it vibrating beneath her skin, demanding to be fed. Her voice, though, was calm when she spoke.

'When this is over, you and I will get together privately and discuss manners. Until then, let go of my arm and step aside, or I'll turn your fat ass into a Jackson Pollock painting right here on the sidewalk.'

Murphy didn't let go.

'You want to carry your nuts home in an evidence bag? You know I can do it.'

He released his grip, seething. 'Any other smartass comments?'

'Yeah. Upgrade your mouthwash.'

Darby walked away, thinking about all the things she could do to him; the sounds he would make when she snapped his joints. It allowed her to put her anger up on a shelf.

Coop stood at the far end of the kerb, talking on the phone and waiting for her. She saw his expression and knew he was about to rip into her for once again jumping into the fray without thinking. It reminded her of a statement he'd made last year in a cheerless airport bar at Denver International, after their flight had been delayed for several hours. They had just finished working a particularly gruelling case in Red Hill, Colorado. He was on his third, maybe fourth, bourbon when he said, *You are, hands-down, the single angriest person I've ever met.* Then his face took on the pale, grave expression of a pallbearer. *I think you've got a death wish.*

'She's right here, I'll call you back,' Coop said to the person on the other end of the line.

Darby held up a hand, cutting off whatever he was about to say. 'I don't want to hear it. Murphy didn't know what he was doing in the lobby, and you know it.'

Coop looked like he was about to argue the point; then he saw the sea of people swarming around him, the crowds getting larger, cell phones and police radios and sirens and flashing lights going off everywhere, and he gently placed a hand on her back and the two of them walked into the parking lot that annexed the station.

'The gunman,' he said, turning his back to the wind. 'What are his demands?'

'He wants a face-to-face with *Mayor* Briggs inside the lobby.'

His brow furrowed. 'Briggs isn't the mayor.'

'I reminded him of that fact. He said he wants Briggs, and he said he wants me, and only me, to escort Briggs, a TV cameraman and a reporter inside the lobby to conduct what I'm guessing is some sort of interview on live TV. When the interview has been conducted to his satisfaction – his words – he said he'd surrender himself.'

'And if we don't?'

'He'll detonate the bombs,' Darby said, her attention swinging back to Tremont Street, to the rising tide of cops, every one of them trying to do something to control the situation, to make it stop or at least pause; and for some reason she couldn't explain, she was thinking of a vacation with her parents in Kennebunk, Maine. It was the morning after a major thunderstorm and they were at the beach, the waves tall and angry. She went to swim with her father, the two of them had been bodysurfing when, all of a sudden, a terrible force pulled her deeper under the water, her body bouncing along the bottom of the ocean until she miraculously resurfaced, gasping for air and discovering she was what felt like miles from the shore. She was thrashing in the water when her father grabbed her and said, *It's me, Darby, I've got you, you're safe.*

Later, when it was all over, when they were on shore and safe and she could breathe, her father said, *The riptide got you. It comes out of nowhere and drags you down to the bottom and tries to kill you. You always need to watch out for the riptide, Darby, the things you can't see.*

Coop said, 'He didn't give you a reason why he wants Briggs?'

Darby shook her head. The fresh air and the adrenaline had helped clear her head, put her hangover on a shelf. 'He told me he planted bombs inside the city.'

His face drained of colour. 'How many?'

'He didn't say. But we have –' Darby glanced at her watch '– we have two hours and forty-two minutes to deliver Briggs, or the first bomb goes off.'

'Oh,' Coop said wanly, punching a number into his cell phone, 'is that all?'

7

+00.45

Street cops, military, elite Special Forces – on day one, before you learned how to handle and shoot a weapon, you were taught the importance of combat breathing. It was the single most critical function you performed when suddenly confronted with a situation in which your every decision could not only affect your life but also the lives and safety of others. You needed to create a bulletproof mind. To do that, you needed to keep your blood pressure low and minimize the overwhelming psychological and physical side effects caused by an adrenaline dump. Ignore your breathing and you allowed the lethal cocktail of stress hormones and chemicals to devour your ability to think and act at peak and optimum levels.

Easier said than done. Even more so when you began your morning with a nearly empty gas tank.

Darby sat beside Coop in the back of the screaming patrol car, focusing on her breathing as she tried to drown out the sirens and Coop shouting on the phone and the voices blaring over the police radio. The patrolman, an old Irish guy probably around the same age her father would have been if he were alive, kept eyeing her in the rearview mirror. He had gin blossoms on his cheeks, and the warm interior reeked of the chemical-induced vanilla odour from the air freshener hanging from a radio knob. She wished she could crack a window, but the back windows in a squad car didn't open.

She ignored the odours packed in the warm air, which was growing hotter with each passing minute, and forced her attention on her breathing, taking in a slow draw through her nose and counting to four, feeling her lungs expanding until they couldn't hold any more air. Then she held her breath and counted to four. Exhaled slowly through her mouth for another four count. Another sixteen, maybe twenty seconds had passed, bringing the time until the first bomb went off to –

No, she told herself – again – and went back to her combat breathing. *Do not play that game.*

The problem – the thing gnawing away at her self-control – was time. It had taken Coop nearly seventeen minutes to find a patrolman who had a nearby vehicle who could drive them to Northeastern University, the nearby college that was the designated ICS command site in the event of a terrorist attack. The campus was less than ten miles away from BPD headquarters, but Boston was a small city with narrow streets, all of which were still clogged with morning traffic. Police sirens and flashing lights couldn't magically widen the streets or make the traffic disappear. She couldn't control any of these things, and it ate at her.

Do your job, Darby reminded herself as she inhaled, counting to four. *That's the only control you have.*

Or, to use one of her father's favourite expressions, this one coined from his Marine days: *Hope for the best, plan for the worst.*

Coop was on the phone, on a conference call with SAC Gelfand and the hostage negotiator, when the patrolman delivered them to the rear of the parking lot, which was already shut down and in the process of being evacuated by Boston PD and college security. The lot needed to be cleared in order to make room for the incoming swell of city, state and federal vehicles.

The patrolman mercifully killed the siren and put the car in park. At the moment, they were the only law enforcement inside the lot. The patrolman turned down the radio a bit, and when she saw him eying her in the rearview again she shifted in her seat and looked down at the floor mat, breathing and counting, breathing and counting, while she reviewed what information she had managed to glean from Coop's conversation.

Gelfand and the hostage negotiator were en route, fighting their way through traffic. The Boston Bomb Squad had been called in to inspect and search any vehicles parked near the station, city garbage cans and any suspicious packages, for explosive devices. The state troopers' bomb people would coordinate their operations with federal bomb experts to see if there was any way to render safe the two IEDs inside the lobby. All information and tactics would flow through the Mobile Command Post, which had been dispatched. Not much could happen until the MCP arrived.

Her gaze landed on the dashboard clock. She saw

the time and before she could stop herself her mind was off and running, doing the calculations.

Seventeen minutes to find the patrol car, then twenty-four minutes and change to arrive here. Call it forty-three minutes. That left them an hour and fifty-nine minutes to find the former mayor and deliver him and the TV crew to the lobby.

It wasn't going to happen.

Even if Briggs were standing here right now, the people in charge wouldn't allow him to go inside the lobby. She didn't blame them. The gunman's true agenda could be to detonate the bombs and kill Briggs and everyone else on live TV. Was that his true endgame? If that happened, his message, grievance, whatever this was about, would ensure global headlines.

Another minute had passed.

Another minute lost.

Stop, she told herself. *You can't control that part.*

Intellectually, she knew that. It made perfect, logical sense.

But that didn't mean she had to accept it.

The inside of the car felt too hot, too close. She wanted fresh air. Because the squad-car doors couldn't be unlocked from the inside, she had to ask the patrolman to let her out.

Darby stepped outside and began to pace back and forth near the chain-link fence overlooking Huntington Ave. Traffic was clogged on both sides, and the Green Line's E-train rumbled down a track in the centre of the street, *clank-clank-clank*, brakes screeching. Her head pounded from the hangover and from not having eaten. She wished she had grabbed something back at the hotel when she had a chance. She wished –

Wish in one hand, shit in the other, and see which one fills up first.

Her father's voice quoting one of his favourite sayings, one he had used when she was younger, railing against some real or perceived injustice and wishing it were different. *Either do your job, Darby, or step aside and make room for someone who can*, he liked to say. Being back in Boston had dusted off all sorts of memories. Here came another one: Big Red's massive frame filling the doorway of the principal's office and Darby feeling the weight of his gaze and judgement as she sat in the chair, indignant, a bag of ice resting on her scraped and swollen knuckles. During recess, Mark Alves had snuck up behind her and snapped her training bra, to the cackling delight of his friends. The laughing died when she broke his nose. Darby was eleven.

Big Red wasn't mad at her about the fight. But he was upset about what happened afterwards: her confrontation with the elderly principal, Sister Agnes, a stern and humourless woman who wore orthopedic shoes and had a face that looked like melted wax. The Catholic nun had asked – no, she had *demanded* – that Darby apologize to Mark Alves for hitting him. Darby refused, even after Sister Agnes had threatened her with a week's detention and then, finally, expulsion from school for two days.

'I'm not saying you shouldn't have popped the Alves boy,' Big Red said as they drove home, Darby sitting beside him, her face still hot with anger. The windows were down, the spring air cool and fresh, but all she could smell was the cigar smoke baked into his clothing and the upholstery of his squad car. 'No one has a right to lay a hand on you. Someone does, you've got every right to defend yourself. And I'm not saying you should have to apologize to him either.'

Darby turned her head to him. Waited.

'You've got yourself a two-day vacation. First thing Friday morning, you're to march into her office and apologize, then serve out your week's detention. If you don't, you don't go back to school – her words, not mine.'

Darby sat up in her seat, indignant. Her body trembled with rage when she spoke, but her voice was clear. 'I did *nothing* wrong. I am not going to apologize to her, and I am *not* going to serve a week's detention all because I refused to say I was sorry for hitting an asshole.'

'Right or wrong, she's the one in charge, and she makes the rules. It's your call, your problem. You're the one who has to deal with it.'

Darby's eyes watered. Tears streamed down her cheeks but she refused to cry.

Big Red pulled the car over on to the shoulder of the road, and sighed tiredly, as if he'd been asked to perform some Herculean task. 'Darby, even when you're right, there are going to be times when it's better to play along in order to get along – even if you have to fake it. The world isn't a fair place; the same goes for people. If you spend your life battling every person who doesn't do the right thing or acts unfairly, you're going to wind up like Sister Agnes: bitter and angry and very, very lonely. You'll always be an outsider.'

The January wind slapped her face. Darby blinked behind her sunglasses, remembering that Friday morning when she apologized to Sister Agnes. Remembered the smug look of satisfaction on the crone's face and remembered how she so badly wanted to reach across the massive desk and punch the woman in the face. Darby had always suspected the nun was, at heart, a bully. Only she wasn't as transparent as someone like Mark Alves. At least Mark had the guts to do it in public. Sister Agnes enjoyed performing her brand of torture behind closed doors, safe from prying eyes.

Darby remembered the bitter taste in her mouth after she left the office. *So this is what defeat tastes like*, she thought. Her mouth tasted that way right now as she recalled another memory, this one new and fresh: Murphy's comment about her and her father.

You think you're so goddamn high and mighty, that you're better and smarter than the rest of us – so fucking righteous. *Your old man was the exact same way.* That's *what got him killed.*

You never spoke out against the tribe. That was the primal rule when you grew up in places like South Boston, Charlestown and Belham; when you became a member of the Catholic Church or part of the Blue

Brotherhood. You kept your secrets and sins at home. Right and wrong never factored into the tribe's decision because the tribe's job was to protect itself, ensure its survival. Disobey or break a single rule and you were banished.

Or, in her father's case, killed.

Darby was watching a news copter flying in the direction of BPD headquarters when Coop's head popped over the squad car's roof, waving at her to join him.

8

+01.11

Coop was still on the phone. It was too windy and too noisy to talk outside, so he ducked back inside the squad car. When Darby slid next to him, she felt better, more in control.

Coop, though, looked a little frayed around the edges. He had juggled multiple phone calls while taking notes in his small Moleskine notebook during the bumpy drive. The writing and shorthand he used was practically illegible.

Darby shut the door as he hung up on his call. 'The commander of the state's bomb squad wants a conference call with you,' he said. 'His name is Ted Scott.'

Darby fished her cell out of her jacket pocket. 'Was that him on the phone?'

'No. BPD's building manager. He's at a remote site where he can access all of the station's security camera feeds. He's got full control of the cameras and all building operations – power, heating and cooling, the phone lines, everything.'

'Good.'

'Not good. There's a problem with the lobby security cameras.'

'What kind of problem?'

'The cameras are working, and the building manager can operate them from his control station, make them turn every which way, zoom in and out, all of that. The problem is the CCTV feeds on his screens; they're full of static. We can't see what the gunman is doing, the lobby or the hostages. We're blind.'

'Just the lobby cameras are down?'

'Just the lobby cameras.'

Jamming unit, Darby thought, but didn't say it. She didn't know how much to say in front of the patrolman, but knew Coop would want to contain as much information as possible, to minimize leaks.

Then, as if reading her mind, Coop turned his head to the patrolman and said, 'Hey, Jimmy? It's Jimmy, right? You mind shutting off the heat? It's like Miami back here. We're roasting.'

The patrolman looked into his rearview mirror as he spoke. 'A gauge or some shit in the heating system crapped out, so it's got only two speeds: off and inferno. Only way to shut it off is to kill the engine.'

'So kill it and open a window. In fact, open two. And go and grab yourself a smoke while you're at it.'

'Thanks. I've been dying for like an hour.'

'No shit. You look paler than my sister does after she stumbles out of a confession box.' Coop had slipped back into his Boston accent: *pale-ah* and *sis-tah*.

The patrolman chuckled as he rolled down both windows just enough to get some fresh air without freezing them out of the back. Darby was always amazed by how easy and natural it was for Coop to break the ice and make people feel comfortable and at ease with just a few choice words – even hard nose piss-and-vinegar types like Patrolman Jimmy here, a street cop from a generation where you treated strangers and outsiders with suspicion and derision.

Coop didn't speak until after the guy stepped outside and away from the car. She realized then he had gotten the patrolman out of the car so he could talk to her alone.

'That device you pulled out of his backpack,' Coop said. 'You sure it was a mobile router?'

'Am I a hundred per cent sure? No. It looked like ones I've seen before, but I didn't see anything to indicate that it was. I told you he painted over any logo, numbers and letters.'

'Was it powered on when you took it out of the backpack?'

'I didn't see any lights to indicate it was. And he didn't ask me to turn it on, just to place it on the counter.'

'So it could very well be a jamming device.'

'Could be. I've seen units that size and shape. They typically have a range of anywhere from thirty to sixty metres.'

'Sixty metres . . . that's just under a hundred feet – more than enough to jam the lobby cameras.'

She nodded. 'He'd want control over all communications, not only video surveillance but cellular frequencies, Wi-Fi, Bluetooth, all of it. Those jamming units are all handheld, though.'

'How big are they?'

'The portable ones? About the size of a walkie-talkie.'

'So he could be carrying one with him, clipped to his belt or something, and you didn't see it.'

'Possible. Why?'

'The building manager reviewed the recorded footage for the cameras posted outside the main entrance,' Coop said. 'At eight thirty-three this morning, the feed for those cameras started experiencing mild static interference. The feed then turned to snow two minutes and thirty-three seconds later. Then it began to gradually abate.'

'So he had the jamming unit turned on as he approached and entered the station.'

Coop leaned closer. 'Briggs lives in Brookline,' he said, his voice low. 'We have two agents who live there. Howie got on the horn and told 'em to hightail it over to Briggs's place. He's not there. No one is. Neighbours are saying he and the family are up north, at their vacation house on Lake Winnipesauke.'

Darby felt her stomach drop. 'You have the number?'

'We have all of them. The home line keeps going to voicemail, and Briggs isn't answering his cell phone, either. Same with the wife. Even if the man picked up right now, he's at least a hundred miles away. That's over two hours by car – more, if it's snowing in New Hampshire.'

'Helicopter?'

'Several, ours and the state police. But we've got to locate the man first.'

*

She pulled back her jacket sleeve and checked her watch.

One hour and forty-five minutes left.

'He's not going to make it in time,' Coop said.

'Let me go in and talk to him, see if I can buy us some time.'

'That's Howie's call.'

'Get him on the phone.'

'Listen to me. The Bureau and BPD have a joint terrorism task force, but Howie's the one driving the bus, so he calls all the shots. That means we're going to be taking all the heat. It means you can't go off half-cocked –'

'You're referring to what I did in the lobby?'

Coop sucked in a deep breath through his nose, steeling himself.

'What should I have done, Coop? Just stand there and watch Murphy waffle his way through a hostage negotiation? He's lucky he didn't get himself shot and killed, the way he was pressing our guy.'

'And that's the word I want you to always keep in mind: *our*. Not *your* guy or *your* case – *our* guy and *our* case. He chose you as his spokeswoman, so now you're involved in this thing even if BPD puts up a fight – and they will, you know they will.'

'Coop, you don't have to explain what –'

'The first sign of trouble, the moment something goes wrong, BPD is going to point the finger at you – at *us*. You want to stay involved, you've got to follow orders even if you don't agree with them.'

'Be a good girl and do what I'm told and shut my mouth and smile.'

'I didn't say that.'

Coop's phone rang.

'I'm not the enemy,' he said, glancing at the screen showing the incoming call. 'I would think you would know that by now.'

Darby sighed. Swallowed. She went to rub her face and caught sight of the time on her watch and felt the lining in her stomach constrict.

Coop put her on the line with the hostage negotiator.

9

+01.27

The Mobile Command Post was a long fibreglass structure without windows and had the look and feel of a luxury mobile home. Developed by Homeland Security, the MCP featured the highest levels of government encryption and surveillance technology. The roomy interior was buzzing with activity and beneath the morning scents of deodorant, shampoo, soap and competing brands of cologne, she smelled new carpet. Darby suspected this was the MCP's inaugural run.

The conference room was in the rear, equipped with a table that could seat six comfortably. She sat next to Coop. Peter Donnelly, BPD's police commissioner, sat across from her with his elbows on top of the speckled grey laminate top and his large hands folded together and resting against his mouth, his jowly face dour as he stared at the conference call unit, a UFO-shaped device with speakers.

On the phone was Ted Scott, the commander of the Massachusetts State Troopers' Bomb Squad Unit. His deep voice sounded crisp and clear when he spoke. 'Tell me again about the sample you collected.'

'White and hard, like putty,' Darby said. She had just

finished walking Scott through what she'd seen on the suicide vest and the items in the gunman's backpack. 'It smelled like bleach.'

'Until the lab analyses it, I'm thinking triacetone triperoxide.'

Darby felt her scalp prickle. 'TATP,' she said.

'You've come across it before?'

'No, thank God. But I've read about it.'

'It's an incredibly potent explosive, the de facto choice for suicide bombers in the Middle East when they can't get their hands on TNT or C-4. It doesn't produce any flames, creates an outward force of 1.5 tons per square inch.'

Darby heard Coop mumble 'Jesus' under his breath as she grabbed the pad and pen in front of her and started writing.

'It's not difficult to make,' Scott said. 'All you need is drain cleaner, bleach, acetone and a few other easily available items. But it's notoriously difficult to mix properly, and it's notoriously unstable. You've got to be crazier than a shithouse mouse to make this stuff, let alone want to use it.'

Darby slid the pad to Coop. She had written a single line: *Do not turn up heat in lobby.* Turning up the heat was a popular tactic with hostage negotiators, to make the gunman feel physically uncomfortable and shed clothing.

Coop got to his feet and darted around the table, heading for the door.

'What if you're a chemist or had a chemistry background?' Darby asked.

'Then you're talking a surprisingly simple process,' Scott replied. 'Like I said, the real danger isn't in making this stuff, it's in handling it. TATP is highly susceptible to friction, shock and heat – that's why they call it the 'Mother of Satan' over there in camel country, the shit is so unpredictable. The fact that this guy carried it in a backpack should say a lot about his state of mind. How close did you get to him when you were in the lobby?'

'Pretty close.'

'You catch a whiff of bleach? See the explosives?'

'I didn't see or smell anything. The coat covered most of his vest.'

'If his suicide vest is made with TATP – he could sneeze and it could blow up. Who's the hostage negotiator?'

'Alan Grove, out of the FBI's Boston field office. I've walked him through my conversation with the gunman.'

'Tell him under *no circumstances* is he to turn up the heat in the lobby. In fact, I'd suggest cutting the heat entirely, let the place cool down. It'll help keep the TATP stable – and that needs to be our top priority. You don't want that shit to go off.'

'I just sent word.'

'You said Commissioner Donnelly is there?'

'He's sitting right across from me.'

'Good. I need to explain to you both what will happen if, God forbid, one or both of those bombs in the lobby go off.

'The lower floors of the station, especially the lobby, were constructed with an explosive-resistant concrete. It has a higher cement count and is mixed with very fine silica sand and sets of narrow steel fibres, giving it a tensile strength roughly ten times higher than normal steel-reinforced concrete. Those blocks of bevelled glass at the front of the lobby contain a new type of woven cloth soaked with liquid plastic and bonded with adhesive – the same stuff used on the president's limo. If the bombs go off, the glass won't explode, and the concrete and tile, which is also bomb-resistant, will absorb most of the blast, and prevent debris from scattering. We're still talking major structural damage, but the explosion can be somewhat contained, which will allow my people and, if necessary, SWAT to remain closer to the building in the event they're needed.'

'Your guys find any IEDs near the building?' Darby had been told that Scott had dispatched bomb-sniffing dogs to search all the cars and city garbage cans.

'The dogs haven't found anything yet,' Scott said. 'But here's the problem: If the guy left an IED using TATP somewhere in a car or in a city garbage can, whatever, that shit's odourless, even the bomb dogs won't be able to detect it. And I don't want my people towing cars and poking in garbage cans because of TATP's inherent instability. We need to increase the evacuation radius, pull people out of the surrounding buildings.'

'It's being done as we speak. Ted, this part about him having the vest hooked up to his heartbeat, is that real or Hollywood movie bullshit?' asked Donnelly.

'Totally real and totally doable. Which brings me to the portable router you saw.'

'I don't know if it was, in fact, a mobile hotspot. It could very well be a portable jamming unit. Did Cooper tell you about the lobby cameras?'

'He did. If the gunman has, in fact, planted IEDs in and around the city, he's got to have a way to communicate with them. He could be using a cell signal or the city's public Wi-Fi – maybe he even tapped into BPD's Wi-Fi.'

'Or he could have armed everything before he walked inside the building.'

'That would be the smart play. But if what he told you is true – that he'll shut down the devices once you bring him Briggs, or if he's killed the suicide vest will go off along with all the other IEDs – then he's got some sort of communication system already in place. There's some way all the IEDs can talk to each other.'

'I don't think he'd rely on Wi-Fi, either BPD's or the city's. I think he's too smart for that. I think he'd know that would be the first thing that we would shut down. *Are* they shut down?'

'We're in the process.'

'And that router, or whatever it was, looked battery-operated. He knows – or suspects – we're going to cut power to the building at some point.'

'I passed along my recommendation to have the governor shut down the city's Wi-Fi in case our man's using it. Right now our EOD vehicles are strategically positioned near the building, jamming everything in that area – cell signals, Wi-Fi, radio frequencies.'

Darby had been told the bomb vehicles positioned near the building were equipped with the same military-grade jamming units used to locate and disarm bombs over in Afghanistan and Iraq.

Scott said, 'If I can get a closer look at his vest, the router and whatever equipment he might be using, it'll give us a better idea of what we're dealing with, maybe even find a way to locate the IEDs and shut them down. Maybe.'

'We're working on something,' Darby said.

'Get back to me as soon as you know.'

'Ted, before I let you go . . . your people, they have access to the building's junction box, right?'

'Yeah. Why?'

'The lobby phones are landlines. We can reverse-engineer the line and turn the phones in there into listening devices, pick up on his conversations.'

'My people are already on it,' Scott said, and hung up.

Darby was already on her feet and moving around the table when Donnelly said, 'We need to talk.'

'We will. Later.'

'We'll do it now. Grab a chair, this'll only take a minute.'

Darby moved past him and slipped through the door.

10

+01.39

Darby ducked into a narrow hall with aeroplane-type bathrooms on either side and stepped into the command area, the heart of the MCP, where half a dozen or so federal agents were seated in front of computer screens and speaking over their headsets to the agents and officers in the field. Boston SWAT officers and snipers, cameras mounted to their helmets and tactical scopes, were positioned a safe distance away from the building, and out of the jamming range of the bomb vehicles, in order to provide encrypted, real-time footage back to the agents in this room. A flat-screen showing a timer hung on the wall, the timer synched to the countdown on her watch.

Darby moved to the baby-faced agent monitoring the lobby cameras. All six feeds were still filled with snow. 'Any change?'

The agent shook his head and moved a can from one ear. 'I keep having the building manager set the cameras to different frequencies, but so far he's got them all jammed.'

'Sound?'

'Nothing. We're still deaf, dumb and blind.'

She thanked him and patted him on the shoulder, feeling the ridge of hard and knotted muscle created from frustration, and then opened the door to conference room B. This one was smaller, boxy and didn't have a conference table, just a narrow desk that faced a grey wall. Howie Gelfand, the SAC for the Boston field office, sat there, hunched forward, his back to her. He was on the phone and she could see him rubbing his forehead.

Gelfand looked over his shoulder, saw her, and motioned for her to join him. He returned to his conversation. She shut the door behind her and turned to the wall-mounted screen tuned to Channel 5 news.

The sound was muted, but the closed-caption scroll was on, the reporter talking about 'the developing siege' at Boston police's main headquarters building at One Schroder Plaza on Tremont. There was no information about the bombs, but the 'sky camera' mounted inside their news copter was providing live, aerial footage of the bomb dogs sniffing the cars parked along the streets.

'Stay right where you are, I don't want your signal to drop again,' Gelfand said into the phone. He had grown up in Long Island, New York, and his voice still carried traces of his accent. He had been the SAC for less than two years. 'I'll make all the arrangements and call you back.'

'Briggs?' she asked, hopeful, after he hung up.

'The man himself. He and his family are hitting the slopes in Vermont – *northern* Vermont, right near the Canadian border.'

'Shit.'

'It gets worse. Vermont's getting clobbered by a nor'easter – the same one that's supposed to hit us later this afternoon. We can't fly him out but we *can* drive him to the nearest helicopter pad.'

'New Hampshire?'

'No, they're getting hit now. The closest pad is on the Mass. border. Probably he's at least two hours from there – probably more like three in this weather. But if we can get him there in time and ahead of the storm, we can fly him out. If we can't, then we're going to have to wait for the man to arrive by car. Under normal circumstances, we're talking a five-hour drive. In this weather, with these road conditions, we're probably looking at more like seven or eight. Some of the roads near the lodge are shut down.'

Seven hours. In that time two more IEDs would detonate with a third one on its heels. Eight hours, and three IEDs would have gone off.

Darby was imagining body counts and severed and missing limbs when she said, 'The gunman didn't ask for a specific reporter or cameraman. If we can get Briggs to go in there, we can have SWAT go in disguised, maybe one of the bomb guys.'

'Way ahead of you, Doc. I talked to Ted Scott, the commander of the Mass. State Troopers' Bomb Squad. He volunteered.'

'One other thing – two things, actually. I want a paramedic with combat experience on standby.'

'Done. What else?'

'An OBGYN who's willing to go into the station,' Darby said. 'I want to be able to bring them both into there to examine Laura.'

'Laura?'

'The hostage. The pregnant woman. I don't know her last name.'

'Okay,' Gelfand said. 'Now let's talk about Briggs. He's –'

Gelfand cut himself off when the door opened.

Boston Police Commissioner Peter Donnelly was impossibly tall – six foot six, a big, lumbering and jowly man who had started out as a beat cop in Lawrence and worked his way up through the ranks, to superintendent, before being tapped for Boston police commissioner. The man had to duck through the doorway.

Gelfand got to his feet, his knees cracking. He was a heavy man with thinning blond hair he combed straight back across his scalp, and he always seemed to have a grin tugging at the corner of his mouth, even when he was angry or, like now, under tremendous pressure.

'Briggs has agreed to talk with the gunman during the drive,' Gelfand said to her.

'Ted Scott is jamming all the cell signals in the area,' Darby said.

'Two choices: throw-phone or a satellite phone.'

'You want me to go back in there and deliver it.'

'You're the one he wants to talk to. You think you can sell our guy on it?'

Donnelly spoke up, 'I can't allow that.'

Gelfand looked at him.

'She's a civilian, for starters,' Donnelly said.

Darby knew the real reason: she had broken BPD's blue wall of silence when she came forward about police corruption and the murder of her father. She couldn't be trusted – and now because she was no longer a member of the tribe, Donnelly couldn't exert any influence over her. That and the fact that the moment the media found out she was involved, it would dredge up BPD's history of corruption, all of which involved Donnelly's predecessor, Christina Chadzynski, may the bitch not rest in peace. The woman had played an integral part in her father's murder.

Donnelly didn't voice this, of course; he was too smart for that. Instead, he threw down the one card he knew would get Gelfand's undivided attention. 'And there's the issue of liability,' he said.

Darby turned to him, anger jumping into her voice before she could catch it. 'We're really going to have this conversation right now?'

Donnelly didn't look at her; he spoke only to Gelfand. 'If she gets hurt or injured – or, God forbid, killed – the city of Boston would be liable. You let her in there without her signing off, then the Bureau is liable, not us.'

Darby brushed past Gelfand and moved to the corner desk.

Gelfand cut to the chase. 'You guys don't want any more shit smeared on your faces, I get it,' he said. 'But the guy elected the good doctor here as his spokesman. If we send someone else in there, it could set him off.'

'Or she could set him off. Dr McCormick is not a professional hostage negotiator.'

'So you want me to send in Grove.'

'The city of Boston can't allow her to go into the lobby until Legal has signed off.'

'Give me the forms.'

'Legal is drafting them.'

How convenient, Darby thought, as she wrote on a pad of paper.

'We have an hour and twelve minutes until the first bomb goes off,' Gelfand said. 'What do you suggest I do? Sit around and do nothing while we wait for the paperwork to come through?'

'Send in a professional hostage negotiator,' Donnelly replied.

'And if Grove goes in there and it provokes our guy to do something drastic, then what? The city will pick up the tab instead of the federal government? Is that what you're proposing?'

On the pad, Darby wrote that she waived all liability, for injury or death, for both the BPD and the Bureau. She slapped the pad against Donnelly's expansive gut and opened the door.

11

+01.50

Darby didn't have to look far for Coop. She found him on his phone in the parking lot, standing near the back doors beside a federal SWAT vehicle.

Almost all the civilian vehicles in the college parking lot had been removed. The sky seemed darker, the air colder, and the traffic sounds from Huntington Ave were drowned out by the steady *thump* of the news copters circling overhead and by the constant throbbing purr of the gas generator powering the MCP.

Coop hung up and turned, surprised to see her. 'I was just about to come get you,' he said. White plumes of breath scattered in the wind. 'That was Ted Scott. His people hit the junction box to reverse-engineer the lobby phones.'

'And?'

'Nothing. The gunman either cut the lines or unplugged the phones.'

Shit. 'The hostage negotiator, whatshisname,' she said. 'Where is he?'

'Alan Grove, and he's waiting for you in there.' Coop jerked a thumb over his shoulder, at the back of the federal SWAT van. His gaze swept across her face. He had known her for a long time and knew how to read the nuances of her expressions and moods.

'No,' he said. 'You can't be –'

'I'm the only one he'll talk to.'

'He's not looking for a business partner. You go back in there, he'll kill you.'

'Trust me, Coop. He won't kill me.'

Coop took in a deep breath, about to mount a defence when she stepped on the van's rear bumper and opened the door. Inside, the back was crammed with shelves holding various electronic equipment and gear, she saw a lithe, bald man seated at a corner table, a phone pressed against his ear. Alan Grove had shut down BPD's automated calling system and voicemail but had kept one line open, hoping the gunman would answer.

Grove moved the receiver away from his mouth. 'He refuses to pick up. That, or he cut the phone lines,' he said. His tone and body language gave no indication that he was feeling any pressure.

Darby told him what Coop had just shared with her about the phone lines. Then she explained what was going on with Briggs and the strong possibility of the gunman using TATP. Grove listened, his expression impassive.

'Howie wants me to go in and talk with him, put him on the line with Briggs,' she said.

Grove nodded. She couldn't read anything in the man's face, couldn't tell how he felt about it. He had a hawkish nose and the colourful tie he wore elegantly matched his finely textured suit. He reminded her of a concierge at a luxury hotel, a man who could satisfy every need or desire with a single phone call.

Coop climbed into the back and shut the door. The truck's engine was no longer running, but the air was still warm and smelled of oil, lubricants and metal.

'How much time do we have?' Grove asked.

'One hour and eight minutes,' Darby replied.

'Then we better get on with it – unless you have any reservations, Dr McCormick.'

'I don't have much of a choice.'

'You can say no – and I wouldn't blame you in the slightest. If this man is, in fact, using TATP in his suicide vest, there's a strong chance that it can go off at any moment – well, I don't have to explain to you what will happen. Does Mr Gelfand want you to wear a bomb suit?'

'He didn't mention it, but I'm assuming he does.'

'My recommendation is not to bother. If one or both of the lobby bombs go off, all the suit will do is ensure we'll find your corpse in one place. The pressure wave will liquefy your organs. You'll be dead before you hit the floor.'

Darby saw Coop shift in his chair. The thought of being in there when the bomb went off made her break out in a cold sweat.

She said, 'The idea of going back in there, frankly, sets my teeth on edge. But I can't just sit back, either, and do nothing. I'm not a hostage negotiator, so if you think it's best that you go in –'

Grove held up a hand, cutting her off. 'Ego has no place in hostage negotiation,' he said. 'Dr McCormick, you and I –'

'Darby.'

'Darby, you and I are after the same thing, so let's talk one professional to another, and then you can make your decision.

'We need to establish a line of communication with the gunman,' Grove said. 'That's our first priority. Our man seems to know a lot about police matters, so I think one of us should go in with a satellite phone instead of the typical throw-phone. It's less threatening, and since the commander of the Massachusetts State Troopers' Bomb Squad Unit, Ted Scott, isn't jamming any satellite frequencies, we can talk to the gunman without Scott having to drop his jamming capabilities. Scott told me about the router.'

'I don't know if it was a router,' Darby said.

'Until we know more, we'll have to assume it is. Be on the lookout when you go in there, see what you can find.' Grove got to his feet and slid a thick black Mont Blanc pen inside the small breast pocket of her leather jacket. 'The pinhole camera is installed inside the front, near the small clip. It records DVR quality audio and video to its hidden USB drive.'

Then Grove turned to the SWAT agent sitting in the passenger seat. 'How's the picture looking, Charlie?'

'Crystal clear.'

'We know he's using a jamming device,' Grove said to her, 'so we set the pen to a low radio frequency. If his device is blocking radio high frequencies, then the video won't work – but the camera should. You don't have to operate it manually. It's already been programmed to take a picture every fifteen seconds. As a backup, I'd like you to use this.'

Grove picked up a small recordable audio device, what the FBI called a FBIRD. 'It's digital and not susceptible to any commercial jamming units,' he said. 'We can tape it underneath your clothes if you want, but it's thin enough to slip it in your breast pocket too, where it will be out of view. Fresh batteries, I've already tested it, it's good to go. Just stick it in your pocket and forget about it.

'I'm aware of your impressive background and credentials, but we still need to go over this next part.'

'Okay,' Darby said.

'Remain calm and nonjudgemental at all times. The key is to make him believe – to keep him believing – that you're on his side. Gather as much information as you can. He'll be expecting that, so whatever you do, don't push. I forgot to ask earlier: did he appear in any way under the influence of drugs or alcohol?'

'He disguised his voice, so I couldn't get a read on his tone. His pupils weren't dilated.'

'Body language?'

'Calm and controlled,' Darby said. 'Gives the impression he has every angle covered.'

'Like he's rehearsed this moment?'

She nodded. 'He also seems resigned to the fact that he might die – but not, I think, before he gets his message out. Could be law enforcement, I don't know. He strikes me as intelligent, as a cold and rational pragmatist, which is the worst kind of person to negotiate with.'

'You're right – which is why I'm reluctant about letting you or anyone else go back into the lobby without Briggs. He may decide to make a display of power to make sure his demands are taken seriously.'

'Killing a hostage.'

'It's a very real possibility. But if he's as intelligent as you say he is, then he'll know that killing a hostage now will effectively destroy any opportunity of us allowing the former mayor to enter the lobby. Briggs is the carrot. You go in there and deliver the phone, saying he can talk to Briggs in exchange for a hostage and for disarming the first IED.'

Darby nodded, thinking, *He'll never agree to that.*

'We have to try,' Grove said, as if reading her mind. 'We just can't sit back and do nothing with a bomb supposedly about to go off.'

'I understand.'

'Do you still want to go in?'

Darby nodded.

'But?' Grove prompted, reading something in her face.

'I was just thinking of what he told me as I left.'

'"There will be blood."'

Darby nodded.

'In these situations,' Grove said, 'there usually is.'

12

+02.01

An Explosive Ordnance Disposal truck made the approach to the building.

Darby rode in the back, standing on the diamond-plated nonslip flooring, one hand holding on to a grab-rail bolted into the ceiling. The door and window-breaching equipment rattled in their wall compartments. Coop stood beside her, Darby knowing he wanted to talk her out of this. He said nothing, though, knowing it was pointless. She had already made up her mind.

The floor thundering beneath her feet and the engine vibrating against her ears, Darby retreated inside her head and went through the script she had quickly rehearsed with Grove. She conjured up various scenarios she might encounter with the gunman, went over her responses and reminded herself to watch her body language. This wasn't a confrontation. She needed him to think, and keep thinking, she was on his side.

The satellite phone vibrated inside her jacket pocket. *Grove must be calling with an update*, Darby thought.

The caller wasn't Alan Grove. A light and airy female voice said, 'Dr McCormick?'

'Who's this?'

The woman didn't answer. Then another person got on the line: Edward Briggs. She recognized the nasal but affable voice, with its thick Boston accent, right away.

'Dr McCormick? Edward Briggs.'

'Hello, Mr Briggs,' Darby said, her gaze bouncing up at Coop.

Briggs said, 'I'm glad I caught you. How you holding up? You okay?'

'I'm fine. What can I do for you?'

'I'm told you're going back inside the lobby.'

'That's right.'

'I just wanted to call and thank you for doing this. The city owes you a tremendous debt.'

Darby said nothing, trying to figure out the true reason for the man's last-minute call.

'Anything you can tell me about this guy?' Briggs asked. 'What his angle is?'

'Nothing beyond what I told the FBI. Did they brief you?'

'They did. Anything you need – and I mean *anything* – you get on the line to either me or Christine.'

'Christine?'

'My personal assistant. Woman who made the call, she's sitting next to me, helping me out. Thank you, Darby. And good luck.'

And then the former mayor was gone.

Darby pulled the phone away, stared at it.

'What was that about?' Coop asked.

'Damage control.'

City police and state troopers had cleared a direct route from Northeastern to BPD headquarters. They made the drive in nine minutes flat.

It felt like nine seconds. Darby blinked, and then the truck had stopped, the driver looking over his shoulder at her, wondering why she was still standing there.

Coop opened the back door to grey light and cold air. He got out, which confused her; he wasn't accompanying her into the lobby. Then he did something that both surprised and shocked her: he offered her a hand. Coop knew she had never cared for displays of male chivalry; she could open her own damn doors and carry her own luggage, thank you very much. So why was he standing there, waiting for her to take his hand and help her down like she was some delicate creature that might topple?

Then she saw his face and knew why: Coop was afraid this was the last time he was going to see her alive. He wanted a moment alone with her, maybe even a quick display of physical affection to let her know how much he cared for her, but he didn't want to embarrass her or diminish her authority with so many eyes watching. He wanted to touch her in case this was goodbye.

She took his hand and a memory resurfaced, one that seared her: gripping her father's baseball-mitt-sized hand as he lay in a hospital bed in a coma. She squeezed his thick fingers and she dug her nails into his calloused palms, waiting for a return signal, some piece of evidence that he was still inside there, fighting to come home, back to her. He lingered in a biological purgatory for three weeks until her mother made the decision to 'let him go'. Right then, at twelve, she had learned that at any moment, and without any warning, love could turn toxic and exile you inside a colourless landscape of grief and pain that would be with you until you drew your final breath. Right then, at twelve, she refused to ever be that vulnerable again.

Coop squeezed her hand and let his grip linger for just a moment before he let go. 'When you're done, come back out to the street and wave,' he said. 'We'll be watching for you.'

'Okay.'

'Make sure you come back to me in one piece, okay?'

'You got it, Cap.'

Darby began to walk. Her legs felt steady, and she didn't look over her shoulder at Coop. She heard the EOD vehicle turn and then drive back the way it came, to get outside the projected blast radius in case the lobby bombs blew.

All the vehicles on this part of Tremont were gone. She didn't see a single soul but knew there were dozens of eyes watching her through sniper scopes and binoculars; through the TV cameras aimed at her from the hovering news copters.

She took the satellite phone out of her jacket pocket and hit the pre-programmed number.

'Can you hear me?' Darby asked.

'Loud and clear,' Grove replied. 'I have Briggs waiting on the other line.'

'I spoke to him a few minutes ago. He called while I was inside the truck.'

'I know, he asked me to speak to you. Gelfand wanted me to tell you he located an OBGYN willing to go inside the station – a woman from Mass. General. She'll be delivered to your location in about two or three minutes, along with a pair of paramedics. One of them is a member of the bomb squad. He's hoping to get a look at the bomb, provided the gunman allows this group in.'

'I'll see what I can do.'

'Just deliver the phone and I'll take it from there,' Grove said. 'One last thing, and this isn't hype or bullshit: you know what you're doing. Trust your instincts and you'll come out of this just fine.'

Just fine.

She didn't want to die, but the idea of dying didn't frighten her; Darby had come to grips with that business a long time ago. She had been shot and beaten. She had been chased through a nightmarish maze of locked and unlocked doors and shifting rooms while a madman stalked her with an axe, a place buried so deep in the earth that not even God himself could hear her prayers. What terrified her – what made her arms shake and her stomach turn to lead when she stepped inside the lobby – was standing there helpless if the gunman decided to kill an innocent.

It could happen.

Might happen.

Don't let that happen, an inner voice said.

In times of great stress, the voice, she noticed, sounded an awful lot like her father.

Darby drew in a deep breath and held it as she opened the door.

13

+02.07

The first part of the lobby felt eerily quiet. She moved to the raised marble planter, her footsteps announcing her, and looked inside the main lobby. From this angle, she could only see the rear part of the reception desk. She didn't see anyone, heard nothing.

Something caught her attention from her right, the side of the building facing the street. She looked at the wall, the blocked-shaped squares of bevelled glass that would prevent a sniper from being able to see inside the lobby.

Then she saw it, a circuit board with an attached nine-volt battery fixed against one of the blocks of glass by a suction cup: a laser microphone surveillance defeater that would prevent the surveillance techs from trying to listen in on their conversations. *You've thought of everything, haven't you?*

Then came the mechanical voice: 'For your sake I hope you brought Briggs. If not, turn around and leave before I do something I regret.'

She had discussed this with Grove. Time to roll the dice.

'I have him,' she replied, blood pounding in her

ears and her heart leaping high in her chest. 'We're coming in.'

Darby had taken only a few steps when the gunman ordered her to stop.

She was still standing behind the raised planter when the gunman turned the right corner, near the X-ray machine. He had the pregnant woman gripped in a chokehold, using her as a human shield. He had duct-taped her mouth and bound her hands behind her back with plastic zip ties. He had also traded his Glock 40 for a hunting knife with a curved blade, the tip pressed against the thin skin below the woman's ear, near her jugular. One swift cut and she'd bleed out in less than two minutes. The baby, deprived of blood, would slowly suffocate in the womb.

The gunman, still wearing the balaclava and the voice-altering device, stood, with his hostage, a few feet behind the body scanner. She wore a new piece of clothing – a bright red fleece scarf tied in a casual knot around her neck – and Darby noticed the coat had been buttoned. The woman's eyes were puffy and wet, the strips of tape across her mouth shiny with tears and snot. Darby could hear the woman slurping saliva and sucking air behind the tape.

'It will be okay, Laura,' Darby said. 'We have doctors standing by who will help –'

'You lied to me,' the gunman said, again speaking through the voice modulator, in the same deep and rumbling robotic monotone

'I have Briggs right here.' Darby held up the satellite

phone. *Don't look at Laura, keep your focus on him*, an inner voice urged. 'He's in upstate Vermont with his family, skiing. We're making arrangements to bring him to Boston as we speak. Until he arrives –'

'Remove the battery from the phone.'

'He's agreed to speak to you and he will –'

'Agreed? He's *agreed*?' The mechanical voice shrill at the end, distorted, and the woman flinched and screamed from behind the tape.

Calm. Stay calm. 'Poor choice of words on my part,' Darby said. 'I've never been in a situation like this.'

'Remove the battery or I'll slit her throat.'

Darby turned the phone over in her hands and found the battery compartment. 'Briggs wants to speak with you – and he will, for as long as it takes, until he arrives here,' she said as she went to work. 'Vermont is getting hit with a major nor'easter – the same one that's going to hit us later this evening. All they're asking for is some additional time.'

'Drop the phone and take off your clothes.'

'Why?'

'Because it's what I want.'

Darby hesitated.

The tip of the knife pierced the woman's neck, her cry muffled behind the tape. Darby saw blood and her hands flew to her jacket.

After she kicked off her boots, she slid out of her jeans and then unbuttoned her shirt and dropped it to the floor. She straightened, dressed in her white tube socks and matching white Hanes bra and underwear.

'Take off everything,' he said.

She did, without hesitation or complaint, saving the watch for last and noting the time until the first bomb went off: fifty-one minutes.

'Now take your clothes and the phone and throw everything out of the front door. Then come through the body scanner.'

When she passed through the scanner, she didn't try to cover herself. She stood tall and faced him, the marble floor cold and gritty beneath the soles of her feet, her skin prickling in the cooling air, her nipples involuntarily hardening.

The gunman's gaze flicked across her body – not in a sexual way, she noticed, but cold and clinical. *He's checking me for listening devices, possibly a concealed weapon*, she thought. He had traded the knife for the TEC-9. He had also removed his overcoat. His suit jacket was unbuttoned, and she could see the shoulder strap for the suicide vest.

'That's an interesting tattoo you have on the side of your chest. It looks like a surgical suture.'

It was. The tattoo was eight inches long and subtle, at least in her opinion, and ran along her ribcage and ended just under her breast. The blue, red and black ink covered a scar left by a man who had tried to kill her inside a dungeon of horrors – the same man who was responsible for the faint hairline scar along her cheek.

She had had the tattoo done last year, at a place in Las Vegas. She gave the artist strict instructions. The black sutures and the tiny initials next to it belonged to the name of the killer. The red sutures and the tiny numbers next to it belonged to the number of victims he had claimed. Darby had found that transforming the scar into a permanent work of art – a reminder of the things she had endured – had acted as some sort of talisman that helped keep away the ghosts of the victims who had often visited her in her sleep.

'Do you feel self-conscious?' the gunman asked.

'About the tattoo?'

'Standing before me naked?'

'Mostly I feel cold,' Darby said.

'You're not afraid of me, are you?'

Darby said nothing.

'Tell me the truth,' he said.

'No. I'm not afraid of you.'

'I could kill you right now.'

'You could.'

'I could also make you get down on your knees, maybe bend you over the reception counter and have my way with you.'

I'd like to see you try, Darby said to herself, looking the man over, trying to see where the detonator for the vest was, if it was within reach.

'Would you bend over to save the life of one of these strangers?'

Darby said nothing.

'I wonder how far you're willing to go,' the gunman said. 'Maybe it's time to find out. Turn around, please.'

Darby didn't move. Said nothing.

'I want to get a good, solid look at you,' he said. 'Now turn around.'

She did, reluctantly, watching him over her shoulder.

'Satisfied?'

'Extremely,' he replied. 'I thought you might be wired. That's why I made you disrobe.'

'I'm not wired.'

'When you came in, I saw a pen sticking out of your front jacket pocket. That wasn't there earlier.'

Darby felt a rush of freezing dread.

'They make all sorts of secret gadgets these days,' he said. 'Did you know they make microphones, even pin-hole video cameras, that can be hidden inside the support wire of a bra?'

'I do now.'

'I warned you not to come back here without Briggs and yet here you are, standing before me, naked and alone. What am I supposed to do?'

'They made me come back in here, to talk to you.'

'You said you wanted to help me.'

'I do – and I *will*. But you've put me in a difficult position. I'm –'

'*No.*' The word echoed and then died inside the cold marble lobby. '*I* didn't put you in this position; *you* offered, remember? No one asked you to step forward this morning, you did that all on your own. I admire your courage, but you're a fool risking your life for these people. They don't care about you. They don't serve us and they place no value on the truth. They're moral and spiritual cowards.'

'Including Briggs?'

The gunman didn't answer. The pregnant woman sobbed, inconsolable.

'Turn to your right and you'll see my overcoat resting on the conveyor belt,' he said. 'Take it. Please. I don't want you to be cold.'

'Thank you.'

'Don't misinterpret my manners for hospitality or absolution. I'm still deciding on whether or not to kill you.'

14

+02.11

The gunman couldn't kill her now – later, possibly, when he no longer had any use for her, but not now. Darby was sure his threat was nothing more than an attempt to keep her afraid. People tended to listen intently and obey without questioning when their life was threatened.

He may not kill you right now, but he may decide to hurt you, an inner voice added.

The overcoat was roomy and warm and smelled like cigars and, she was sure, Old Spice aftershave. It was like wearing one of her father's old coats. She still had one in storage, a down vest he seemed to live in during the fall and winter months, even when he was inside the house; but the cigar and cologne smells had long since faded.

The gunman was staring curiously at her. 'Go behind the reception desk and bring a chair here so you can sit. You might as well be comfortable.'

Darby didn't want to sit. She did, however, want to check out the phone situation.

Access to the reception area was by a swinging counter hatch in the back. As she approached, she saw the other two hostages sitting on the floor with their legs out in front of them and their backs propped up against the lobby wall. They had been bound and gagged like the pregnant woman. Unlike the pregnant woman, tape covered their eyes, and their ankles were secured together by multiple plastic ties.

Darby moved behind the desk. It was exactly as she had feared: the gunman had cut the lines to each of five phones. Without the cords, the phones couldn't be reverse-engineered to listen into the lobby.

She pushed a rolling desk chair across the tiled floor, manoeuvering it around the coffee spills and other detritus.

'Who has been put in charge of my party?' the gunman asked.

'The FBI.'

'And the name of the ringleader?'

'Howard Gelfand. He's –'

'The SAC for the Boston field office.'

'You know him?'

'Just what I read in the papers. What about Peter Donnelly? Was he at the Mobile Command Post?'

Again Darby considered the possibility the gunman was or had been law enforcement. He knew about the Mobile Command Post, and he had used the term 'SAC,' cop speak for 'Special Agent in Charge.'

'Donnelly was there,' she said.

'And what did Boston's newest police commissioner have to say?'

'Not much.'

'Ever the stoic.'

'How do you know him?'

'Let me save you some time: I'm not a law enforcement officer. Never was.'

'Then what are you?'

'Free,' the gunman said. He motioned to the chair. 'Sit. Please.'

'I brought the chair for Laura,' Darby said, nodding to the pregnant woman. 'She needs to get off her feet and rest.'

'If I wanted her to sit, I would have provided her with a chair.'

'Her water could break. She could go into labour.'

The man's cold blue eyes seemed to glow around the balaclava.

'I have an OBGYN on standby,' Darby said. 'Let them come in and take a look at Laura and her baby, make sure –'

'Whatever happens to her and her baby is in God's hands.'

'Do you believe in God?'

'What I believe doesn't matter. What I know for certain is something else entirely.' His gaze narrowed into slits. 'Don't waste time trying to appeal to my spiritual life; I no longer have one. Bring the chair closer and then step away.'

After he had helped the woman into the chair, he rested the TEC-9 on her shoulder and pointed the barrel so it was aimed at her stomach.

'Do you have children?' he asked Darby.

'No.'

'Why not?'

'Never had the urge.'

'Married?'

'No.'

'Same sex partner?'

'Nope. You?'

The gunman didn't reply, but she saw his face flex underneath the skintight balaclava, as though he were smiling.

'Let the paramedics examine Laura,' Darby said. 'Please.'

'What happened to your father? You didn't tell me how he died.'

The sudden shift in conversation threw her for a moment.

'If I tell you, will you let the paramedics in here?'

'I'll consider it,' the gunman said.

'He was shot.'

'Did he die on the way to the hospital?'

'No. They rushed him into surgery and stopped the bleeding. But he had already lost too much blood and went into a coma. Belham Union Hospital could only do so much, so they transferred him to Boston, to Mass. General.'

'And then he died.'

'No. He . . . '

'What?'

'He lingered,' Darby said, and saw her father's enormous frame, all six-foot-five-inches of him, lying in a bed and covered in a white sheet, his jaw hanging open to make room for the machine to help him breathe; the room filled with mechanical bleats and beeps.

After the shooting, Darby had refused to go back to school. She sat by her father's bed and spoke to him, and when she ran out of things to say she read to him Homer's *The Iliad* and *The Odyssey*, his two favourite books. When her mother insisted she go back to school, Darby took the bus and then the T into Boston so she could be with him.

'He was brain-dead,' Darby said. 'The doctors told my mother he would never wake up, so, after a couple of weeks, she decided to let him go. To disconnect him from life support.'

'Where you there during his last moments?'

Darby nodded. She had insisted, against her mother's wishes.

'How old were you?'

'Thirteen.'

'I'm sorry for your loss.'

'Thank you.' She paused for a moment, as a display to show that she appreciated his words. 'Now, about the paramedics –'

'No,' the gunman said, tightening his grip on the knife. 'I asked you to bring Mr Briggs here and you didn't,' the gunman said. 'I told you what would happen if you came back here without him.'

15

+02.14

'You strike me as a reasonable and intelligent man.' Darby let the words hang in the air before she continued. 'Someone as reasonable and intelligent as yourself would know that there are things beyond anyone's control. Things like the weather. Briggs is in the northern part of Vermont, and right now a nor'easter is pounding the state. That same storm is already moving through New Hampshire and making its way here.'

The gunman did not answer.

Darby spoke into the silence. 'If you really want Briggs to come in here, then you've got to show them you're a reasonable man. If you allow that bomb to –'

'How do you know Mayor Briggs is in Vermont?'

'He's skiing there with his family.'

'But how do you know?'

'We located him. The Vermont state police are on their way to the ski lodge. They're going to bring him here.'

'A long drive – especially in this weather.'

It was maddening to have to listen to him speak in that robotic monotone. She was denied vocal inflections and tone, the nuances of emotion; she had no idea if he were simply stating a fact or mocking her.

'It is a long drive,' Darby said. 'Which is why the Vermont staties are going to drive him to a helicopter pad on the Mass. border and fly him here.'

'Provided they can get ahead of the storm.'

'Yes.'

'Odd that he picked this weekend to take the wife and kiddies skiing, don't you think?'

'Not if you like to ski. Briggs offered to talk to you on the phone, for as long as you want, and you –'

'I didn't ask to talk to him on the phone, I want to talk to him here, in person.'

'Then maybe you shouldn't have picked a day when you knew he wouldn't be at home. Or was that part of your plan?'

The gunman said nothing.

'If Briggs were at his Brookline home, then he would be here right now,' Darby said. 'But he's in Vermont. The FBI found and located him, and they're moving mountains to bring him here to meet you.'

'And if he decides not to come?'

'I'll make him.'

'Brave talk from a brave woman. But that's all it is: talk.'

'I can turn up the heat so he can't squirm away.'

The gunman tilted his head to the side, his piercing blue eyes with their thick lashes narrowing in thought. Curiosity.

She didn't provide the details.

Made him ask.

'How?'

'By giving me some insight into what your grievance is,' Darby said. 'Clearly he wronged you in some way. If you tell me what happened, I can help you make sure he's held accountable.'

'You've already lied to me.'

'When?'

'That pen stuck in your jacket pocket. It was a recording device, wasn't it?'

Darby went with the truth. 'It was.'

'Yes. I thought so.'

'They made me wear it.'

'We always have choices, don't we?'

'We do. And I chose to help you. But you need to work with me.' Darby paused, waited for him to speak. He didn't, and then she said, 'I'm telling you right now, if you allow that bomb to go off, you'll never get your face-to-face with Briggs.'

'He won't come, no matter how many people die today. Mark my words.'

'I don't believe that.'

'You don't know him.'

'And you do?'

'The man is a skilled liar. Ask him about Levine and see what he says. I bet he denies it.'

'Who's Levine?'

The gunman didn't answer.

'If you're so certain Briggs wouldn't come,' Darby said, 'then why hijack a police station?'

'Anything worthwhile is ultimately achieved through violence. History, Doctor, only remembers blood. You and I would still be under British rule if it weren't for a group of brave rebels who demanded a better way of life. If what you've shared about former mayor Briggs is, in fact, true –'

'It is.'

'Then I'm willing to be reasonable.'

'I'm glad to hear you say that.'

'Don't be so sure,' the gunman said. 'What's about to happen next is entirely your fault.'

16

+02.17

'The bomb or a hostage,' the gunman said. 'Choose one.'

Darby straightened, shivering beneath the coat.

'You have thirty seconds to decide.'

'Give me both,' she said. 'Show them that you're –'

'Twenty-six seconds.'

'If you want the truth to get out, I'm your best and only shot.'

'Twenty-three seconds.'

'Go through with this and I won't help you.'

'Twenty-one seconds.'

Darby wanted to lunge. She wanted to grab him and snap his neck. She wanted to leave.

Then leave, a voice said.

'Nineteen seconds.'

She couldn't leave. It would show weakness.

'They'll kill you,' she said.

'I'm already dead – and you will be, too, if you don't make a decision. Seventeen seconds.'

He can't disarm the bomb from in here, she thought. Every radio and cell signal in the area was being jammed, and he had cut all the phone lines in the lobby. Or was he going to give her the location of the bomb and the means to disarm it?

Another voice piped in: *What if it's a trap?*

'Fourteen seconds.'

Think.

The gunman's true agenda lay with the Boston Police. She suspected his plan for revenge or whatever this was about didn't entail killing a bunch of innocents with a bomb. If that was true – and she believed it was –

'Eleven seconds.'

– was it possible that the first bomb was designed not to kill but demonstrate his power and reach, to show that his demands were to be taken seriously? What if he had set the first bomb someplace where no one would be killed or hurt? What if the first bomb was nothing more than a warning shot across the bows?

'Six seconds.'

There was no way the gunman would have left Briggs's whereabouts to chance. Darby felt sure the man knew Briggs wouldn't be at home today, maybe even knew that the former mayor was skiing with his family in upstate Vermont – and would be delayed there if not outright trapped by the storm. If that was true, it meant the gunman *wanted* the first bomb to go off. It meant it was part of his overall plan.

'Time,' the gunman said. 'What's your decision?'

The bomb. I'm willing to bet you put it someplace that, when it goes off, it won't hurt anyone. But if I'm wrong, I won't be able to live with the knowledge that innocent people died or were maimed.

'I want the bomb,' Darby said. 'And the hostages.'

The gunman said nothing.

Removed the TEC-9 from the woman's shoulder –

'I'll take a hostage,' Darby said.

The gunman aimed the weapon at her face, his arm steady. All he had to do now was squeeze the trigger.

You won't feel a thing, a voice added.

That was probably true. What she felt right now was numb. Physically and emotionally numb.

Coop's words last year at the Colorado airport bar came back to her: *I love you, but you've got a death wish.*

The gunman tossed the knife on the floor.

'Take the black woman and leave,' he said. 'Drop the knife when you're finished.'

Darby picked up the knife. The gunman followed her as she moved to the rear corner of the lobby, wheeling the pregnant woman with him. The woman had gone silent and still, and stared blankly into space. She was in shock.

The gunman watched Darby as she cut the plastic cuffs binding the black woman's ankles and wrists. All it took was three quick snips. Cutting through the layers of duct tape covering the woman's eyes was more difficult.

'Come in here again without Briggs and the only way you'll leave here is in a body bag,' he said. 'Do you understand?'

Darby nodded.

'Say it,' he said.

'I understand.'

'Don't forget her cane. And leave my coat.'

Cold and naked, she escorted the black woman across the lobby. She had reached the metal detector when he called for her.

'Darby.'

She turned to him.

'The FBI, the press,' he said. 'They'll need to call me something besides "the gunman".'

'What do you want to be called?'

'Call me Big Red. After your father.'

17

+02.22

Darby had to ask the woman three times to go outside and retrieve her clothes. When she finally did, the woman moved slowly, and she couldn't stop blinking, like a flash bulb had gone off in front of her eyes. She seemed confused and her arms shook and not once did she try to pull at the tape covering her mouth.

Darby dressed quickly. She saved the watch for last but refused to check the time. She stuffed it in her pocket, saddled with the bitter knowledge that she had failed, that she was powerless to stop what was happening, what was about to happen.

Outside, in the roar of cold wind and rotors from the copters watching and recording, as she collected the pieces of the satellite phone, the memory of her last day with her father returned, and she saw herself at twelve, squeezing her father's hand and digging her nails into his skin, drawing blood. It felt warm and sticky, a good sign – an excellent sign; it meant he was alive. It meant his heart was still pumping, and once his brain realized the machine was no longer pumping air into him, his brain would tell his body to go to work, to breathe on its own.

And he would, she was sure of it. Big Red was strong; his lungs would restart, and he would begin to breathe on his own, without the machines, and then soon – maybe not today or tomorrow or the end of the week, but *soon* – he would heal and then wake up, and when he did, she would be sitting right here beside his bed, holding his hand and smiling when his eyes fluttered open. There was still so much she needed from him. So much she needed to know. He knew that and wouldn't let her down. He wouldn't leave her alone.

She didn't realize she was crying until she wiped at her face, felt the tears stinging on her cheeks.

Darby shook her head and slid her arm around the woman, feeling the frail bones beneath the heavy jacket, and escorted her towards Tremont, where the EOD vehicle was already waiting for them. Darby tried to pick up the pace but the woman was having trouble standing and walking.

The EOD's rear doors flew open, and she saw Coop rush out to help.

There were no chairs in the back of the vehicle, so Darby helped the woman to the floor and sat beside her. Coop shut the doors and the woman jumped as though a shotgun had gone off.

The engine was loud and the SWAT officer riding in the passenger seat kept shouting into his phone. Darby had to yell over the noise. 'You're safe,' she said, rubbing the woman's back. 'It's over.'

The woman was staring blankly at a gun cabinet

mounted against the wall. She still hadn't touched the tape. Darby asked for a pair of gloves and a bag.

As she began to work the tape from around the woman's mouth, about to ask if she had heard anything about the bomb or its location, the hostage started rocking back and forth, mewing. Then the tears came and when she started to sob into her hands, some of the knuckles already twisted from arthritis, Darby placed the duct tape in the evidence bag Coop had given her and then held the woman against her chest.

Coop stood over them, gripping the side railing as the vehicle bucked and swayed. She knew the question he wanted to ask, and shook her head.

The hope vanished from his eyes. He sucked in air through his nose and, defeated, glanced at his watch before dialling a number. Darby, not knowing what to do with her hands and needing something to do, put the satellite phone back together.

Her name was Anita Barnes and she was fifty-nine years old and lived alone on the top floor of a triple-decker she owned in Dorchester. That was all the information Darby got before the woman started hyperventilating.

Barnes sucked deeply from an oxygen mask. It was strapped across her mouth and nose by a strong elastic band, but she held on to it with both hands as though the mask might fall off and disappear.

Darby sat with her on the gurney in the back of an ambulance, one of six parked at the command centre. She had asked the EMTs and agents to give them a moment. The woman was frightened, seemed to shrink under their heated questions and desperate stares. Barnes needed some time to collect herself.

Darby couldn't collect herself, and she found it difficult to sit still. She felt for the woman but wanted information – *now.*

A frightened witness was not a reliable witness. Best to let her calm down.

Commotion outside the ambulance and voices she couldn't quite make out were shouting. Had the bomb gone off? There was nothing she or anyone else could do at this point but wait.

And pray.

Darby had reset her watch during the drive back to the campus. She was staring at it when the woman spoke, her words muffled behind the mask.

Darby turned to her. 'I'm sorry, I didn't catch that.'

Barnes pulled down the mask with a trembling hand.

18

+02.44

The woman licked her lips. Swallowed.

'He was nice about it.'

'Nice,' Darby said.

Anita Barnes nodded. She was a baby-faced woman with soft features and an even softer voice. Darby had to lean close to hear her.

'He kept saying he was sorry, after you left the first time. We couldn't talk back because of the tape he put over our mouths.'

'What else did he say?' Darby asked, fighting the terrible urge to rush through the questioning. Stay calm or Barnes might shut down again.

The woman wiped at her face with the back of her wrist. 'He said he didn't want to hurt us – and wouldn't, as long as we cooperated. He –'

'Sorry to interrupt you, Miss Barnes, but were those his exact words, or yours?'

'His. His exact words. He sounded real sad when he said it.'

'How could you tell?'

The woman looked at Darby for the first time. 'What do you mean?'

'How could you tell he sounded sad when he was speaking to you through that voice modulation device?'

The woman seemed confused by the question. Then her eyes brightened. 'Oh. Oh, I see. He turned that off after you left and spoke to us normally. His voice was all, you know, pinched tight. Husky.'

Interesting, Darby thought. It suggested that the gunman didn't want to harm an innocent – and reinforced her theory about the first bomb being a message and set at a remote location where no one would get hurt or killed.

'He apologized again after he put the tape over our eyes,' Barnes said. 'He didn't speak very much after that point. Everything got real quiet.'

'Did you recognize his voice?'

'No. Why would I?'

'Tell me everything he said and did after I left the lobby the first time. Walk me through it, step-by-step.'

It took the woman a moment to gather her thoughts.

'Well,' Barnes said, 'first he had us all go over to the corner where you found us. He took those plastic things out of his pocket and told the other woman, the one with the white hair –'

'Did she say her name?'

'No. We didn't talk, he told us not to talk. He tied me up with the plastic things and then the pregnant lady and then he tied up the white-haired woman. He asked us if we were comfortable, I remember that . . . then he shut off that voice-thing and apologized again, and when he taped our mouths he thanked us for cooperating.

He apologized again when he put the tape over our eyes.' She swallowed several times, her eyes growing wet. 'That was the worst, not being able to see. I didn't know if he was going to kill us or not.'

'Did you see anything before he taped your eyes?'

'Like what?'

'Did you see him remove anything from his backpack? Did he call anyone?'

'I don't think so. I mean, he might've, but I was busy praying – not just for me but for all of us. But I don't think he was listening.'

'The gunman?'

'No, God. The day String Bean was born, I prayed to Him morning, noon and night. I –'

'String Bean?'

'My grandson,' Barnes said. 'His birth name was Tae Jonah Fallows but we all called him String Bean because he was this skinny weed of a thing, no matter how much he ate. He was that way since the day he was born. That's why I was there at the po-lice this morning, to talk about String Bean's case.'

'What happened to your grandson?'

'God broke His promise to me again, is what happened,' Barnes said heatedly. She seemed abashed at having spoken the words out loud. She took in a deep breath and then swallowed, her voice contrite when she spoke again. 'String Bean was taking his afternoon nap when the neighbourhood gang-bangers decided to have a shootout. I was in the kitchen getting dinner ready when the bullet came through String Bean's bedroom window and hit him in the head. The doctor who did the thing on his body afterwards, the what-chamacallit, the coroner, he told me my baby didn't feel a thing. That was kind of him, lying to give me some comfort, but I know String Bean suffered 'cause he died alone, no one there holding his hand.' She wiped at her face. 'He was four years old.'

'I'm truly sorry for your loss,' Darby said.

'Day I took String Bean in as my own, God warned me to move on up to the third floor where we'd be safe – warned me more than once. My neighbourhood, you hear gunshots so much you get used to them, as crazy as that sounds. Still, it would be safer to be living higher up, and what did I do? I ignored Him. I ignored Him because I was only thinking of myself. I've got really bad knees and type 2 diabetes. I didn't want to do that walk up every day, and my grandson paid the price.'

The back of the ambulance opened and Coop poked his head in, his expression grim. She could tell he wanted to talk to her alone. *He has news about the bomb.*

'Miss Barnes,' Darby said, 'the FBI is going to want to ask you some questions, probably the same ones I did. You could be here awhile. Is there someone you'd like me to call to come here and sit with you?'

'Everyone's in Pine Valley now.'

'Where's that?'

'Cemetery. Ain't no one in my family left.'

'I'm sorry,' Darby said, because she didn't know what else to say. 'What about a friend or a neighbour?'

Barnes thought it over for a moment. 'I should probably call Rosemary, let her know what happened to me,' she said. Coop had a pen and pad out, ready to write.

'What's Rosemary's last name?' he asked.

'Shapiro.'

'The lawyer?'

'Yes, sir. You know her?'

Every cop and federal agent knows her, Darby thought. Rosemary Shapiro had made a career – and a small fortune – suing the city of Boston. Her specialty was civil suits. She represented prisoners who had been wrongly convicted and was the go-to person for the families of victims who had been shot and/or killed by Boston cops.

Coop took over the questioning. 'Why did she want to meet you at the lobby?'

'She said she had some information on the people who killed String Bean and wanted to talk to me about it this morning at eight thirty, at the police headquarters,' Barnes replied.

That doesn't make any sense, Darby thought. Shapiro wouldn't meet with a client inside the lobby of a police station.

'Told me to go to the reception desk and ask for her,' Barnes said.

'She told you this?' Coop asked.

'That's what her assistant told me last night.'

'Her name?'

'Not a she, a *he*. It was hard to understand him, though. He kept coughing and his voice was really hoarse. He kept apologizing, said he was getting over a bad cold and had laryngitis.'

'He tell you his name?'

'No.'

'You're sure?'

Barnes nodded emphatically. 'All he said was that he was Miss Shapiro's assistant.'

'Tell me about your conversation.'

'It was real short, and like I just said I had to ask him to repeat himself a few times. He said Miss Shapiro had some information on String Bean and asked if I could meet her in the lobby at po-lice headquarters on Tremont. I said yes, of course, and he told me to be there at eight thirty.'

Darby and Coop exchanged a look. Without speaking, he ducked back outside and shut the door.

The woman's expression turned quizzical. 'Something wrong?'

Not wrong, just odd, Darby thought. She shook her head. 'I'll call Miss Shapiro, tell her you're here.'

'Her number's in my handbag. I left it back there, at the station. My handbag.'

'We'll find her number. Let's get the EMTs back in, make sure your blood sugar and pressure are doing okay.'

'I'm going to say a prayer for you, keep you safe.'

'Thank you, Miss Barnes.'

'You be careful around that man in the lobby.'

Something in the woman's tone caught Darby's attention. 'What makes you say that, Miss Barnes?'

'I've lived a long time, seen all sorts of misery – my own and others. There's something wrong in that man's eyes. Way he was looking at you back there . . . There was this man I'd seen once in our neighbourhood late at night, and he was standing there on the sidewalk with the rest of us watching one of the houses that caught fire, just kept staring and staring. That man in the po-lice lobby got those exact same eyes. People like him don't care, they just love watching things burn.'

19

+02.56

When Darby stepped out of the ambulance, she saw Coop standing several feet away in the big parking lot. His back was to her, and he was still on the phone, a hand pressed against his ear.

She ducked around the side of the vehicle and took out her satellite phone and dialled the pre-programmed number for Grove.

'I need you to connect me to Briggs.'

'You got it.'

'*Wait.* Is this line being recorded?'

'It is.'

Good, Darby thought.

'I won't be on the line with you, but I'll be able to hear everything,' Grove said.

'That's fine.'

A brief silence followed on the other end of the line. Darby glanced around the back corner of the ambulance and saw Coop. He was still on the phone.

Then she heard Briggs's deep voice burst across her receiver: 'Dr McCormick?'

'I'm here,' Darby said.

A sigh exploded against her ear.

'Thank God you're okay, I was worried,' Briggs said. 'How did it go?'

'Good, I think. Made some headway. The hostages are still alive.'

'Excellent. What's our next step?'

'Do you know a woman named Anita Barnes? Had a grandson named Tae Jonah Fallow, everyone called him String Bean?'

'No. Why?'

'Anita Barnes was one of the hostages. Her grandson was killed by a stray bullet.'

'What does that have to do with the gunman?'

'What about someone named Levine?'

'Levine? I don't think so. Why are you asking me these questions?'

'The gunman told me he knows you.'

Silence greeted her on the other end of the line.

'You're sure you don't know anyone named Levine?' Darby asked. 'The gunman seems to believe you do.'

'The name doesn't ring a bell. Do you have any information on this person? Man or woman? Is Levine his or her last name or first?'

'I don't know. I was hoping you would tell me.'

'Let me look into it – Levine and Anita Barnes, her grandson, see what I can find. My memory isn't what it used to be. I'll be in touch shortly.'

'One last thing,' Darby said. She knew she was being recorded, didn't care. 'If I find out you're lying to me, I will jam my foot so far up your ass you'll choke to death. I'll make it my personal mission. Do we have an understanding?'

'We do. We're both after the same things, doctor. Again, thank you for what you're doing for the city. You're a brave woman. You always were.'

And then Briggs hung up.

Darby joined Coop, who was still on the phone. They fell into step together, heading for the MCP on the opposite side of the parking lot, which was packed with every single conceivable emergency and disaster recovery vehicle, lights flashing everywhere.

Her head felt stuffed from her conversations with Briggs, Anita Barnes and the gunman; and the adrenaline dump and lack of food had left her feeling hollow and jittery and weak. Her morning hangover had switched over to a pounding headache and, coming up on its heels, a wave of nausea. Breathing wouldn't help; she needed food and water – lots of water – and aspirin, preferably Excedrin.

'That was Shapiro's office,' Coop said. He stuffed the phone back in his jacket pocket as they darted around a crowd of anxious firefighters waiting for the call about the bomb. 'Her secretary, personal assistant, whatever, is a woman. Said Shapiro didn't have anything on the books with Anita Barnes – hadn't heard the name before. The name isn't even in her database.'

'What about Shapiro, you talk to her?'

'She called in sick this morning with the flu. Secretary can't give out the phone number to anyone – Shapiro's orders – so she said Shapiro will call me back. You thinking what I'm thinking?'

'That the gunman called Barnes last night and asked her to be in the lobby this morning? Yeah.'

'I don't think it's a coincidence, the woman being there.'

'Neither do I. First, we need to rule her out as an accomplice.' Darby didn't believe it, but they still needed to exclude her. 'She's from Dorchester. Her grandson's name is Tae Jonah Fallows. Kid got hit by a stray bullet when he was taking a nap in his bedroom.'

'Cop shooting?'

'No. Gang-thing, I think.'

'How old?'

'Four.'

'Jesus.'

'I know. Barnes said the killer or killers were never caught or identified.'

'What's this business about the gunman wanting to be called Big Red?' Coop asked.

'Classic misdirection,' Darby said. 'He doesn't want me thinking about or focusing on him, so he throws me off with all these questions about my father, what happened to him.'

'Did he?'

'Did he what?'

'Throw you off.'

'You think my head's not in the game?'

They had reached the door for the MCP.

'Of course not,' Coop said.

Darby saw that this was true.

'I'm just checking in, see how you're doing with it,' Coop said. 'Coming back here and now talking about your old man – it's okay if you're feeling a bit rattled.'

'Anything on the bomb?'

'Don't know anything yet, but I have some news on the pen Grove gave you. He didn't get a single picture or video or audio recording. The jamming unit the gunman's using must be covering radio frequencies.'

'What about the FBIRD?'

'Nothing.'

'That's not possible. There's no commercial jamming equipment that can –' Darby cut herself off, already knowing the answer.

'You're right, the commercial stuff, all of which is illegal, all of which comes from overseas, doesn't contain any of the frequencies the Bureau uses on their devices. But there *is* military-grade equipment out there that can scramble *all* frequencies. Our guy must have somehow got his hands on one. I love dealing with psychopaths who are smart.'

'He's not a psychopath.'

'Then what is he?'

'Determined.'

Fire and ambulance sirens pierced the air. Both she and Coop started at the sound, the combined wail of the sirens hammering into her skull like nails. Darby threw open the door, thinking about the gunman, how meticulous he was.

And that makes him dangerous as hell.

20

+03.04

The MCP had a tiny galley right off the main door. Darby ducked inside and squeezed her way past another agent who was pouring coffee and grabbed a banana from a fruit plate. As she wolfed it down, she opened the refrigerator and grabbed an ice-cold can of Coke and a pre-made sandwich wrapped in plastic.

The trailer walls were insulated and soundproofed, but she could still hear the sirens. Everyone inside could. As she trailed Coop down the narrow hall, she felt the ground shaking under her boots as her imagination began to conjure up all the grisly scenarios that happened in the aftermath of an explosion: people with missing limbs, people trapped underneath rubble and screaming for help, some fighting for air, everyone bleeding and in pain. Frightened.

She hoped to God her initial theory was correct, that the gunman – *Call me Big Red. After your father* – had chosen a 'soft target' for the site of his first bomb, to display his power: someplace where people wouldn't get hurt.

Darby stepped into the middle of the cramped control

area and saw Howie Gelfand standing in the centre, a phone pressed to his ear, his face looking bloodless underneath the canister lights. The flat screen on the wall was playing shaky camera footage recorded by the Channel 5 Sky Copter. Darby saw an aerial shot of herself throwing her clothes out the front door of the station.

Gelfand put his hand on the receiver, looked to Darby and Coop. 'Reports are flooding in from Quincy about an explosion.'

Darby felt her stomach tighten, then sink. Gelfand's gaze darted to the man seated to his right, a federal agent with a blond crew cut who looked like he had just stepped out of a Marine recruitment poster. 'Jeff, show 'em what we got.'

Jeff tapped at his keyboard. Darby moved behind him and, looking over his shoulder at the computer screen, saw BPD camera footage of the area just outside the station's front doors. A Metro City taxi with a dented rear bumper pulled up against the kerb. She couldn't see the driver or who was sitting in the back.

Three seconds passed, and when a back door opened – the one behind the driver – the footage turned fuzzy.

Jeff froze the frame. Advanced the footage slightly. Paused.

'Here you can see he's walking with his head down, and he's wearing a black hat,' Jeff said. 'This is probably the best shot we have of the guy.' He resumed the normal playing. The screen practically turned white. 'When he enters the lobby . . . here, the interference for the outside cameras begins to settle down and then slowly turns back to normal eight to ten seconds later.'

Coop said, 'So he turned on the jamming device before he got out of the taxi.'

On the screen, the static abated and then disappeared. The taxi was trying to pull away from the kerb, the driver waiting for someone to let him into the heavy morning traffic. When it finally pulled away, Darby caught a flash of the rear licence plate.

Coop said, 'Can you enhance that?'

Gelfand answered the question. 'Already did,' he said, and handed Coop a folded piece of paper. 'Track down the driver. Doc, you're with me.'

Darby took a large bite of her sandwich, chicken salad loaded with too much mayo on cold and soggy bread, and had drained half the can of Coke by the time Gelfand closed the door to the conference room. He left the lights off, and he didn't sit.

'Where's Donnelly?' Darby asked.

'Fielding phone calls from the mayor and governor. I don't have a hard address for the bomb yet.' He rubbed his forehead for a moment, then studied his fingers. 'Looks like this guy wasn't bluffing.'

'He's the real deal.'

Gelfand's gaze jumped up.

'He's intelligent and well organized,' Darby said. 'And he's prepared to see this thing through to the very end.'

'You think he's suicidal?'

'I think he's willing – and prepared – to die for his cause, but that's not the same thing as being suicidal. Coop tell you about the FBIRD?'

'Yeah, he did. That, and this shit about this lunatic deciding he wants to be called your old man's name. What's that about?'

Darby told him, then said, 'You reset your watch?'

'Unfortunately, yes. But let's check times to see that we're both properly synched.'

'Howie, that bomb was going to go off no matter what we did.' Darby wondered who she was trying to convince – herself or Gelfand. 'He needed it to go off. That first target, whatever it is, is key to his agenda.'

Gelfand's phone buzzed. He ignored it. 'I realize that,' he said. 'But it doesn't make it any easier to swallow.'

'Any abandoned buildings in that neighbourhood? A location that isn't near any homes?'

'I don't know. Why?'

'I think the first bomb was designed to serve as a warning – a display of his power. He's using the bombs to ensure Briggs's cooperation, force him into a face-to-face in the lobby.'

'Then he's one stupid son of a bitch because there's no way Briggs is going to walk in there, not after what just happened.'

'And what if Briggs agrees to go in? Will you let him?'

'He'll die if he goes in there.'

'His senate bid will die if he doesn't.'

'Which is why we're going to keep the gunman's request under wraps for the time being.'

Of course, Darby thought. 'The gunman isn't going to kill Briggs.'

'You suddenly develop psychic powers I don't know about?'

'The fact that he wants the interview to run on live TV suggests he wants to embarrass Briggs on a national platform, get some confession out of him. What better way to do it than on live TV? I'll tell you something else about him. The gunman is playing us.'

'That shit about the taxi pulling right in front of the station.'

Darby nodded. 'He knew the cameras were there, recording him. He wanted us to see him, find the plate so we can start the process of tracking him down.'

'You're the one with a PhD in nut-jobs. What do you think?'

'He's already put external pressure on Briggs by telling us he'll give us the hostages and disarm the remaining bombs, however many of them there are, if Briggs agrees to the live interview. Now he's going to apply *internal* pressure. Supply us with clues as to what his agenda is by dropping breadcrumbs – tracking down the taxi and this stuff with Anita Barnes.'

Darby filled him in on her conversation with Barnes. Saw his eyes widen when she mentioned Rosemary Shapiro.

'What the hell does Shapiro have to do with this?' Gelfand asked.

'She's the go-to lawyer for suing the BPD. How much has she won in judgements?'

'Too much to count.'

'I'm sure she's gone head-to-head with Briggs on more than one occasion. We should bring her in – the gunman wants us to bring her in, ask questions. What can you tell me about Briggs?'

'I don't know about any skeletons in his closet, if that's what you're asking.'

'No scandals?'

'Nothing comes to mind.'

'Would you tell me if you knew anything?'

Gelfand straightened a little, looking like he was going to hurl an insult her way. Then he chuckled.

'Doc, I'm gonna give you a free tip,' he said slyly. 'You want to tickle a guy's balls first, you know, create a rapport, get him all relaxed before you give 'em a squeeze.'

'Clock's ticking, so foreplay's off the table.' Darby took another bite of her sandwich.

'Day Briggs was inaugurated, Boston had one of the highest homicide rates in the country. Every good politician is interested in statistics, so he was heavily involved in homicide cases, applying pressure to the police commissioners and other department heads to increase their clearance rates and improve the safety in high-crime areas like Roxbury, Dorchester and Mattapan. And he achieved that. Did he bust heads along the way? Goes without saying. That's life, the cost of business. But if you're asking me about some scandal or incident, I don't have anything to tell you – you probably had more interactions with him than I did, back when you were still in the BPD's good graces.'

'Mainly I avoided him.'

'I can't wait to hear this.'

'Nothing much to tell, other than he's the textbook definition of someone who suffers from narcissistic personality disorder: arrogant, grandiose and believes the world centres around him.'

'You two sound like a match made in heaven. I'm surprised it wasn't love at first sight.'

'He also lacks empathy for others and displays psychopathy and Machiavellian tendencies.'

'In other words, the perfect politician.'

'The mentally ill always rise to the top spots. How did you rise to the top, Howie?'

'Results and people skills,' he said. 'You get results, but you lack people skills. You've got the personality and warmth and subtlety of a wrecking ball.'

'Thank you. Seriously, I mean it.' Darby ate the last of her sandwich.

Gelfand, grinning, gave her the finger as his phone rang again. This time he answered it.

As he listened to the person on the other end of the line, he picked up a remote and fumbled with the buttons. The wall-mounted TV turned on, and then he flipped over to Channel 5, where a news copter was showing live aerial footage of a suburban neighbourhood, the banner at the foot of the screen reading: BREAKING NEWS: EXPLOSION IN QUINCY.

The TV had been muted. Gelfand didn't turn up the volume – didn't need to. The images of the house practically torn off its foundation and looking like a molar tooth cracked in half, the damage to the surrounding homes, the emergency personnel – police, fire, paramedics, even some civilians – scrambling through the smoke and the debris lining the lawns and streets told them everything they needed to know.

Gelfand, she saw, was no longer on the phone. His attention was locked on the screen when he said, 'I don't have any solid information yet – who the target was, casualties.'

Darby felt as though her midsection had disappeared. Her theory about the gunman/bomber choosing a soft target for his first IED was wrong.

She swallowed dryly and sucked in a deep breath through her nose.

'There's something else we need to consider, Howie.'

Gelfand tore his eyes away from the destruction. 'What's that?'

'If the gunman didn't call Anita Barnes, someone else did – someone who could be working in tandem with the gunman.'

'That crossed my mind, too,' he said sombrely. 'And you know what? I keep hoping to God I'm wrong.'

21

+03.17

Coop had made quick work tracking down the taxi driver, who had no problem remembering the soon-to-be gunman. The man had tipped generously – twenty bucks on top of a thirty-dollar fare. Federal agents, along with a sketch artist, were on their way to Metro Cab's main office in Allston to interview him.

Darby needed to talk to the man herself and did so while riding shotgun in the Bureau car, a black Ford Explorer with tinted windows. Coop drove, following the lead car, another Explorer that had its lights flashing and sirens wailing to clear a path to Jackman Square in Dorchester, the place where the cabby had picked up the gunman. The EOD vehicle that had delivered her to BPD headquarters followed in the rear. Gelfand wanted the bomb squad in Dorchester in case any suspicious packages or items were found. Like Darby, he wondered if the gunman might be sending them into a trap.

Most witnesses act and speak like they're on their way to a firing squad. Not Michael Friedrich. The sixty-two-year-old cab driver wasn't in the least bit reticent or disturbed by the fact that he had delivered a terrorist to the front steps of the Boston Police station this morning. In fact, he sounded downright excited by his part in the unfolding drama.

'Guy didn't give off a bad vibe, didn't look or act weird, nut'in',' Friedrich said on the other end of the line, then snapped his gums for emphasis. 'He was just standing there alone on the corner of Dumont and Parsons, waiting and looking relaxed even though he's *the* only white face in that neighbourhood. I don't mean any disrespect or to sound, you know, racial or politically incorrect or any of that crap, but that neighbourhood is . . . let's just say a different class of people live there now, okay? I grew up in Dot, and back then, in that neighbourhood I'm talking about? You could walk anywhere you wanted, day or night. You can't do that now, even if you're wearing a bulletproof vest out and about in the daylight, you're still taking your life in your hands, understand what I'm saying?'

Darby knew the Dorchester neighbourhood all too well from her BPD days: alleys full of crack vials and buildings spray-painted with graffiti; homicides that were as predictable and steady as the sunrise; witnesses with bloodshot eyes; and tired and weary black and brown faces who were eager to close the door on the police, or not answer the door at all.

'Describe him to me,' Darby said.

'He looked like a, you know, a regular guy. And he was white, like I said. I don't know how tall he was – average, I guess – and I couldn't tell you if he was thin or fat because he was, you know, all bundled up 'cause it was freezing out this morning.'

'What was he wearing?'

'He had on one of those overcoats that business people wear over their suits. He was also wearing a hoodie underneath it.'

'A grey sweatshirt, right?'

'No, it was black. Definitely black.'

Same as the gunman, Darby thought.

'He had the hood on and tied, you know, underneath his chin. He also had on, like, a ski hat underneath the hood, one of those knit things. That was black, too. Oh, and sunglasses and a scarf. The sunglasses were all black, including the lenses, and the scarf was . . . a dark blue, maybe. I'm not sure.'

With the exception of the sunglasses, the man Friedrich was describing was a dead ringer for the gunman. 'When he got in your cab, did he take off his hat or sunglasses?'

'No,' Friedrich said. 'He stayed all bundled up, even though I had the heat on in back.'

Some cabbies had diarrhea of the mouth; they didn't want to make conversation necessarily, just enjoyed hearing themselves talk. Darby suspected Friedrich was one of those types.

'Did you talk to him?'

'Sure I talked to him,' Friedrich said. 'I mean, he didn't tell me what he was planning to *do*, if that's what you're asking – *and* I didn't get no hint that something, you know, *bad* was about to go down.'

'What did he say?'

'Not much. He couldn't really talk on account of his cold or laryngitis or some shit, I forget.'

Which was pretty much the same thing Anita Barnes had told her about the man who had called her last night pretending to be Rosemary Shapiro's assistant.

'I went through the usual song and dance – "Hey, how are yeah, how's it going." Typical chitchat,' Friedrich said. 'So I asks him about the nor'easter that's coming, asks if he's all stocked up and ready, all that stuff. He didn't speak, just nodded.'

Her thoughts shifted to Briggs, the focus of the gunman's agenda. Was it possible the gunman knew Briggs would be in Vermont today?

'After that he kinda lapsed into silence,' Friedrich said. 'We were, like, six blocks or so away from the station – I could see it from the window – and we're sitting in dead stop rush hour traffic when I says to him, "You wanna get out and walk? It's not that far." Guy shakes his head. Couple of minutes pass and then I ask him again because, truth be told, I *wanted* him to get out 'cause there ain't no good fares out that way, and I didn't want to be stuck in that traffic trying to get back into the city. If I got him out, I could've turned around and headed on over to South Station, you can always pick up someone there coming off the train. But it was all good 'cause he tipped me real nice, a double saw-buck.'

'The twenty he gave you, you wouldn't happen to –'

'Yeah, I got it right here in my envelope. He didn't

wear gloves when he touched it, either, I'll swear to that on a stack of Bibles. Told that to the FBI man I spoke to a few minutes ago, whatshisname, Cooper. Told me to leave it alone, not to touch it.'

'The federal agents on their way to you will need to take your fingerprints for –'

'Comparison prints,' Friedrich said proudly. 'I watch all the *CSI*s and *Law & Order*s so know *all* about fingerprints and handling and securing evidence. Everything's good and safe. Oh, and in case any reporters ask, I live at Sixty-two Alabaster, the old sawmill building in Watertown that was converted into condos.'

'I'm sure Agent Cooper already explained the importance of not sharing any of this information with anyone – and no posting on Twitter, Facebook or any other social media platforms.'

'I sound like an eighteen-year-old girl to you? Like I got to get online and share everything that happens in my life?' Friedrich chuckled. 'Don't you worry, ma'am, my lips are sealed.'

'Thank you, Mr Friedrich. You've been very helpful.'

Darby hung up, knowing that the news was going to get out soon, if it wasn't out already. Michael Friedrich was no doubt the talk of his taxi company right now; someone there had most likely already called or shot an email to his or her spouse or a friend, maybe even posted something on Facebook or Twitter.

Coop took a hard right off the Southeast Expressway, following the lead car as it headed down the ramp for Dorchester Ave. Darby braced herself against the sway and then, as she leaned back in her seat watching the flashing lights, the sirens piercing her skin and flooding her veins, she felt like throwing open the door and running.

Coop cocked his head to her. 'You all right?'

'I feel like Don Quixote tilting at the windmills.'

'You've lost me.'

'This is exactly what he wants.' Darby thought she saw a few snowflakes floating through the air, but she wasn't sure. 'He doesn't want us to sit still and think. He needs to prove to us – and fast – he's not the real monster.'

'Briggs,' Coop said.

Darby shrugged. 'Maybe,' she said. 'I think he's the catalyst to get things rolling. I think our guy has the power to raise the dead.'

'On what?'

'That's what he wants us to find out.'

22

+03.21

Dorchester, in Darby's opinion, had always gotten a bum rap. Boston's largest neighbourhood reminded her a lot of Belham, the city where she'd been born and raised: hard-working middle-class families who, at one time, were predominately Irish and lived in small homes and triple-deckers that were crammed next to each other. Mostly everyone parked in the street, and those people who had a front lawn – always the size of a postage stamp, always protected by a chain-link or picket fence to keep away the dogs and kids – took a lot of pride in keeping it neat and clean, and planted shrubs and plants with flowers that bloomed from early spring until late fall.

Pride was the key word. People took pride in their homes and in their neighbourhoods, their town. You knew your neighbours and everyone looked out for each other. A kid – five years old or fifteen, age didn't matter – could play in the streets or ride their bikes or walk day or night without fear of getting caught in gang crossfire, because gangs and drugs and the homicides that went with them were, more or less, strictly limited to the projects.

Then a crack cocaine epidemic flooded Boston in the early nineties, and everything changed. The neighbourhoods went downhill, as did the schools. People fled, looking for the implied safety of suburbia. Then, before the dawn of the twenty-first century, another terror invaded the city, this one far more powerful than crack cocaine: gentrification. Successful and prosperous gay men had already taken over South Boston and transformed it into a real-estate seller's wet dream. Properties that once upon a time couldn't be given away were now selling for millions of dollars. People with big jobs and even bigger bank accounts devoured neighbourhoods of historic homes and helped pave the way for antique stores and upscale dining and a Starbucks on every corner. Real estate prices skyrocketed, taking property taxes with them, and suddenly the middle-classes and Baby Boomers and retirees could no longer afford their homes and were forced to either move out of the city, where real-estate prices were just as high, or go live in the already less desirable areas with people who were already pissed off and angry at life. Dorchester, like Belham, was now divided into two categories: parts that were very, very good, and parts that were very, very bad.

The business district in Jackman Circle, though, had its own special category: hopeless. The stores here catered to the neighbourhood clientele: cheque-cashing and cash for gold; rent-a-furniture stores advertising no money down; discount liquor stores and cheap Chinese food restaurants and dive day-drunk bars advertising chicken wings and dollar-draught beers specials in bright neon signs that glowed behind windows protected by steel-mesh screens. The area was also ground zero for homicides, most of which were gang-related. Standing on the corner where the taxi driver had picked up the gunman, Darby could recall at least nine homicides she had worked on around here back when she worked for BPD.

Why had the gunman chosen this spot to be picked up? Darby felt there was a strong purpose behind the man's decision.

A social security office, a small building with windows made of bulletproof glass, took up the corner. It had an attached parking lot with six spaces, all of them occupied by high-end luxury cars – BMW, Mercedes, Lexus. The parking lot was sectioned off by two other buildings, both tall and made of brick, the sides marred – or, one could argue, decorated – with a colourful mural of a Spanish woman with gigantic cleavage smoking a blunt, along with messages: 'Lost Boys', 'RIP Lost4Boyz', and 'Down with the Sickness'.

Coop emerged from the office's front door, behind a heavy-set white woman holding a toddler and speaking on a phone. She was south of twenty-one, had bleached hair and long fingernails encrusted with fake diamonds, and wore a leather coat with a collar lined with fur. She shot daggers at Darby then focused her attention on helping her young son into the backseat of a new Mercedes SUV.

'I wouldn't tangle with her,' Coop said. 'I bet she's packing.'

'I bet she's not the only one,' Darby added. It was past noon on a workday, and everywhere she looked she saw groups of young men huddled together on the corners, bundled in oversized goose down North Face and FUBU jackets, their half-lidded eyes darting between her and the EOD vehicle and the six bomb-sniffing dogs that were moving along the streets, checking the parked cars and city garbage cans. Lots of hoodies here, and baseball caps worn sideways, their pristine $300 LaBron and Jordon high-tops worn with the laces undone, their baggy, wide-legged jeans sagging well-below the waist to reveal the brand name of the designer stitched prominently on the waistband of their boxer shorts or boxer briefs.

'Any luck with the office cameras?' she asked.

Coop nodded. 'Our guy was standing right about where you are, right here in front of the entrance for the lot at seven thirty this morning. He wore sunglasses and that black cap of his was pulled down over his ears and forehead, and not once did he ever turn his face to the cameras.'

'Because he knew exactly where they were.'

'And he didn't use the jammer this time. We don't have a good shot of his face, but there wasn't any interference in the feed.'

'Which way did he come from?'

Coop pointed across the street, to Drummond Ave., another busy corner. They saw a lot of hostile faces aimed at them. Lots of illegal firearms, too, she suspected.

'We should have worn vests,' Coop said, reading her

mind. 'There's no way our guy lives in this neighbourhood.'

He was right. A white male wouldn't be welcome here – wouldn't *survive* here.

'He chose this place for a reason,' Darby said, more to herself than Coop.

'If we keep standing out here, we may not live long enough to find out what that reason is. I feel like I've got a target scope painted on my back. Let's get back in the car.'

'Ask patrol to canvas the streets and check all the parked cars,' Darby said after she shut the door.

'For what?'

'A watcher. Our boy may not be working alone, remember? Have them target anyone sitting in a car parked nearby – man or woman, young or old, it doesn't matter. Tell patrol to pull their licences, have them flag anyone who doesn't live in or around this neighbourhood.'

'You think our guy is local?'

'Has to be, if he's got a beef with BPD.'

'Right, but what I meant was, if our guy isn't from around here, that means he had to come here from somewhere else. Either he drove here and parked, or he took public transportation.'

'All the MBTA stops have cameras.'

'Howie's got agents working with the subway's transportation people on that.'

'Where's the closest station? The Red Line at Fields Corner?'

Coop nodded. 'It's about three, maybe four miles from here,' he said. 'I don't see him walking that far – not through this neighbourhood, not in this weather.'

'Let's take a drive down Drummond, see what's there.'

'What are we looking for?'

'A bus stop.'

'Buses still aren't equipped with any security cameras.'

Coop was right. While the MBTA had security cameras posted on all their T stations, bringing the same level of security to their busses was slow because of – surprise, surprise – lack of government funding.

'We know our guy made the taxi driver pull right up in front of the BPD so the taxi would be caught on camera,' Darby said. 'Now we've found where the driver picked him up – right in front of a government office where he *knowingly* got caught on camera.'

'There aren't cameras at the bus stops, either.'

'I realize that. But our guy knows about the cameras, and in this neighbourhood some store or whatever has got to have a security camera, and he'll be on one of them, I guarantee it. Our guy wants us to find him – to find out *everything* about him.'

23

+03.27

Coop hit the lights but not the sirens. 'I feel like I'm involved in a circle jerk,' he said, pulling away from the kerb.

'You speaking from personal experience?' Darby asked.

'I'm serious. If this guy is dropping breadcrumbs like you said, all we're doing is running around and tying up our resources, and for what? What's the reason?'

'He's doubling down on his investment.'

'His *investment*?'

'What he's put into motion is the culmination of his life's work – his life's *purpose*.'

'And it's all centred around Briggs.'

Darby nodded, held on to the door as Coop did a hard U-turn. 'He knows there's a good chance that Briggs won't come into the lobby – that'll we'll prevent him or that Briggs will try to worm his way out of it, whatever. So what does he do? He picks a day when he knows Briggs is going to be out of the state to make his stand and to make sure he's caught on camera so he can lead the FBI on a tour of BPD or government corruption or whatever this is about.'

'Why not just tell us what it's about? Why the theatre?'

'Because saying the truth isn't as powerful as discovering it.'

Coop turned right on to Drummond. To her left Darby saw what looked like an abandoned department store. It took up a good part of the block, the rows of missing windows reminding her of a mouth full of broken teeth, graffiti everywhere.

Then she looked out the front window and at the far end of the street and standing high in the air was a sign for The Gate of Heaven. Darby recognized the name, remembered reading about it. The Catholic church had recently been sold off by the Boston Archdiocese to help pay for the victims of sexual abuse from paedophile priests who, for decades, had been knowingly shuffled from parish to parish before being uncovered by a group of reporters from the *Boston Globe*. The ringleader, Cardinal Bernard Francis Law, the Archbishop of Boston at the time, had, according to law enforcement circles, left the city for Italy before state troopers arrived with subpoenas seeking his grand jury testimony. The Pope, aware of Law's transgressions, appointed Law as Archpriest of the Basilica di Santa Maria Maggiore in Rome.

Across the street from the entrance of the church was a bus stop, the small, outside shelter consisting of a Plexiglas roof and three walls covered with stickers and posters and spray-painted messages.

Coop pulled up to the front so they could read the

small words printed on the MBTA sign. Darby was looking at a rainbow-coloured backpack sitting underneath the bench. She got out of the car and left the door hanging open.

Squatting on her haunches, she examined the backpack without touching it.

Then she looked over her shoulder and said, 'The straps are duct-taped to the post.'

'I'll call the bomb squad.'

Darby shut the car door. As she made her way across the street, Coop pulled into the church parking lot.

Darby stood in the cold air, next to a sign put up by the Miller Construction Company that advertised a new condo development that would take the place of the church.

Four corners here, and a four-way stop. Behind the bus stop, a small parking lot, this one big enough to hold one, maybe two cars max. It was empty. Across the street from the stop, two stores: a local convenience store called 'Timmy J's' and a hair salon called 'B Luxe' that offered blowouts and ten-dollar manicures. Standing here under the grey sky, cold, the snow on its way to bury them, she realized how much she ached for home – for any home.

Darby checked the hair salon first. It didn't have a security system. The convenience store did. The camera posted behind the front corner also overlooked the bus stop across the street.

The young African American guy working behind the counter asked to see her ID. He was glassy-eyed and wore baggy clothes and had fake diamond earrings the size of dimes in each ear. She could smell beer on his breath.

She didn't have a shield and told him she was working with the FBI. He wouldn't allow her into the back room to let her look at the security camera.

Coop's FBI credentials changed that.

The security system was hooked up to a Dell laptop that sat on a cheap, pressboard desk in the corner of the cramped back office located across from a bathroom and a pay phone that was missing its receiver. The kid gave them the password to unlock the screen. The trashcan was packed with empty Miller High Life cans, and there was a container of mouthwash sitting next to the keyboard. *He came back here when it was quiet to pound a beer or two to relieve the boredom of his job.*

Their years of working together had exposed them to all kinds of different security systems. This one was easy – a boxed system that could be picked up at the price clubs for two hundred bucks and recorded everything to the computer's hard drive. He didn't need her for this.

'What's the latest on Briggs? What's his status?'

'Howie's on it,' Coop replied, focusing on the security software.

The satellite phone was in her jacket pocket. She took it out and began to dial the pre-programmed number for Alan Grove.

He didn't pick up.

'You have Briggs's direct number?' she asked Coop.

'Why?'

'I want to talk to him about the first bomb site, see if he knows anything.'

That broke his concentration. Coop shifted in the chair, clearly uncomfortable.

'Christ,' she said. 'Are you serious?'

'I don't have his number. Even if I did, the answer would be no.'

'We need to talk to him.'

'*We* are.' Coop looked away from the screen, his face serious. Stern. 'Howie is in touch with Briggs, will be the only one who will be in contact with Briggs from now on. And why is that, you ask? Because the former mayor didn't take too kindly to you threatening him.'

'I didn't threaten him.'

'You said – and this is a direct quote – that you'll jam your foot so far up his ass he'll choke to death. What would you call that? A pickup line?'

'I don't have time for his bullshit. And if I find out he's lying to me, I *will* –'

'This isn't about *you*, Darby, there is no *you* in this situation.'

'Really? I didn't see anyone else willing to walk into the station.'

'That was *your* choice. I'm not arguing with you about this. Let Howie handle Briggs. Now let's focus on the job.'

The job.

That was the fundamental difference between them. What they were doing right now, all the cases they worked together, the endless days and night spent hunting and searching for evidence and witnesses, the bodies that piled up day after day – this would always be a job to him and nothing more. He did his job well, no question, had always pulled his own weight and went to the mat for her. But when he wasn't on the job, he transformed himself into a present-day Bacchus who could wash away his anger and frustration and whatever other emotions he always kept in check with shots of Irish whiskey and pretty women, all of them interchangeable objects, each one more than happy to slip between the sheets and be used as nothing more than vessels of sexual gratification. For as long as she'd known him, Coop had surrendered to an unassailable fact of life, one she knew was true but could never accept: that at the end of the day, what they did for a living didn't make a difference. The dead were still the dead, and the dawn that greeted them each morning would always be fraught with some new horror or terror.

She secretly despised him and admired him for it.

Darby watched Coop fast-forwarding through the colour footage on the thirteen-inch screen. The office door was open, and from the corner of her eye she caught blue and red lights flashing across the grungy white wall and bathroom door. She ducked her head out into the hall and, looking across the top of the display racks to the street, saw the bomb truck along with a pair of BPD cruisers, flashes of blue uniforms moving across the sidewalks. Patrol was working on clearing the area.

She glanced at her watch.

Two hours and twenty-seven minutes.

'Darby.'

She looked at him from the doorway.

'I found Big Red,' Coop said, nodding with his chin to the computer screen.

24

+03.33

On the screen, an MBTA bus pulled up next to the stop across the street. No one was waiting at the stop. The camera didn't provide any sound, but from inside the store she heard the bell mounted on the front door ring, and then a woman's voice ordered the kid working the counter to leave the store *now*.

Darby leaned over Coop's shoulder. She could smell the hotel soap on his skin and the citrus-scented shampoo in his hair.

Now she watched as the bus doors opened. Only one person got out: a tall white male wearing an overcoat over a suit and tie; black trousers and black Oxford shoes and thin black gloves; sunglasses with dark lenses and a black knit hat that covered his ears and most of his forehead. He was carrying a backpack, the same one she'd seen inside the station.

'That's our boy,' Coop said.

The gunman stepped on to the sidewalk. He stood there, looking around as if to get his bearings. When the bus pulled away, he walked into the street then stopped and, looking directly at the camera, removed a cell phone from his jacket pocket.

'It's a burner,' Coop said.

'How can you tell? I can barely see it.'

'Howie called right after I got off the phone with the bomb squad. The call that came into the taxi dispatch, the number belonged to a burner.'

As the gunman began to dial a number, a BPD patrolwoman appeared in the doorway. 'Bomb squad wants to deploy the robot for that backpack,' she told them. 'We need to clear the area.'

'Tell them to hold off for a minute,' Darby said, watching the screen as the gunman, his back now to the camera, began walking up Drummond, heading for the social security office.

'That backpack underneath the bench,' Coop said. 'He didn't plant it.'

The gunman hung up but he didn't put the phone back in his pocket. Instead, he held it somewhere in front of him, reading the screen or maybe dialling another number. They couldn't see what he was doing.

Then, further up the street, he turned to a city garbage can chained to a streetlight. His back was still towards them, but they saw him glance over his shoulder, as if to check to see if he was being watched or followed. Then he leaned forward and shoved something down into the trash, one quick movement.

'He dumped the burner,' Coop said.

'That, or he left something else for us.'

He noted the tone in her voice and turned his head to her. 'You think he planted an IED in there?'

'No. No, I don't.'

'So what's bothering you?'

'EOD guys are going to want to check out the garbage can. To do that, they'll need to suit up and get the bomb robot ready, their equipment. That's going to eat up time.'

'Not much of a choice.'

'I know, I know.' There was something else bothering her, though, something she couldn't put a finger on. 'Who's handling the evidence, you or BPD?'

'Us,' Coop replied as he dialled a number on his phone. 'We've got two Evidence Response Teams on standby.'

There are strict procedures to follow when dealing with a potential IED. The procedures cannot be skipped, and they can't be rushed. There are no shortcuts.

Charlie, the bomb disposal robot, was a hydraulic, bendable arm attached to a massive chassis with six ATV wheels that could climb over kerbs and up stairs. Darby waited in the back of the EOD vehicle and watched the monitor as Stu Lewis, senior bomb disposal engineer for the Mass. State Police, remotely controlled Charlie to look inside the garbage can. The video feed mounted above the retractable claw provided high-definition clarity; she could see the ribbed edges of a used condom stuck to a Dunkin' Donuts coffee cup.

'You guys have no idea what he might've put in there,' Lewis said. A statement, not a question.

'We think he might have dumped a cell phone in there, but it could be anything. We couldn't see what it was.'

'We'll have to check everything, then.'

Charlie had brought along a plastic garbage can and had set it up next to the city one. Darby watched as *he*, as Lewis insisted on calling the robot, pulled out the coffee cup with its dried condom stuck to the side and dumped it into the plastic can.

Charlie went to work on the next item, Lewis examining it closely before picking it up and hauling it away, the same procedure repeated over and over again.

Darby kept time in her head. Each item of garbage, from examination to disposal, took anywhere from one to three minutes.

It was maddening to wait. She didn't want to wait but she had to. There was nothing she could do. On the screen, she examined the artwork on the brick wall behind the cans. Some of it was quite detailed. In the midst of big cartoon characters, and gangster and rap phrases like 'Don't Believe the Hype' and 'Fuck the Police' someone had painstakingly drawn, using spray paint, a big fat white baby with a black heart and, next to it, the portrait of a scowling black man wearing a dark green hoodie that shrouded his eyes, doves flying above his shoulders painted with purple wings and above his head, two lines of text: 'Sean Ellis, Never Forget".

When the graffiti no longer held her attention, Darby closed her eyes and rubbed her forehead. In her mind's eye, she saw the second hand of a clock spinning wildly, like a roulette wheel.

The back door opened. Coop was standing there, motioning for her to join him outside.

They stood on a sidewalk in a cordoned-off street four blocks away from where the bomb robot was working.

'Got some preliminary info on what's happening in Quincy,' Coop said. 'Given the blast patterns, the bomb guys think the IED used dynamite. Bomb site is a residential home, belongs to a BPD detective.'

'Who?'

'Danny Hill.'

'Mr Murder?'

Coop nodded. Everyone knew Hill. The detective had an unbelievable clearance rate on homicides, had solved some of the city's toughest cases over his nearly three-decade career. He loved the press, and the press loved him, nicknaming him 'Mr Murder.'

'Hill is still on active duty, works out of the Kenmore district now,' Coop said. 'He called in sick this morning. Bomb guys found his personal car and unmarked car, what's left of them, in the driveway. They're sifting through the rubble as we speak. They also found part of a leg on a car roof a couple of blocks away.'

'It's definitely Hill?'

'No positive ID yet, but yeah, it looks like it's him. Blood type matches Hill, and there's a small and slightly faded Marine crest tattooed on the upper thigh – exact same one Hill has, according to people who know him.'

'Any other casualties?'

Coop nodded sombrely. 'Next-door neighbour,' he said. 'Elderly woman who lives alone, they think she had a heart attack when all her windows exploded.'

'Any connection between Hill and Anita Barnes's grandson?'

'I'm working on it.' Coop studied her face for a moment. 'What is it?'

'We're several steps behind this guy. We need to find something we can use as leverage.'

The EOD's back doors opened.

'I've got something for you,' Lewis said. He was looking directly at Darby.

They all looked at the monitor. On the screen was a rolled-up brown paper sandwich bag, the kind given to you at a deli or liquor store. Across the bag, two words written in thick black block letters:

DARBY MCCORMICK

25

+03.48

Darby rode with Coop in the back of another vehicle, this one an Evidence Response Team van owned by the Boston FBI. An ERT agent sat across from her, a man with black curly hair and fingernails bitten down to the quick. They didn't talk – couldn't, over the wail of sirens – but the agent, whose name was Sonnenberg, kept looking at her.

Darby kept her attention on the pair of sealed evidence bags sitting on the floor between the man's legs. One held the cell phone the gunman had left for her inside the garbage can. The other evidence bag contained the phone's SIM card, which the gunman had snapped into two peices.

The van took a hard right. Darby grabbed the armrests. Her head swam and she felt slightly nauseated, as though she was experiencing motion sickness.

The gunman hadn't stopped to write her name on the bag on his way up Drummond Ave. Her name was already written on it when he wrapped up the cell phone and then shoved the bag deep inside the garbage can, which meant he had intended to include her in his plan from the very beginning. It meant he had been thinking about her for some time. Thinking and planning and dreaming. About her.

But how did he know she was going to be in Boston this weekend, and how did he know she was going to BPD headquarters this morning? Her BPD friend and colleague, Anna Lopez, had asked her last night at the wedding reception to come by this morning.

Had the gunman been following her?

Stalking her?

Was he at the wedding?

What if this whole thing centred on her and not the former mayor Briggs? What if the gunman had waited not for Briggs to be out of the state but until *she* was in Boston?

Word had no doubt gotten out about the gunman leaving behind evidence with her name written on it. That kind of news travelled fast; no doubt BPD Commissioner Donnelly was grinning ear-to-ear like some goddamn Cheshire cat. Now that evidence had been linked to her, she couldn't work the case. Now there was a clear conflict of interest. Howie Gelfand didn't have a choice: he had to bench her.

Darby was jostled out of her thoughts when the van came to a sudden, jarring stop. She checked her watch. Two hours and eleven minutes until the second bomb went off.

When the back doors opened, she expected to see Donnelly waiting for her. No one was there. Coop motioned with his head for her to follow him. She did, ducking and weaving through the emergency vehicles and personnel crowding the lot. She caught sight of the MCP and wondered what was going on in there, if Briggs's special convoy was getting ahead of the storm or was caught in it.

SAC Gelfand was waiting for her by the back steps for the mobile lab. A young female agent with a round face and flawless skin, her blonde hair worn in a ponytail, stood with him.

Here comes the boot, Darby thought, straightening.

All eyes were on her when Gelfand said, 'You touch or handle any of the evidence?'

'No, nothing,' Darby replied.

'Good. You know I can't let you work the evidence or do the documentation – conflict of interest and all that. Cooper's going to be hung up in the lab, and I need someone to consult and report back to me. Hang back, take notes, feel free to advise on any forensic matters, but under no circumstances are you to touch the evidence or the equipment.'

'Understood.'

'This lovely young lady standing next to me is Agent Marion Kelly. Kelly here's going to put her Yale law degree to work and stand by your side, make sure everything's on the up-and-up so we don't get any blowback later from BPD or the city. She's going to record everything. When you're finished, she'll take you to the MCP and we'll reconvene. Get to work everyone.'

Howie had more than enough causality to sideline her. Instead, he had created a flimsy legal loophole for her to slip through, to keep her front and centre of everything involving the case.

But why? Darby wondered, as she followed Coop into the trailer. Was Howie throwing his support behind her because he needed her? Or was he using her as a pawn to play some sort of political angle?

The same company that built the MCP had constructed the mobile lab. Darby saw the same grey flooring and aluminium walls. The counters and surfaces, though, were a bright white, and there was plenty of light to work with.

Coop removed his overcoat and suit jacket and looked to Agent Kelly. 'Is the recorder set to the correct date and time?' he asked.

'Set and ready.'

'Good. Once you start recording, don't stop it or pause. Keep everyone in frame at all times.'

Coop looked at the digital video camera and introduced himself and everyone standing inside the room. He described the items that were recovered and where they had been found. Then he gave the date and time just in case there was a trouble with the recording, or a mistake. They couldn't afford either. Every single step and moment needed to be documented in the event a lawyer tried to contest the procedural handling or validity of entered evidence.

Darby shadowed Coop as he brought the brown paper bag to a large white counter where two agents stood, waiting. One had a forensic camera, the other a clipboard. A microphone hung from the ceiling to augment written notes, but it wasn't necessary as both audio and visual were being captured on the digital recorder.

Coop cut the piece of clear tape on the bag and then slid the contents on to the counter.

'One SIM card, snapped in half, a pair of Samsung rechargeable batteries, and a Samsung cell phone that, at first glance, seems to offer basic calling and nothing else.' His gloved hands worked quickly, placing the forensic rulers beside each item. Then he stepped away to give the photographer room to work.

Darby was going to suggest that he perform a swab-DNA test on the phone's mouthpiece, to collect the epithelial cells that were expelled on a person's breath, but Coop had already grabbed the necessary equipment from the counter behind him.

A true DNA sample would take two days. A Polymerase Chain Reaction analysis – and from what she could see, the lab had the appropriate equipment to do PCR – could take the smallest trace of DNA and amplify it in just under four hours to produce a DNA fingerprint suitable for a search inside the federal DNA database, CODIS.

The photography done, Coop leaned forward across the counter and looked through an illuminated light magnifier to check the phone for any possible trace evidence – a hair or fibre that might have been caught between the keypads or in one of the crevices of the hard white plastic shell. Finding nothing, he swivelled the magnifier to the agent standing next to him, and as the man went to work examining the inside of the paper bag, Coop used what was essentially a big Q-Tip to swab the phone's mouthpiece. He performed a second, separate swab against the receiver to collect possible DNA that might have been left behind by the gunman's ear.

Coop cocked his head to her. 'The keypad?'

'On the convenience store video he was wearing gloves when he dialled. But if he used the phone on a previous occasion and used his fingers . . . DNA will help us with a conviction, but if he has a record and we're looking for an ID, we're better off going with fingerprints than through CODIS. I'd hate to swab it for DNA and destroy evidence when he might have left a print behind.'

'Agreed,' he said. 'Let's check for prints.'

26

+04.04

First, Coop bagged the broken SIM card.

'We'll deal with this last,' he told the group. 'Agent Kelly, make sure you record the seal on the bag, right here – and record me initialling it.'

Then he made Kelly record him bringing the SIM card over to the evidence locker. He signed the form hanging on the clipboard in front before locking it away inside the cabinet. He was taking no chances with evidential procedures. He didn't want anything to come back and bite him in the ass.

Coop placed the phone and the paper bag in separate trays. The group followed him to another counter where a portable super glue chamber had been set up. Dusting the phone with black powder would have been quicker, but fuming with cyanoacrylate, the main chemical ingredient of super glue, would keep the print stable for dusting and allow him to make numerous lifts off the same print without destroying the latent.

After he stood the phone on a nonporous block of laminate, one of the agents handed him a small plastic cup of warm water, which would rehydrate the prints on the phone's plastic shell. Coop pulled apart the developer and clipped the sheet of cyanoacrylate to a plastic hanger inside the centre of the chamber, then pulled down the plastic sheet and tucked it in along the bottom of the base. It could take up to thirty minutes for the cyanoacrylate to react with the fatty deposits left behind by fingers and palms.

An agent stood next to the chamber, watching as Coop took the second tray and moved further down the length of the counter. He needed some room to work on this next part.

He cut the paper bag along the seams so he could lay it flat on the counter. Then he placed the appropriate rulers for comparison and measurement purposes next to the bag and moved back away from the table to let the evidence be photographed, recorded and documented.

Coop turned to the lab gear folded on top of the chairs, all of it chemical-resistant: clothing, lab coat, goggles, a breathing mask and a box of nitrile gloves. Nitrile was thicker and offered better protection against harsh and toxic chemicals like Ninhydrin, the go-to method for detecting fingerprints left on paper. The chemical was especially toxic to the eyes and lungs. Darby wondered if he was going to spray the paper bag or try to minimize his exposure by using either dipping or painting the paper.

Coop spoke as he worked the protective clothing over his own. 'Take multiple pictures of the writing, then move the rulers next to it so we have exact measurements,' he said. 'Kelly, make sure you get a close up on it – I want everything documented, every single step. There a photocopier in here?'

'Yes,' replied the agent manning the clipboard.

'Good,' Coop said. 'After you guys finish, make several copies of the writing – and make sure you wipe down the copier plate before you do it. We'll all need to walk to the copier so Kelly can keep everyone in frame.'

Darby couldn't take her attention off the bag. Seeing her name written there set off a high, ringing sound in her head and made her feel cold all over.

Who are you?

And what do you want with me?

After the writing was photocopied, the bag was handed to Coop, who carried it in a tray with him back to the counter where one of the agents had already set aside a photographic developer tray containing the chemicals Coop had called ahead for. Coop carried everything with him into a small, ventilated room equipped with a fume hood.

Agent Kelly didn't have to be told what to do next. She carefully moved back until she had everyone and the evidence in the frame of her recorder. She needed to capture it all, in real-time, without a single interruption in the recording; otherwise, a lawyer could contest the validity of what had happened in here. She didn't need to enter the room with him in order to record his work; a thick glass window allowed her to watch him.

Coop preferred fresh-mixed solutions, as they were more dependable than premixed pump spray dispensers and aerosol cans. Inside the photographic developer tray he mixed Ninhydrin with ethyl acetate and acetic acid. Darby was glad to see him add one litre of heptane to the solution, as using heptane made inks less susceptible to running or dissolving.

The fume hood running, Coop dipped the entire bag inside the solution. Then he clipped the bag to the pair of hooks mounted underneath the hood to allow it to dry. Ninhydrin reacted with the proteins and peptides left behind by fingerprints and left a telltale and easily identifiable deep blue or purple colour known as Rhuemann's purple.

They gathered in the space between the portable fuming chamber and the door for the ventilated room so Kelly could record them and, if needed, show that no one had been moving around the trailer while they waited for the prints to be processed.

Minutes passed.

Darby checked her watch.

One hour and forty-eight minutes until the next bomb went off.

And where was Rosemary Shapiro?

Was Briggs ahead of the storm? Would he make it here in time?

Coop leaned into her and said, 'If I find a good-quality latent print, I'll transfer it to the fingerprint card and send it into IAFIS. People on the other end are expecting it, so it will go in fast. If he's in the database, we'll know in twenty minutes or less.'

Darby could see he wanted to ask her about why

the gunman had deliberately left evidence behind for her. He didn't ask, though, because they were being recorded. He didn't want any of her responses as part of the record.

Twenty-two minutes passed until the fingerprints were visible on the cell phone.

'Give it a few more minutes,' Coop said. 'I want to make sure the glue sets.'

Darby stared at the palm prints and latent fingerprints. The gunman hadn't wiped down the phone before placing it inside the bag.

He left prints behind so we could identify him.

Not we – you, an inner voice added. *He left this evidence behind for* you.

Coop removed the phone and dusted the white plastic shell with a black granular fingerprint powder called 'Black Widow'.

'Got two, possibly three latent prints to work with,' he said, examining the phone underneath a magnifier. 'More than enough to get a hit in our system, provided he's in it.'

He's in the database, Darby thought. *I'm sure of it.*

27

+04.35

Darby quickly made her way through the MCP. The people in here, mostly federal agents, most of them men, all stopped what they were doing to look at her. Some just glanced at her while others outwardly stared. She could tell by their expressions that the news about finding evidence with her name written on it had already made its way through the ranks.

She wondered how long it would take for the media to find out. Surely someone had leaked it.

The door to the conference room was closed, but she could hear Gelfand talking on the other side of it, discussing the possibility of SWAT feeding an odourless gas into the lobby vents that would induce sleep. The problem was the gas wasn't fast-acting. When the gunman noticed he was feeling groggy, he might put two-and-two together and decide to detonate his vest – and the remaining IEDs he planted in and around the city.

Gelfand had launched into a second possible plan, this one involving drugging bottled water and having it delivered to the lobby, when Darby opened the door.

The overhead lights had been turned off. Gelfand

stood near the wall on her far right, next to a TV screen playing shaky aerial footage of the bomb disposal robot approaching the backpack taped underneath the bus stop bench. The sound was muted. The robot, she saw, was armed with a shotgun.

A puff of smoke from the gun barrel and then the backpack exploded, painting the sidewalk and the sides of the bus stop in a rainbow of bright colours.

'Two teenage jerkoffs stuffed the backpack full of spray paint cans and taped it there,' Gelfand told her. 'They were going to call in a suspicious package when the bomb squad showed up. Pure coincidence. Patrol caught 'em sneaking out of that abandoned building on Drummond. They stuck around so they could film the paint can explosion on their phones, post it later on YouTube.'

Gelfand turned on the lights. Commissioner Donnelly was seated at the head of the table. Flanking him were two older African American men she had never met personally but recognized, both impeccably dressed and already groomed and made-up for TV: Boston mayor David Finch and Massachusetts governor Stewart Vaughan.

'Gentlemen, this is Dr McCormick, the one who made contact with the gunman. She's working with the Bureau in an advisory capacity.'

No introduction was needed. Darby could tell Vaughan and Finch knew exactly who she was. They regarded her with the barely contained contempt given to someone who had crashed a private party and refused to leave.

'You have an update on the evidence you found?' Gelfand asked.

Darby nodded and slid into her seat. 'We pulled several quality latent prints off the phone and the paper bag. Agent Cooper is transferring them to print cards to run through IAFIS. The SIM card can *possibly* be repaired to a point where the techs can extract the data from it, but it will take time. The fact that the gunman included it suggests there's something on there he wants us to find.

'The phone contains an accelerometer, a device that measures the force of acceleration caused by either movement or gravity,' Darby said. 'That's good news for us because it means we can track the movement of the phone, show where it travelled and how *fast* it was travelling, meaning we'll know when the gunman was walking and when he was driving. With any luck, we may find out where he lives.'

'How long until they have that data?'

'The software they're using is sophisticated but slow. Could be an hour or two, maybe more. That's all I have on that front.'

'Cooper told me about Danny Hill. Anything new there?'

'Nothing at the moment,' Gelfand said.

'Where do we stand with Briggs?'

'He crossed the Vermont border into New Hampshire

about ten, fifteen minutes ago. Storm's moving through New Hampshire right now but the troopers feel confident they can get him to the helicopter pad in time. He's willing to talk to the gunman.'

'Face-to-face?'

'Briggs says he's willing to go through with it.'

Governor Vaughan was shaking his head. 'I told you: that's not going to happen – especially after what just happened with Detective Hill,' he said to Gelfand. 'Briggs goes in there, this crazy lowlife will kill him on live TV, blow up the entire building.'

'He's not crazy,' Darby said. Crazy was a word she didn't like to use. It was a throwaway label that meant nothing.

All eyes had turned to her.

The governor took the lead. 'Then what is he?'

'Extremely intelligent and ruthlessly determined.'

'The traits of a psychopath.'

'Or a good politician or CEO. I'm not speaking pejoratively. The gunman is wedded to his goal and determined to see it through.'

'And what, *exactly*, is his goal? What does he think he's going to accomplish?'

'Psychological destruction,' Darby said. 'He wants to psychologically destroy Edward Briggs.'

'And then kill him.'

Darby shook her head. 'If killing Briggs was his true objective, the gunman would have done it by now. We wouldn't be sitting here – and he wouldn't have gone through the fanfare – seizing the lobby, the hostages and the bombs, requesting the meeting. He's gone to these great lengths because he wants everything on public record, wants Briggs and the people associated with him to suffer.'

'But he killed Detective Hill.'

'I wouldn't be surprised to learn that was accidental. Hill was supposed to be at work today and called in sick; he wasn't supposed to be home. He wants us to take a closer look at Hill, see how he's connected with Briggs. Is there anything you can tell us?'

Headshakes all around the room.

'Have you asked Briggs about Hill?' Darby asked.

'We will, after this briefing,' the governor replied.

'Good. I can't wait to speak to him.'

Governor Vaughan turned to Gelfand and said, 'Howie, if Eddie Briggs goes in there, the gunman has got to relinquish the suicide vest and the other IED he's got with him. He also has to tell us the location of *all* the other devices. Once they've been disarmed, then and only then, will we be amenable to having a discussion on whether or not we're going to allow Ed to go in there with a camera crew.' Then his gaze cut back to Darby. 'You need to go back into the lobby and tell the gunman to disarm the second bomb.'

'He threatened to kill me the next time I walked in there without Briggs.' Darby suspected that would suit the governor just fine. The mayor and Donnelly, too.

'He issued that same threat the first time and he didn't kill you,' Vaughan said.

She detected an undercurrent of contempt in his voice and body language. 'Your point?'

'I think it's rather obvious. He deliberately left evidence behind with your name on it – *and* he wants us to call him Big Red, the nickname of your father. Clearly he wants to keep you involved, so he can't kill you. He needs you to help carry out his vendetta against us.'

'Which is?'

The governor's face darkened. 'I don't care for what you're implying, Doctor McCormick.'

'Vendetta is a very specific word.'

The governor waved it away. 'Semantics.'

'If there's something you want to tell us, now would be a good time, Governor.'

Vaughan regarded her from across the table. Before becoming governor, he had been the vice president of a global soda company. He had successfully managed to keep soda machines carrying his product in the poorest of schools in the country, and he had been an instrumental figure in defeating former New York Mayor Bloomberg's health crusade to fight adolescent obesity by limiting the size of soda drinks. In turn, the soda lobbyists had financed his campaign for governor. The man's twenty-one million net worth didn't hurt, either.

'You've had two private meetings with him,' Vaughan said. 'We have no idea what transpired during those two interactions.'

'I told everything to SAC Gelfand. If you're looking to corroborate what I said, you can talk to the witness the gunman released.'

'Anita Barnes, I'm told, was blindfolded. She couldn't have seen anything.'

'Are you suggesting, sir, some impropriety on my part?'

'The FBIRD you were wearing had no record of your conversation.'

'The gunman is using an audio jammer that utilizes either federal or military-grade technology.'

'Did you see this jamming unit?'

'No, but that's the only way he could prevent the conversation from being recorded.'

'We'll have to take your word for it, then.'

'Meaning?'

'Maybe you . . . forgot to turn it on?'

'I'm sure SAC Gelfand explained to you that the gunman had me strip down and throw my clothes out the front door because he suspected I was wired.'

'And the security camera at the convenience store?'

'What about it?'

'You found that rather fortuitously.'

Darby scratched the corner of her lip. Her voice was calm when she spoke. 'Are you suggesting that I'm working in collusion with the gunman?'

'I'm not suggesting anything.'

'Good. Because you would look rather silly leaving this meeting holding your teeth.' Darby didn't give the governor or anyone else a chance to rebuke. She swung her attention to Gelfand and said, 'Did you ask Briggs about Anita Barnes?'

Gelfand didn't get a chance to answer. Governor

Vaughan said, 'Howie, she needs to sign the forms, as we discussed.'

'We have –' Darby glanced at her watch '– one hour and seventeen minutes until the next bomb goes off, and we're talking about paperwork? *Again?*'

'You have an inherent bias against BPD and the city of Boston.'

You're goddamn right I do, Darby thought. *You people murdered my father, and when I uncovered the truth you murdered my career and tried to murder my reputation.*

'And your priorities are uncannily aligned with the gunman's,' Vaughan said. 'As such, we're concerned that you may take advantage of what's going on –'

'Choose your words *very* carefully, sir.'

'– and may use it to further your cause, personal vendetta, whatever you want to call it, against the city. It's not unreasonable for us to protect ourselves.'

'You mean cover your asses.' She looked to Howie for support.

'You have to sign the papers.' Gelfand looked sad when he said it. 'That's not coming from me. Those are the orders from Above.'

Vaughan said, 'Did you tell Howie about what you were doing inside the lobby this morning?'

'I was there to meet with Anna Lopez with CSU. She asked me to consult on a case she's working on – those two retired cops who were murdered last year, Ventura and Owen.'

'So you've seen the case files?'

'No. Lopez only told me about the case last night,

she didn't get into any specifics. I haven't seen any materials.'

'I see. And Rosemary Shapiro?'

'What about her?'

'Did you tell Mr Gelfand you hired her to bring a civil suit against the city?'

'Shapiro isn't my lawyer.'

'But you met with her to discuss a possible civil suit against the city.'

'I met with her once a year or so ago, but I didn't hire her.'

'Have you hired another lawyer?'

'No, but this conversation is making me wonder whether or not I should change my mind,' Darby said. 'Howie, have you talked with Shapiro?'

Gelfand shook his head. 'She hasn't called back, and she isn't answering her cell phone,' he said.

'The secretary said she was home sick.'

'I know. Shapiro has three homes – the Cape, Beacon Hill and a ski house in northern New Hampshire. We've sent agents to Beacon Hill and the Cape.'

A cell phone rang – Howie's. He studied the incoming call on the screen.

'Excuse me,' he said, heading for the door. 'I've got to take this.'

'What's going on?' Vaughan demanded.

'I'll be right back.'

Stewart Vaughan had no intention of remaining seated like some schoolboy. He got to his feet and adjusted the cuffs of his monogrammed shirt, complete with gold cufflinks, and moved around the table with the urgency of someone who believed in his own importance.

The mayor, not to be outdone, also stood to leave. He shot her a withering look designed to intimidate her. Darby winked at him and took out her cell phone. Commissioner Donnelly remained seated.

28

+04.46

Donnelly spoke after the door clicked shut.

'I don't think they're fans.'

'I'd say that was a safe bet,' Darby replied, tapping her finger against the screen of her iPhone. 'What's the connection between Briggs and the first hostage, Anita Barnes?'

Donnelly didn't answer. He placed his meaty hand on the thick manila folder in front of him and joylessly pushed it across the table.

The folder was bound together by an elastic band, the stack of papers inside it at least two inches thick.

'I'm not signing anything,' Darby said.

'That's your choice. If you don't, you'll be excluded from the investigation. We'll have someone drive you back to your hotel.'

Darby placed her smartphone on the table. 'Who's going to go into the lobby with Briggs? Grove?'

'He's the most qualified.'

'If you send anyone else in there, you're sentencing those hostages to death.'

'You're probably right. But that's a chance the governor and mayor are willing to take. Howie and I have a different opinion. We want you involved in this, but our hands are tied.'

'By the mayor and governor.'

'By the banks,' Donnelly replied. 'The banks and the insurance carriers and underwriters. There's going to be a lot of property damage when this is over and – and I hope to God I'm wrong about this next part – a lot of deaths. We're talking major civil suits against the city. Sure, the suits will drag it out for years, but lawyers cost money – a lot of money – and the city hires the best money can buy. What they really need is a scapegoat: you.'

'There's a newsflash.'

'In the end, someone always has to pay, be held accountable. It sure as hell isn't going to be Vaughan or Finch. They don't take the blame, they assign it.'

'Let me guess,' Darby said. 'Because I took charge of the situation in the lobby this morning, and because the gunman nominated me as his mouthpiece and then purposely left behind a bag with my name written on it – ahead of time – a lawyer will argue collusion.'

Donnelly nodded solemnly.

'Small problem,' Darby said. 'I have no idea who this son of a bitch is.'

'Maybe.'

'No, not *maybe*. If I knew who he was, you'd have his name.'

'Let me be real clear on this,' Donnelly said. 'I'm not even remotely suggesting that you're withholding information. What I *am* suggesting is that it *is* possible you *might* know him. Did you get a solid look at his face while you were in the lobby?'

'No.'

'And in the video evidence we collected so far, we can't see his face – and you haven't heard his actual voice. Is it possible he's disguising it *because* of you? Because you may know who he is?'

Darby said nothing, knowing exactly where Donnelly was leading her. She felt a shiver along her spine that tightened her scalp.

'If the gunman ends up walking out of there alive and you do, in fact, know him, you're screwed,' Donnelly said. His tone was cold, matter of fact. 'If you don't know him but he says you do, again, you're screwed. Either way there will be an investigation. A grand jury will be formed and more than likely criminal charges will be brought forth – not because the charges will have any merit to them, necessarily, but because our mayor and governor need a scapegoat, like you said.'

'Maybe I should ask Rosemary Shapiro to represent me.'

'Maybe you should. She's good, and she gets results – especially when it comes to going up against the city. But, as I'm sure you know, lawyers like Rosemary Shapiro charge big money to defend criminal cases. That kind of defence will bankrupt you. Best-case scenario is she takes you on pro bono in the hope that, after your criminal trial, she'll be able to mount a civil suit against the city. And let's say she wins and gets you a nice payday. We're talking years, maybe even a decade or more, until you see a single penny. And you want to know the worst part?'

'Absolutely.'

'The worst part is that your reputation will be destroyed,' Donnelly said. 'This consulting gig you're doing? Gone. All your hard-won experience, your Harvard degree – no one is going to want to hire someone who may or may not have been working in collusion with a gunman/serial bomber using your *father's* name. Perception is the law of the land. No one in their right mind will hire you to investigate so much as a parking ticket because no one in their right mind is going to want to draw that kind of publicity to themselves – and you already know that kind of publicity will haunt you, thanks to the internet.'

Donnelly sighed. His shoulders slumped as he leaned forward in his chair and folded his hands on the table. 'What I'm saying is that the truth doesn't matter. Nine-eleven, what happened right here in Boston with the Marathon Bomber – the public never knows the full truth. They're fed what we're willing to feed them, and we only feed them a fraction of what really happened – just enough to fill their bellies so they'll be satisfied and turn their attention back to their lives or on to some other fresh new horror, like what's the latest and greatest with Kim Kardashian and her stepfather, Bruce Jenner – or is he now her stepmother?'

Darby said nothing. Waited for the rest of it, thinking about the papers, how if she didn't sign them they'd boot her from the case – and yet the governor and mayor could still turn around and try to make her their scapegoat. If she signed the papers, she could stay on the case in an advisory capacity – and yet the mayor and governor could still use her as their scapegoat. It didn't matter how this thing flushed out. She was dealing with men who took out people with a pen or a phone call.

'I'm trying to be a friend here,' Donnelly said.

'And just how much is this friendship going to cost me?'

Donnelly opened his mouth to speak. It hung open for a moment until he sat back in his chair, as if recoiling from a noxious odour.

Darby grabbed her phone. She pressed the button and the screen came to life. The app she had opened previously, one that used the phone to record conversations, was still running.

'However this thing unravels, at some point it will end,' he said. 'You'll go back to your life, and the rest of these people will sit back and think about how they're going to destroy you.'

'They're already doing that. They have the time and the resources and the venom. Signing those papers isn't going to change that.'

'Why did you get involved in this?'

'Murphy didn't know what he was doing.'

'And you do?'

'I didn't want the gunman to start shooting. You're welcome.'

'You think you maybe jumped in because you saw a chance to get back at us?'

Darby got to her feet. 'Good luck with the gunman.'

The door opened and SAC Gelfand came inside, alone, his face wan when he said, 'Big Red has made contact.'

29

+04.52

'Made contact?' Darby said, confused – and alarmed. There was no way the gunman could have made contact with *anyone* by phone, email or text because the bomb squad was jamming all cellular, Wi-Fi and radio frequencies in the area, and had shut down the BPD internet and the phones inside the lobby. 'Made contact how, and with whom?'

'I don't know the *how* yet,' Gelfand replied, frustrated. 'As for *whom*, Big Red contacted – or I should say, the pregnant hostage made contact with a reporter for the *Boston Globe*. Guy named Dave Carlson.'

Out of the corner of her eye she saw Donnelly visibly stiffen.

Dave Carlson covered city and state politics, but his specialty was uncovering corruption. He had won a Pulitzer for his work on the Boston Catholic Church sex abuse scandal and was awarded another one just last year, for his in-depth reporting on former BPD Commissioner Christina Chadzynski's decades-long reign of behind-the-scenes corruption and terror involving Boston's most notorious Irish gangster turned serial killer, Frank Sullivan. Carlson had been the go-to reporter because he had an unnamed source close to the investigation. Darby knew who the source was because she was the one who had provided Carlson with the necessary details and information he needed to make sure neither BPD nor the city could spin the story for their benefit.

'Carlson broke the story about ten minutes ago on Twitter,' Gelfand said. 'So far, he sent out four tweets, all of them allegedly from Big Red.'

What did surprise her was how the gunman got access to Twitter when every single line of communication coming from the station had been shut down. And why hadn't Donnelly given her the boot?

Gelfand read from the screen of his BlackBerry. 'The man who is holding myself and another woman hostage is Big Red. Big Red wants a peaceful resolution to the situation and promises not to detonate any more bombs or harm the hostages or my unborn baby as long as former mayor Briggs promises to come inside the lobby and talk openly and honestly on live TV.' He looked up. 'That's it.'

Donnelly's face was mottled red when he spoke to Gelfand. 'You *assured* me the area was locked down.'

'It *is* locked down. I just got off the phone with the bomb squad guy, Ted Scott, and he assured me – *again* – that there is no way in hell the gunman could have made contact with the reporter – with *anyone*. Every single goddamn cell phone and Wi-Fi signal in that area is being jammed, and we shut down the internet and phones inside the lobby.'

Then Gelfand looked to Darby and said, 'He made you toss the satellite phone and its battery out the front door of the station. That's what you told me.'

She nodded. 'I gave it to Grove after I helped Anita Barnes into the back of the EOD vehicle. Where's Carlson? Have you talked to him?'

Gelfand shook his head. 'I sent agents out to the *Globe*'s office and to Mercy Park on Cabot Street.'

'Why there?'

'That's where the media is congregating.'

'So the gunman has got to be using his own satellite phone. That's the only way he can be making contact with the outside.'

'That's exactly what Scott just told me.'

'That portable router I saw – it was misdirection. He wanted me to see it because he wanted us to think he was operating the bombs on either a cell signal or Wi-Fi frequency. He didn't want us to know he had his own satellite phone with him.'

'And if that's the case – and I believe it is – then we've got a major problem,' Gelfand said. 'Jamming a satellite signal takes specialized equipment – military-grade equipment that Scott doesn't have access to. He will have got to appropriate it from a military base – provided they have it on hand.'

'Where?'

'He's making some calls. Scott thinks the Parsons base in Portsmouth, New Hampshire, might have the equipment. If they do, we're talking a good hour or so until they arrive.'

Donnelly added, 'Allowing him to call whomever he wants.'

Gelfand sucked in air through his nose. 'Correct,' he said.

'He could be controlling the bombs from that phone.'

'Gee, thanks, Peter, I hadn't thought of that.' Gelfand glared at him for a moment, then his expression turned dour. 'Look, if he is using a satellite phone, bottom line is we have no way to shut it down until the appropriate equipment arrives.'

'Or we take him out.'

'And how, exactly, do you suggest that? There aren't any windows in the lobby, so the snipers don't have a clear shot – even if they did, there's that little matter of the suicide vest being hooked up to a heartbeat monitor. I talked through the scenario with our guys – you were there, Pete – and they said even if they were lucky enough to get off a single headshot and put him down, that would leave them thirty seconds to a minute before his heart stopped. That's not enough time to figure out how the bombs are all connected together – or where they're located. Even if we didn't go that route – if our plan was to take him down and then get the hostages and our SWAT people out of there – there's no way they can get to safety in a minute's time, and a minute is being generous. The two IEDs he has with him inside the lobby, the pressure wave from the blast will kill them.'

'We're assuming this heartbeat device of his works.'

'You think he's *bluffing*? We already had one explosion in Quincy. What makes you think that there won't be a second IED? A third and a fourth? Who knows how many of these things this guy is using.'

'There is one solution,' Darby said.

Both men looked at her.

'Deliver Briggs and the camera crew.'

'And watch him and everyone else get killed on live TV,' Gefland said. 'Great solution. Wish I had thought of that.'

'He's not going to kill Briggs. He wants Briggs to live so he can suffer publicly for his sins. That's what your man wants.'

'Correct me if I'm wrong, but you also said that the first bomb would be used someplace where no one would be killed or hurt, that he was going to use it to make a statement. Well, he sure as hell accomplished that. That IED he left in Quincy killed two people.'

'That target has some significance to him. The others will too. No matter which way you look at it, he's got you guys cornered.'

Gelfand caught her tone and said, 'What's with this "you guys" shit? You abandoning ship?' Then he saw the expression on her face. 'You didn't sign the forms?'

Commissioner Donnelly answered the question. 'The paperwork's in order,' he said, reaching into his pocket to answer his phone.

30

+04.58

SAC Gelfand, veteran of bureaucratic wars, backstabbing and finger pointing, knew better than to speak about sensitive matters when other people were nearby. Every person represented a possible leak, and he couldn't take any chances. He waited until they had stepped outside the trailer to tell Darby about the remaining contents of his phone call.

'This way,' he said.

She followed him around the corner of the MCP, to a narrow space between the trailer and the chain-link fence overlooking Battery Park. An awning had been extended to give privacy from the helicopters that were constantly hovering and recording. They were also out of view from the mix of law enforcement and emergency personnel anxiously milling around the lot.

Commissioner Donnelly was not with them. He had stayed behind in the conference room to take a phone call from the governor who, along with the mayor, was on his way to a press conference.

Why had Donnelly deliberately lied to Gelfand about the papers being signed? What was Donnelly planning? What was his angle? His agenda?

'That plastic explosive you collected underneath your fingernail? Lab confirms it's TATP,' Gelfand said, turning his back to the wind, his hands stuffed deep in his pockets. The awning flapped like the snap of a canvas sail caught in a storm, and the steady *chop-chop-chop* of the helicopter's rotors from high above droned through the air. 'Chemical mixture the gunman used was spot on. Ted Scott says he's never seen anything like it – says our guy has to be a chemist or have a strong chemistry background.'

Darby nodded, watched the traffic coming and going, coming and going.

'If the situation isn't resolved in the next few hours, Hostage Rescue is going to take over,' he said.

'By the time they fly out, the nor'easter will be in full swing here.'

'Which is why the HRT was put on alert status an hour ago. They're already airborne, to get ahead of the storm.'

'Why are we standing out here freezing our asses off?'

'Because our boy Cooper has information he wants to share with us privately, and because I need one of these.' Gelfand held up a pack of Marlboros. 'Just don't tell my wife, okay?'

'I didn't know you were married.'

'Ten years with wifey *numero dos*.' He wrapped his lips around a cigarette and pulled it from the pack.

'I seem to remember you hitting on me at Jim Delaney's retirement party.'

'I wasn't hitting on you, Doc, I was trying to get you to lighten up, maybe even help dislodge that broomstick you've still got jammed up your ass.' He grinned around the cigarette, lit it with a cheap lighter and inhaled deeply. 'You're serious twenty-four seven. I've met death row inmates who are more relaxed than you.'

'I've got to come clean about something.'

'That you're madly in love with me? Don't worry, I already know.'

'I didn't sign the papers. I don't know why Donnelly didn't tell you.'

Gelfand exhaled, looked at her through the smoke.

'Donnelly's not a bad guy,' he said after a moment. 'At the end of the day, he wants to do the right thing. He might need you when he takes over this thing – and he will, probably, before the day is done, because I can't establish a nexus of terror, and I can't stall him forever.'

'Nexus of terror?'

'New federal buzzword. Means that we, the FBI, have to concretely prove that what's happening falls squarely into a terrorist act aimed at the federal government and not some sort of local grievance.'

'That's a helluva grey area, Howie.'

Gelfand grinned slightly. 'Designed that way on purpose,' he said. 'With these things, someone has to pick up the tab for the destruction and loss of life. Federal government doesn't like picking up the check, know what I mean?'

'The Bureau thinking of throwing this to Donnelly?'

'Not if I have anything to say about it,' Gelfand said. 'But if this mess does end up falling into his lap, he may need you, so he showed you he's a fair guy by not forcing you to sign the papers right away.'

'But he will.'

'Oh yes indeed, make no mistake about that.'

Darby turned away and searched the parking lot for Coop, wondering what was taking him so long. Gelfand searched the darkening sky.

'My old man told me the only person you can never escape is the person you see every day in the mirror,' Gelfand said. 'I cheated on my first wife and treated her like a doormat. I deep-sixed my marriage, drank bottles of Absolut like they were water, and my two kids, my son and daughter, they never forgave me for it – nor should they. But I always think of my kids when I look in the mirror now. As corny as it sounds – and I *know* it sounds corny – I want to be able to tell them I did the right thing. Not the correct thing, necessarily, but the right thing.'

'Are we having a moment here?'

Gelfand's hand swept over the parking lot of flashing lights. 'This carnival? All this military firepower we've got here? It's all window dressing. If this jerkoff wants to blow himself up, kill the hostages, whatever, we can't stop him.'

'When did you get so fatalistic?'

'I've got stage three metastatic prostate cancer. It gives you a certain perspective.'

Darby was taken back by his sudden candour.

'I found out a couple of days ago,' he said in a surprisingly casual tone. 'Nobody knows yet – and don't tell me you're sorry or any of that other crap; I've had a good life. A great life, actually. You know what I'm gonna miss the most, besides seeing my kids grow up?'

Darby knew the answer. 'This,' she said, pointing with her thumb over her shoulder to the parking lot. 'The carnival.'

Howie nodded and sucked greedily from his cigarette. 'Does that make me some kind of monster?' he asked.

'No,' Darby replied, watching Coop as he fought his way through the crowds. 'I feel the exact same way.'

31

+05.04

Coop didn't have an expressive face, but that wasn't unusual. In Darby's experience, children of Irish Catholic parents learned early on the importance of keeping one's true feelings hidden. You were taught to swallow your emotions and bury them someplace deep within yourself, and if you went to Catholic school, as she and Coop did, the nuns and priests helped further your emotional education by letting you know that neither they nor God, Jesus, Mary and Joseph gave two shits about your feelings because your purpose in life was to smile and obey – *especially* in times of great personal stress and suffering. When you reached early adulthood, you were a walking toxic-waste dump, bitter and angry about everything in your life.

Her father, thank God, had spared her from that fate.

Coop, though, had one telltale sign when he was troubled, pissed off or deeply hurt: he'd scratch the corner of his right eye like he was doing right now. Pinched between the fingers of his other hand was a folded index card.

'Prints we pulled off the disposable cell phone came back with a match,' he said.

Gelfand's eyebrows jumped in surprise. 'That was quick,' he said.

'I narrowed the search parameters to focus on suspects from Boston first, then widen out to the rest of New England. The prints on the phone, along with a couple of prints on the paper bag, belong to a retired Boston cop named Trey Warren.'

Now she understood why Coop had asked to speak privately with Gelfand. If Donnelly knew about this, he would have sufficient evidence to pull the case from the FBI.

'No arrest record,' Coop said. 'His prints were just loaded into IAFIS, as every law enforcement officer is required to do.'

'Stats?' Darby asked.

'White male, sixty-eight years old, five-foot-eight.'

'He's not our guy. The gunman was at least five-eight. Where does he live?'

'Twenty-two Fodor Road in Quincy. I wrote it down for you.' Coop handed the card to Gelfand, who already had his cell phone out, ready to dial. 'And I already sent someone over to check out Warren's place, Jerry Pike. He was already at the blast site.'

'Please tell me you told him to bring along some people from the bomb squad, have them check out Warren's house before he goes inside.'

'I told him.'

'Good boy.'

'Quincy,' Darby said. 'Same city as Mr Murder.'

'Warren retired in ninety-three,' Coop said. Then he

looked pointedly at her and added, 'His last job was the head of the latent-fingerprint unit.'

'Oh Jesus,' Darby said under her breath.

Gelfand's gaze flicked between them. 'What am I missing, kids?'

Darby motioned to Coop to explain.

'In the eighties and nineties, forensics wasn't what it is now, at least in Boston,' Coop said. 'BPD's fingerprint unit was a known dumping ground for problem officers – mainly officers who were unfit for street duty. When Warren took over in the late eighties, he had no formal training in prints. What he did have, from what I was told, was a well-known and well-documented history of anger management issues, substance and domestic abuse – and witness intimidation.'

'Where did he work before that?'

'Homicide.'

Gelfand beamed. 'How much you wanna bet Hill and Warren were partners at one time or worked together in the same unit?'

'Rumour is the department forced Warren to retire in ninety-three because he either deliberately mishandled or falsified evidence.'

'Which case?'

'*Cases*,' Coop replied. 'I don't know any names – Warren was long gone by the time I came on board in ninety-nine. Then, five years later, the fingerprint unit underwent a massive overhaul, started hiring qualified forensics personnel. Now let's talk about Anita Barnes for a moment.

'I searched NCIC for her grandson's case. It's not listed – and it should be listed because, if what Barnes told us is true, that the person or persons who killed her grandson weren't caught, then it's still an open case.'

The FBI's National Crime Information Center operated under the concept of shared management. Local, state, tribal and federal data providers and systems users entered information into the NCIC, while the Criminal Justice Information Service (CJIS), which owned and operated NCIC, served as merely the custodian of NCIC records.

'So it's possible the case didn't get placed on NCIC,' Gelfand said. 'No big deal, happens all the time. Besides, even if the record *was* there, all it gives us is the so-called 'positive response', and that's not probably cause for any law enforcement officer to take action. NCIC policy requires we make contact with the agency of record to verify the information and then check to see if it's up to date – and I don't want to do that here because if we request the information from BPD, that tips them off to where we're looking.'

'They already know about Anita Barnes's grandson.'

'Right. But if I ask them to see the case file and materials, we lose the nexus of terror angle, which mean BPD can take this away from us, and I can't allow that to happen. I'll tell you something else. I have a hard time believing the gunman, who is white, is doing all of this because of some black kid from Dorchester.'

'The gunman wants to expose BPD corruption,

mishandling of evidence – whatever this is, Anita Barnes's grandson is the starting point,' Coop said. 'He wants the Bureau to investigate this case and the others that are going to follow so we can get everything on record.'

'Well, if he wants us to do that, he's got to give us something more because Donnelly and his cronies want to take the case away from us – and they will, it's only a matter of time. Right now, they've got Anita Barnes's case. They've got a dead cop, Danny Hill. And they're going to find out about Trey Warren, a problem cop who may or may not have botched cases. We give them any more probable cause, we'll have to pack up.'

'Not if we can show a conflict of interest here.'

Darby said, 'Put Briggs on the phone with me.'

'Why, so you can aggravate the shit out of him again?' Gelfand said. 'All we have right now is supposition and hearsay. We have nothing concrete to prove he's involved in this – we don't even know *how* he fits into this yet.'

'Which is all the more reason why we need to get him on the record. Does he know about Danny Hill?'

'You want me to depose him over the phone?'

'I want you on the phone when I speak to him. Coop, too. I want more than one witness to hear him say he doesn't know anything. I want more than one person to hear the answers to his questions.'

'How about I just record the conversation while we're at it and not tell him?' Gelfand shook his head. 'Briggs is a politician, he knows how the game is played. Right now he's being Mr Cooperative. I want to keep it that way for the moment. I don't want him to lawyer up.'

'He will. You can take that as a given.'

'But he won't play that card until he has to. Doc, I know what BPD did to you and your old man, I get it. And I'm sure on some level you're wondering if Briggs might have been involved in your old man's death in some way, maybe helped to bury the whole truth about what went down. If I were in your shoes, I'd want to nail his ass to the wall, too. Right now, though? Right now, I don't want to tell him anything. I don't want to tip our hand in any way. Let's gather the facts and then *we'll* talk to him together, here, face-to-face, and on the record.'

Coop's phone rang. He answered the call without bothering to check the screen, listened for a moment.

'Hold on,' he said to the person on the other end of the line.

Then, to Darby and Gelfand: 'Warren's dead.'

32

+00.00

Darby and Gelfand took out their phones so Coop would conference them into the call.

The federal agent on the other end of the line was named Jerry Pike, and he had a lot to say about Trey Warren.

'Guy was shot in the back of the head, about fifteen, maybe twenty feet away from his front door,' Pike told them. He definitely wasn't from Boston – or New England, for that matter. Darby heard the faint traces of a Texan accent in the man's voice.

She took over the questioning. 'Are you inside the house, Agent Pike?'

'No. Bomb squad is still examining the perimeter, the doors and windows, to see if anything is booby-trapped – Ted Scott's orders. I'm standing in the side yard, with a pair of binoculars, looking through the downstairs window at the late Trey Warren.'

'You're sure it's Warren?'

'White guy, about five-nine, bald, late sixties. Guy looks like a scrotal sack attached to a Q-Tip. Oh, and his face matches the photos I pulled up on this internet thing called Google.'

It appeared Gelfand hired agents who shared his same brand of sarcasm.

'Warren's dressed in a bathrobe, a wife-beater and a pair of boxer shorts,' Pike said. 'Judging from the position of the body and the blood spray patterns, I'd say he was shot in the back of the head first and then, after he collapsed against the floor, shot a second and final time at pointblank range against the temple. Given what I'm seeing, I'm guessing the homicide is recent, within a few hours. I checked the rest of the windows and don't see anyone else in there.'

'What about shell casings?'

'None on the floor from what I can see, and I also checked out near the front door. I think the guy picked up his brass. No sign of forced entry either or any signs of a struggle. Everything points to Warren knowing the killer. Warren answered the door, saw the guy and invited him in. Then, when Warren turned around, he got shot once in the back of the head and then had what was left of his brain splattered across the floor. Given the exit patterns, my money's on a nine-millimetre hollow-point round.'

'How far away is Warren's home from Danny Hill's?'

'I was wondering that too, so I Googled it. It's sixteen point nine miles.'

'Are there bus routes in that area?'

Pike was quiet for a moment. 'None that I can see from where I'm standing, but I'll check it out,' he said. 'Neighbourhood is geezer central – blue-hairs and Buicks. Homes here are packed pretty tight together, so

I'm sure someone must have seen something, provided he or she was wearing their glasses. And hearing aid. We're going to start canvassing for witnesses.'

'BPD?'

'Not here yet. The EOD guys are a mix of ours and staties.'

'Pull his phone records, see who may have called him this morning.'

'Already on it. Howie, you still on the line?'

'Still here,' Gelfand said.

'If you can spare ERT, I'd recommend having one of the vans here ready and waiting for when the bomb guys release the house to us. That way we can get in and secure the scene, document everything hard and fast. After that, we can loop in BPD.'

Murder wasn't a federal crime. Jumping on a homicide without first informing BPD would be a violation of protocol – and cause a major uproar. Gelfand, however, had some leeway. He could always tell Donnelly that the gunman, who was still considered a terrorist, committed the shooting. Darby, though, wasn't sure the gunman was behind it, at least not yet.

'A couple of our ERT vans, they're unmarked, right?' Pike asked.

'Yeah. I'll send one over,' Gelfand replied. 'I want them inside the house the moment you get the go-ahead.'

As Gelfand began to discuss the operational logistics, Darby pulled the phone away from her ear. She tapped it against her thigh as she gazed out at the early afternoon traffic moving beneath the darkening sky.

No criminal wants to get caught. The reality is that most have the IQ and organization and planning skills of a cucumber. They're lazy and act on impulse, leaving a trail of breadcrumbs that lead right back to their doorstep.

All the cases Darby had worked on during her career revolved around two undisputable facts: the perpetrators were of at least above-average intelligence and they went to immeasurable lengths to make sure they didn't get caught. They wanted to remain hidden, in the shadows, for years, if not decades, so they could do what they loved most: torture and kill with impunity.

But they all showed patterned behaviour. When threatened, they either adapted or they'd get caught.

Here, the perpetrator was front and centre. Here, the pattern was already known, and the perpetrator was deliberately spoon-feeding information to them. The gunman had seized control of the BPD lobby by force and taken three hostages. One of them, Anita Barnes, had been asked by an unknown male to meet a well-known attorney with a history of suing the city inside the police lobby to discuss the death of her grandson, a cold case dating all the way back to the early nineties. The suicide vest strapped to his chest, he claimed, was wired to his heartbeat, and one of several bombs he claimed he had planted around the city had detonated and killed Danny Hill, one of Boston's most well-known, successful detectives.

And now there was another dead cop, a former detective, a man who, according to Coop, had a history of witness intimidation and evidence tampering. Instead of being booted from the force, Trey Warren had been made head of the Latent Fingerprint Division. Such a revelation would surprise the general public, but it didn't surprise her. BPD, like any good law enforcement agency, had their fair share of problems. And like any good law enforcement agency, BPD would want to keep their sins private because at the end of the day what mattered most wasn't right or wrong or punishing the guilty but keeping up appearances. She had the mental and physical scars to prove it.

Darby was watching a pair of pigeons fighting over what looked like the scrap of a hamburger bun when out of the corner of her eye she saw Gelfand pull the phone away from his ear and then rub the corners of his mouth with the back of his hand.

'The gunman killed Danny Hill from a distance,' she told them. 'He didn't get up all close and personal. Someone else shot Warren.'

'Like Big Red's partner?' Gelfand asked. He and Coop had moved closer to her.

'We don't know if the gunman does, in fact, have a partner,' Darby said. 'If he does, then they'd be working in unison, not against each other – and the gunman left evidence behind to lead us to Warren.'

'Not us. You. That's an important distinction, Doc.'

'He wouldn't leave evidence behind with fingerprints on it to lead me to a dead body. He'd want Warren to suffer publicly just like Briggs, just like Danny Hill.'

'Hill is dead.'

'Hill was an accident. He wasn't supposed to be home today – he called in sick, right?'

'That's what Donnelly said.'

The bigger of the two pigeons wrangled the scrap of food from the smaller one and then it jumped, its wings flapping, and took flight. Watching the bird, Darby found herself thinking back to the events this morning in Dorchester.

'So if the gunman didn't kill Warren, then who did?' Gelfand asked. 'Any theories?'

'I don't know. But I'm telling you it wasn't the gunman. It doesn't fit his pattern or agenda. He deliberately left –' Darby cut herself off, straightening.

Gelfand was about to speak when Coop silenced him with his hand.

Something was circling her mind, something to do with what happened this morning in Dorchester. What about Dorchester?

The phone, an inner voice answered. *What about it?* He placed it deep inside a city-owned garbage can. First, he placed the burner inside a bag that already had her name written on it. Warren's prints were on the phone and on the bag. Either the gunman knew Warren or he had followed Warren – and why did Warren own a burner?

That same inner voice spoke to her again: *The burner doesn't matter.*

Okay, fine. But why?

The answer wouldn't come to her. *Don't chase it. Wait for it.* But she couldn't wait. Time was moving forward and they had forty-seven minutes until the next bomb went off. Knowing that – thinking about it – didn't help matters. The answer slipped away like a snake retreating from sudden daylight.

Gelfand's phone rang and he answered it. Darby closed her eyes for a moment and tried to shut out all the noise, tried to focus on the gunman walking up the street. The man had called for a taxi. Then he hung up and wrapped the burner in a paper bag with her name written on it. Then he stopped at a city garbage can and –

No. No, he passed another garbage can first, remember?

She did. She did remember. On the convenience store's security video she saw him pass another garbage can. Why would he do that? Why place the burner in a *specific* garbage can, what was there? A sidewalk and a brick wall painted with graffiti. Meaningless words and a mural – a big mural of a black man wearing a hoodie with doves flying around his shoulders and something else there, too, a name: Sean Ellis.

Darby was about to tell Coop to run a name through NCIS when she cautioned herself to slow down. She wasn't sure, not yet. *Don't run anything thought NCIS or the BPD computers until you know for sure.*

Phone in hand, she called up the Google app. A search of 'Sean Ellis Dorchester' came back with a page of headlines, all of them having to do with a Dorchester man who was seeking a new trial. One headline jumped out at her: 'Judge To Rule On Possible 4th Trial For Man Based on Trouble with Fingerprint Evidence.'

Darby tapped the Google 'images' tab on her screen. She saw a mix of white and black faces, but mostly black, several of which bore a strong resemblance to the mural.

Darby turned to Gelfand and said, 'What's going on with Rosemary Shapiro?'

'Still not answering her phone,' Gelfand replied. He stepped closer, pulling back his cuff and shirtsleeve to check his watch. 'We have thirty-one minutes until the next bomb. If you've got something, Doc, we have –'

'I'm well aware of how much time is left, you don't have to remind me,' Darby snapped. She wasn't irritated at Gelfand and he knew that, so there was no need to apologize. 'I need to talk to Shapiro's secretary first, see if I'm right.'

33

+5.16

Coop dialled the secretary's phone number and then conferenced them into the call.

The woman's name was Deborah Young. After Coop did the quick introductions, the woman informed him that Ms Shapiro still hadn't called the office and asked if something was wrong. Coop told her they didn't know anything yet and shuffled her off to Darby.

'Does Ms Shapiro represent an African American man from Dorchester named Sean Ellis?' Darby asked.

Young had a matronly voice and spoke in a crisp, cold tone that reminded Darby of her grammar school principal, Sister Agnes. 'Mr Ellis is – or *was*, I should say – a client. He died last year, in November.'

'Died where?'

'MCI Cedar Junction Prison in Walpole. That information is available on the internet, so I'm not speaking out of school.'

'Family? Where do they live?'

'They're dead, all of them. Mr Ellis's mother was the last to go. There's no one left here, as far as I know. You'll have to ask Ms Shapiro. Have you located her?'

'We're working on it. Did you see the news about Detective Hill?'

'Yes,' the woman replied, her voice pinched tight. 'On the Boston.com website. It keeps crashing.'

Darby imagined the woman clutching her string of pearls. 'What about a former Boston detective named Trey Warren? He's retired now, worked in Fingerprints.'

'If this is in regard to the Sean Ellis case, you'll have to ask Ms Shapiro. I can't discuss such matters.'

'All I'm asking is for –'

'I know what you're asking, and the answer is no, I can't discuss any case details with you even if the client is deceased.'

'How about a client named Levine?'

'I'm assuming that's the last name?'

'I don't know.'

Darby heard the click of keys on the other end of the line.

'There's no one in our database with that name,' the woman said. 'I don't mean to be curt, but I need to get back to work – the phones are ringing off the hook. Call me back with any additional questions, and I'll help you in any way I can.'

The beauty of working with people for a long time was that you developed your own rhythm and shorthand; you didn't have to waste time explaining what and what not to do, what you needed. When Coop nodded and walked away, Darby knew he was going to take care of obtaining all the case information on Sean Ellis without alerting Donnelly or BPD.

With Coop out of earshot, Darby turned to Gelfand and said, 'Send me.'

'Send you where?'

'Back inside the lobby. He won't kill me.'

'He'll have to deliver on his threat or he'll appear weak. Groves was emphatic on that point.'

'He can't kill me if I make myself part of the story.' Darby told him what she wanted to say to the reporters gathered at Mercy Park.

'That's a solid idea. Clever,' Gelfand said after she finished. 'Still, it's a gamble. And I'll need to involve the media people, get them to sign off on it.'

'You want to waste time running this up the flagpole?'

'Those two cases you were going to consult on, those cops who were murdered last year, whatstheirnames?'

'Frank Ventura and Ethan Owen. I haven't read the case files.'

'But the governor asked you specifically if you had.'

'I noticed that too, which is why I asked Coop to very quietly see what he could find out without tipping our hand to BPD.'

'Nothing much slips past you, does it?'

'Ventura, Owen and Trey Warren were all retired – and lived alone. Ventura and Owen, before they were suffocated, someone worked them over with a blunt object. You torture someone for one of two reasons: to obtain information or because you enjoy it. I was told there wasn't a sexual nature involved in the killings, and because both victims were males – and former cops – it falls squarely in the camp of a revenge killing.'

Gelfand rubbed the corner of his mouth with the back of his hand, thinking. 'So we've got two dead cops connected to the gunman – Hill and Warren. Ventura and Owen from last year may or may not play a part, we don't know yet, and we've got a dead child and a guy placed in prison and possibly convicted by wrong fingerprint evidence.'

'And represented by Rosemary Shapiro, whom Anita Barnes was supposed to meet inside the lobby this morning.'

'And Big Red, who is white, is out for revenge based on the death of a black kid and a black guy wrongly convicted? This isn't just some racial thing, there's got to be another connection here – something to do with Warren and Hill, maybe even those two cops from last year.'

'I'll be sure and ask him when I'm inside the lobby.' She saw the doubt flicker across his face. 'We've got a chance to go in and gain leverage, get him to release at least one of the hostages and stop the second bomb, maybe all of those things.'

'And what if he decides to kill one of the hostages? Have you thought of that?'

She had.

'Then we'll both regret it for the rest of our lives,' Darby said.

34

+05.19

Gelfand insisted she go in wearing a bomb suit. The bomb squad units for the BPD, state police and the officers inside the Bureau's Boston field office all used the same top-of-the-line suit that had saved the lives of more than one EOD military officer in Iraq and Afghanistan. The suit was also made of bullet-resistant Kevlar, and the helmet and face shield offered similar protection against gunfire.

Darby insisted she go in wearing her civilian clothes. The suit, she reminded him, was bullet-*resistant*, not bullet*proof*. It also weighed eighty pounds and would require two men and a half an hour's worth of time to put on her. Because of its bulk, the suit would prevent her from running – and if the lobby bombs went off, it wouldn't protect her from the blast's pressure waves. If the gunman wanted to kill her, he would. Better to go in looking strong and confident. Appearances were important. She wanted the man to know she wasn't afraid.

Gelfand tried to convince her to wear SWAT tactical armour: a Kevlar vest and trousers with thigh and shin inserts containing ceramic plating. It was a prudent move, she agreed, but ultimately useless; the gunman could always go for the headshot. She compromised by agreeing to wear a tactical vest.

A federal SWAT officer led her to the 'Bearcat', an Armoured Response Vehicle equipped with night-vision optics, a gas-injection system and a battering ram. The tiny windows were tinted to prevent anyone from seeing inside, and a black matte finish covered the ballistic plating.

After Darby hopped into the back, the agent shut the door and then pounded a fist twice against the side, the signal for the driver to go. She gripped the grab-handles then opened one of the overhead aluminium-finish cabinets and rooted through the vests until she found her size.

Carrying the vest, she made her way to the front of the ARV, passing the ladder leading up to the turret, and entered the area right behind the driver – the place where the hostage negotiator sat on a mounted swivel chair at a counter packed with communication equipment. It was cold in here; she could see her breath. She could also see out the front window: another BPD caravan of flashing lights and sirens was waiting for her beyond the entrance of the parking lot.

The vest was too bulky to fit underneath her leather jacket. She'd have to leave it here.

As she began to click the vest straps into place, a random memory flashed through her mind: her father sitting beside her in the roller-coaster car at Canobie Lake Amusement Park in Salem, New Hampshire. She was eight or so, and it was her first time on a roller coaster. She remembered the metallic click of the bar that locked them against the seat, and she remembered the sickening and sinking feeling in her stomach as the car crawled its way up to the first drop, *clank-clank-clank*. She remembered looking behind her, back at the platform, back where it was safe.

Everything will be fine, her father had told her. *If it gets too scary, just shut your eyes.*

She wasn't eight any more, and she couldn't shut her eyes.

The Bearcat picking up speed and the outside sirens piercing the ARV's protective walls, Darby searched for something to hold her attention. The wall-mounted whiteboards were bare, and all the communications and tactical equipment was bolted and strapped down to the counters and wall-compartments. The view out the tiny window above the scuffed counter showed nothing but traffic. It was only early afternoon and the sky was dark. She could see the snowflakes swirling in all the headlights.

The voice of the gunman's parting words came to her: *Come in here again without Briggs and the only way you'll leave here is in a body bag.*

She had made a will not that long ago. With no husband, children or surviving family, she had named Coop as the sole beneficiary of her life insurance policies, savings and investments. The will was filed with a Boston lawyer who, oddly, had been recommended to her by Rosemary Shapiro. She had told Coop the name of the lawyer, but what if he forgot? She needed to remind him.

The counter where she sat had drawers on the right secured by locking clips so they wouldn't open during transport. Darby unlocked one and pulled it open, hoping to find a paper and pen. She found them, along with a small microcassette recorder.

The gunman's jamming unit had scrambled the BPD lobby cameras and prevented her conversation with him from being recorded on the FBI's FBIRD. The FBIRD was a digital recorder; the microcassette was analogue, a totally different – and much older – technology. Most jamming units didn't cover analogue.

When she pressed the PLAY button, a tiny light turned green and she saw the cassette wheels go round and round. She pressed STOP and then slid the recorder with the microphone sticking outwards into an empty breast pocket on her vest. She tucked the flap underneath it so there wouldn't be any interference.

Darby was writing her last will and testament along with the contact information for where Coop could find her will when the driver called out. His voice startled her.

She didn't hear what he'd said. She finished writing, then ripped the piece of paper from the pad, folded it and then pushed herself out of her seat.

Holding on to a grip bar, she knelt behind the driver. She had to yell over the sirens.

'Can you repeat that? I didn't hear you.'

'I said Gelfand just called.' The driver had a thick moustache and long black hair flecked with grey, and he smelled of cigars, like her father had. She pegged his age somewhere in his mid to late fifties. 'He wanted me to tell you they located Rosemary Shapiro and that she's okay.'

'Where?'

'House down the Cape. That's all I know. He didn't get into any details.'

'Okay. Thanks.'

'One other thing,' he said. 'Mercy Park is gonna be a feeding frenzy, like sharks circling a bleeding seal. I were you, I'd address them from the turret. That way they can't claw at you.'

It was a good idea, strategic, but a bad image on TV, her poking her head out of an armoured vehicle and addressing the crowd like she was George Patton with breasts. She wanted to look into all those TV cameras and show the gunman she wasn't afraid of him – of anyone.

'I'll be fine,' Darby said.

'Your funeral.' The driver meant it as a joke. Then he remembered where he was taking her after the press conference and added, 'Sorry, bad choice of words.'

'In case I don't come out of the lobby, I want you to give this to Special Agent Jackson Cooper.' Darby reached across the man's shoulder, and handed him a folded piece of paper. 'SAC Gelfand knows who he is, you can give it to him.'

She returned to her seat, feeling as though she was

strapped inside another roller coaster – only she couldn't see where she was heading.

There was no way to stop it now. All she could do was hang on and hope and pray that her instincts were right, that the gunman would let her live long enough to see his final destination.

35

+05.24

Darby had given her fair share of press conferences over the years, but when she looked through the ARV's tinted window and saw the media crowd gathered behind the sawhorses on the dead winter grass at Mercy Park, the limbs above them stripped of leaves, she understood why the driver suggested she speak from the turret.

The ARV pulled up against the kerb along with the pair of BPD cruisers that had escorted them. A dozen or so blue uniforms were already standing on the sidewalk, their breath steaming in the cold air, snow dusting the brims of their caps. She went out through the back doors, alone, and the moment the patrolmen saw her they formed a protective barrier between her and the sawhorses sitting on the edge of the park.

The flashing blue-and-whites and the sight of the armoured truck shaped like a tank had drawn the crowd's attention; some reporters and cameramen were already running towards her. Others quickly followed suit and within seconds she saw a tornado of limbs and bright camera lights scrambling in her direction. For some reason it triggered a memory of a story her father had once told her about his father, Michael, who had grown up during the Great Depression. He had been standing in a government bread line when the news got out that there wouldn't be enough to feed everyone. Fights broke out, everyone clawing at each other, including women and children, to get their hands on the food scraps.

Darby braced herself, squinting against the combined glare from all the camera lights and wishing it was still daylight out so she could wear her sunglasses; she felt exposed and vulnerable, like she was about to undergo the psychological equivalent of a rectal exam. She couldn't hide behind sunglasses; she couldn't hide at all. She had to look into the cameras when she made her statement; the gunman might be watching the live coverage on his satellite phone.

The shouting began at once, everyone jockeying for position behind the sawhorses:

'Why has the gunman requested to see former mayor Briggs – and why isn't he here?'

'Why is the gunman referring to himself as Big Red, the nickname of your father, Thomas McCormick?'

'Is it true the gunman contacted Globe *reporter David Carlson?'*

'How many bombs has Big Red planted in the city?'

'Why did Big Red choose you as his spokesman – and what were you doing inside the lobby this morning?'

'Is it true the gunman deliberately left evidence with your name on it this morning in Dorchester?'

Hearing that, Darby flinched internally but kept the

surprise from reaching her face. Someone had already leaked the information – not all that surprising. What did surprise her was how fast the press had found out. She wondered if Commissioner Donnelly or the governor or current mayor had slipped that to the press, the first step in their campaign to shift blame for what was happening and whatever was about to happen to her.

Darby motioned for everyone to be silent and still.

Then, when the uproar died down: 'I have a statement to make,' she said. Flashbulbs exploded in her face and everywhere she looked she saw microphones and recorders and smartphones and TV cameras aimed at her. 'The gunman, who identified himself as "Big Red" to Mr Carlson, a *Boston Globe* reporter, has released one hostage, and I believe he is about to release another. I'm about to head back into the lobby to speak with him. He has promised me my safety and the safety of the hostages. He has requested an audience with former mayor Edward Briggs, who is currently en route to Boston from upstate Vermont where he was skiing with his family.

'At the present time we don't know why the gunman wants to talk to Mr Briggs, but the gunman has assured us that he will surrender himself and also disarm and give us the locations of the remaining explosive devices after he has aired his grievance with Mr Briggs. As a show of good faith, he has agreed not to detonate the second and third explosive devices.'

Those were the words she had rehearsed with

Gelfand and Alan Grove. Darby decided to add a few of her own.

'Mr Briggs has agreed to speak with the gunman when he arrives. I'll accompany him inside the lobby. I'll have more information for you when I return from the police station. Thank you.'

Darby turned her back to the crowd and darted to the ARV as reporters shouted questions.

Their voices were mercifully silenced when she slammed the heavy steel doors shut.

Now the ARV was moving away from the kerb, the engine rumbling beneath her boots, on her way to see the man who had promised to kill her if she didn't return without the former mayor.

Her parting statement had ensured that Briggs wouldn't be able to slither away. Hopefully.

Thinking about Donnelly, Mayor Finch and Governor Vaughan screaming at their TV screens made her smile. Gelfand would catch heat but she would make it a point to tell the Boston trio it had been her idea and not Gelfand's.

Now she wondered about her current course of action concerning the gunman.

What if her instincts were wrong this time?

What if the gunman carried through on his promise to kill her?

In her mind's eye she saw herself writhing in pain on the lobby's cold marble floor, clutching a bullet wound on her stomach as she bled out, choking to death on her own blood, dying alone in the place where she had given fifteen years of her life; dying inside the belly of the same institution that had given the orders to murder her father. What a fitting and ironic end.

Darby closed her eyes and leaned back on the bench where dozens of SWAT officers had sat before her, praying and preparing, about to risk their lives. She didn't think about the gunman, or Briggs, or Coop or anyone else. Who she thought about, who she always thought about in these situations, was her father, and it was always the same question: If he was alive and in her position, what would he do?

There was no pause or need to think. The answer came swiftly and smoothly, like the lapping of a wave against the shore: Her father would go back into the lobby and use every last scrap of his God-given and hard-won talents to try to save a life. To get at the truth. No matter what happened, he'd go down swinging. Better to go out fighting for what you believed in than to fade away.

36

+05.31

Darby used the short walk from the ARV to the station to fortify her courage. The snow danced across her face and vision, but she could make out the SWAT officer crouched by the corner not far from the front door, waiting for her. The sky was getting darker and again from high overhead came the thumping of two, possibly three news copters.

The lobby doors were growing larger, her legs were fluttering with anxiety, but there was some hope there too, she *was* hopeful, and she saw the SWAT agent holding a suitcase phone. He leaned in close to her ear to speak.

The unit was already hooked up, he told her. All she had to do was deliver it. He handed her the receiver.

Standing at the front doors now, she gripped the handle, the steel cold against her calloused fingers and palm, and took in a deep breath. The vest was snug and she could feel her heart beating against the ceramic plating.

The agent, crouching, held the door open an inch or two as she walked inside, the wire connected to the receiver unspooling behind her. The right part of the lobby near the bevelled windows was partially lit up by the streetlights. No windows past the checkpoint, in the heart of the lobby; it was black in there, the power turned off. No sounds coming from there either. No breathing or crying, just the roar of blood pounding in her ears.

Darby moved to the raised marble planter, stopped. It came up to the midsection of her chest. Carefully, she draped the phone and wire over the planter and then stared into the darkness, waiting for him to speak.

Finally, he did, his voice still distorted by the voice modulator. 'For your sake I hope Mr Briggs is with you.'

'Briggs hasn't arrived yet.' Darby hurried into the silence. 'I brought a throw phone. It was my idea. They didn't want me to come back here without Briggs, either, but I insisted.' She felt cold all over, her throat bone dry, but her voice sounded calm and clear. Strong. 'I found the evidence you left for me in the garbage can.'

No response.

Darby kept staring into the darkness, trying to find him. 'They pulled the prints off the burner, just like you wanted them to,' she said. 'Why did you leave evidence behind with my name on it?'

'Surely I've made my meaning plain, Doctor. You can imagine my excitement when you showed up inside the lobby this morning.'

'How did you know I'd be there?'

'I didn't.'

'But you knew I was in town. How?'

'The blessings of social media,' the gunman replied. 'Everyone loves sharing their meaningless thoughts, as though we matter. I know you're not on Facebook, but your friends are particularly chatty, especially when it comes to things like weddings. Have you had a chance to see some of the pictures they posted of last night?'

'I've been busy.'

'You should really dress up more. You looked stunning.'

Then Darby heard a sound, the kind a rolling chair would make. She was expecting to see the pregnant woman, Laura. Instead, she saw the other hostage, the woman with the curly white hair. Her mouth and eyes were taped shut and, Darby noticed, the woman was wearing the gunman's scarf.

'I gave a press conference right before I came here,' Darby said. 'I assured the public that you want a peaceful solution – that all you want to do is talk to Briggs on live TV. I also told them you've agreed to release the hostages and disarm the remaining bombs.'

Big Red began to remove the scarf with one hand, the other holding his weapon. 'Why would you say such a foolish thing?'

'Because Danny Hill and Trey Warren are dead.'

The hand working on removing the scarf paused for a moment. Then Big Red whipped the scarf away with flourish.

'Look at the woman's neck,' Big Red said.

Darby already was. The woman was wearing a steel collar, the metal about three inches wide.

'You can watch her suffocate to death – or not,' Big Red said. 'I don't care.'

'They believe you killed Warren,' she said.

'Of course they do.' Big Red turned something behind the woman's neck, but he didn't take his eyes – or the gun – off Darby.

'I believe Hill was an accident,' Darby said.

The woman sucked air greedily through her nostrils as she tried to fight off the gunman; but she had been bound to the chair with tape and plastic cuffs.

'Hill wasn't supposed to be home today, called in sick,' Darby said. 'They found part of him inside the rubble.'

Big Red twisted the lever or whatever it was behind the woman's head.

'*Listen to me*,' Darby said. 'I don't believe you killed Trey Warren. I'm the only one who believes that.'

'I didn't kill him. But I will admit to killing the two retired homicide cops last year, Frank Ventura and Ethan Owen. I tortured and killed them.'

Another twist of the lever and the woman bucked against her restraints as Darby said, 'I was the one who came here. If you want to torture anyone –'

'I am torturing you.'

Then Darby made a hard, tactical decision. 'We can't find Rosemary Shapiro. No one can,' she lied. 'That was the other reason why I insisted on coming back here, alone. Do you have any idea where she might be? What might have happened to her?'

Big Red said nothing.

Turned the lever again.

The woman was gasping. Choking.

'I also found the second piece of evidence you left for me,' Darby said. 'The mural for Sean Ellis. That's why you left the burner in that particular garbage can.'

'You're very clever. You should be a detective.'

The metal was digging deeper into the woman's neck and her face was a deep, dark red from lack of oxygen; she was going to suffocate. Darby had her hands on the edge of the marble planter, wanting to jump it, wanting to help the woman and knowing if she did the gunman calling himself Big Red would shoot her and kill her – but she couldn't just stand here and watch and do nothing.

'You've set all the chess pieces in motion, but I think someone else is taking them off the board,' Darby said. 'I'm the only one who believes that, by the way.'

The woman's nostrils flared, trying to suck in air as she gagged behind the tape, choking.

Dying.

'If you kill her, I'm done. I won't –'

The gunshot exploded against her ears and slammed into her skull and she dropped to the floor, on to her stomach. Had she been hit? Where? She couldn't feel anything through the spikes of adrenaline, and she heard a second gunshot and screaming. Her limbs were working and there wasn't any pain and she was scrambling and clawing her way to the SWAT agent crouching low and holding the door open for her with the toe of his boot, the man behind him looking down the tactical scope of his MP6 submachine gun, ready to fire, ready to rush inside.

But they couldn't rush inside because of the bomb, didn't want to rush inside, wanted to get the hell out of there now. They grabbed her roughly by the arms and as they pulled her to her feet she heard tinny voices exploding over their headsets, heard another gunshot and the anguished cries of the hostages behind her before they dragged her towards the road, to the waiting ARV, the helicopter lights shining down on them like beacons from heaven.

37

+05.43

When Darby returned to the campus, she entered the MCP through the back and immediately went to the rest room across from the galley. The bathroom was modelled like the ones found on aeroplanes: small and nearly claustrophobic with barely any room to move. But it allowed her a moment of privacy to collect herself.

All the way here she kept choking back the image of the woman slowly suffocating to death, blind and bound, *bam-bam-bam* as the gunshots went off. All the way here she had choked back tears.

There is no greater sin a female law enforcement officer can commit than crying in front of a man. The moment you show weakness, you are ostracized. It had taken her years to prove she was more than just a pretty face. She was smart and she could hold her own with any of them – mentally *and* physically. But at the end of the day it was still a boys'-only club, and some of them – a good majority of them – wouldn't see past her tits.

She locked the door and kept splashing cold water on her face, feeling the aching spots inside her stomach and on her body from where she'd hit the floor, from where the SWAT agents had roughly handled her. Once they got her into the back of the ARV, they had checked her over for places where she might have been shot. Sometimes adrenaline could be so powerful you didn't know you were hit until well after the fact; she had seen it. She was okay, at least physically. Psychologically she was numb, scaled with failure.

Darby shut off the water and grabbed the edges of the tiny vanity mirror, water dripping off her face and pinging softly inside the stainless-steel sink.

She had made the call to go back inside the station, and now one of the hostages was dead. Her fault. She had gone in there without Briggs. She had made the call. Her fault. When this was over, she would visit the woman's family and loved ones and face each and every one of them and tell them that she was partially to blame for what had happened, that she was sorry. The better, more prudent course of action would be to keep her mouth shut in case the family decided to sue. That was what her lawyer would tell her. Mistakes weren't allowed in this new world of lightning communication and TV shows where DNA results were discovered after a three-minute commercial break. The public – the voters – demanded swift and clean justice in easy-to-digest sound bites. Someone had to pay.

But she wasn't built that way, to run and hide. And she couldn't hide now, either. Time to accept what had happened and face it head-on and accept responsibility. She quickly dried herself off with the rough paper towels and unlocked the door.

The walk to the command room seemed long and had the sombre air of a police funeral. The agents in attendance, their faces pale and drawn in sorrow and anger and contempt, saw her coming and immediately lowered their voices and averted their gazes and went back to their work. If things had gone according to plan, there'd be high-fives all around, claps on the back and shoulder. But it had gone to shit, and now she had to be shamed. Failure in law enforcement is as contagious as a hot zone virus; she had to be cast out or they would be infected. That was the law of the blue jungle.

Darby searched herself, searched for some hard-won wisdom to steady her legs and voice, didn't find any. All she had was the same talisman she always relied on: her father. His duty and sense of obligation. His unwavering loyalty. A stand-up guy.

And what did all that get him? Murdered. Dead at forty-five.

Her age now.

She opened the command room door to low voices and grim faces.

38

+05.46

Seated at the conference table were Gelfand, Coop, and Alan Grove, who had his portable negotiator phone unit with him. It sat inside what looked like a small, bulky suitcase, and he had plugged it into a speaker-phone unit that sat in the centre of the table and also another pair of phones, both of which had no keypad or buttons, just an orange shell of hard plastic.

Grove knew the question she was about to ask and shook his head. The gunman hadn't called.

Darby slid into a chair, her gaze sliding to the TV, the sound muted. She saw herself speaking to the reporters and then came a smash cut of aerial footage showing her being dragged through the lobby door. The banner below it read: 'BREAKING NEWS: MULTIPLE GUNSHOTS FIRED INSIDE LOBBY.'

Gelfand answered the next question on her mind. 'We don't have any eyes in the lobby yet, so we don't know who was shot, how bad it is,' he said sombrely.

Darby folded her hands on the table and studied her thumbs. The room felt uncomfortably warm and reeked of cigarettes and mistakes. Hers.

She licked her lips.

Swallowed.

Said, 'He killed one of the hostages.'

'Which one?' Gelfand asked.

'The one with the curly white hair. I don't know her name.' Then she told them about the device strapped around the woman's neck. How she had suffocated to death.

Gelfand scratched the corner of his lip with his thumb and stared down at the table. Coop picked at a hangnail. Grove studied the TV playing more shaky aerial footage showing SWAT officers sprinting through the snow and away from the building, assuming it was going to blow.

'We heard most of your conversation with the gunman,' Gelfand said after a moment.

Darby was confused.

'When you entered the station, SWAT used a shielded audio device that picked up your conversation with Big Red,' Gelfand said. 'We managed to hear most of it, but there are some parts that we'll have to get enhanced. I just want to be sure I heard this next part correctly: he said he *didn't* kill Trey Warren, but he *did* say he killed those two retired officers last year, Frank Ventura and Ethan Owen.'

Darby nodded, glanced at her watch. Twelve minutes until the next bomb went off.

Grove turned away from the TV and looked directly at Darby from across the table. When he spoke, his voice trembled with anger. 'Dr McCormick, I want to go on record saying that what you did . . . It was aggressive, but it was the right call. Let me say that again: you made the right call. We had to try something – we just couldn't sit back and continue to wait. And you –' he tapped his finger repeatedly against the table for emphasis '– *you* were the one who risked her life, no one else. Anyone who says otherwise or gives you any grief is a goddamn fool and an asshole. I'm referring to Police Commissioner Donnelly.'

She appreciated the dry vote of confidence, but it didn't change how she felt, even when Coop and Gelfand nodded in agreement. 'Where *is* Donnelly?' she asked.

'Off somewhere having a heart attack,' Gelfand said. 'He was watching your press conference, and when you added that part about Briggs promising to go inside the lobby, Donnelly looked like an aorta had exploded inside his chest.'

'I added that part in case the gunman was watching the news coverage on his satellite phone. I wanted him to think everyone had agreed to play ball with him, that we wanted –'

'Cut the shit,' Gelfand said. There was no heat or anger in his voice, just a sad and weary acceptance. 'You want Briggs to go into the station and shame himself on TV just as much as the Big Red does. That's why you went off script and said that.'

'I don't even know what Briggs is guilty of, how he fits into any of this. Where is he?'

'New Hampshire, about half an hour from the Mass. border.'

'So there's no way he's going to get here before the second bomb's due to detonate?'

Gelfand sighed heavily. Shook his head. 'We located the reporter, Carlson. The call from the hostage, it came directly to his cell number. He spoke to the woman but said she couldn't answer any questions, just read off those lines. We've got a pair of agents with Carlson in case the gunman calls again, so we don't have to learn about any breaking news developments on Twitter.'

'Shapiro?'

'On her way here. Power went out last night on the Cape and her cell phone didn't charge so she couldn't call.'

'And Sean Ellis, what did she have to say about him?'

'She said she can't discuss any aspect of the case because the city asked for – and received – protective orders to keep depositions and documents sealed, including depositions given by former officers. But she did suggest we might want to take a look at the fingerprint evidence used to convict Ellis.'

'So, they're all connected somehow – Danny Hill, Trey Warren and the two dead cops from last year.'

'And Shapiro.'

'And the former mayor,' Darby said. 'He's at the centre of this. He have anything to add, Howie?'

Gelfand shook his head. 'Did Big Red say why he suffocated those two cops last year? We couldn't hear what he said.'

'No. He just confessed to killing them.'

'I can tell you one thing: Anita Barnes's grandson, String Bean? Danny Hill was the lead detective on that case.'

'The evidence files and murder book?'

'On their way here.'

'What about the Sean Ellis case?'

Gelfand now looked uncomfortable.

'I served BPD with a federal subpoena to turn over all the files, on the basis we may be dealing with a corruption issue or possibly a criminal enterprise.'

That took some balls, Darby thought.

'Agents are at BPD's Hyde Park storage facility gathering everything as we speak,' Gelfand said. 'The subpoena also covers the personnel files of the officers involved, but the lawyers and police union will fight us on those. Donnelly is still fighting to take this away from us, claiming we're using the Ellis case as a bullshit stalling tactic to keep this thing with the gunman on our side of the court.'

The phone nestled inside Grove's portable hostage negotiating unit rang.

'Let it ring,' Grove said to them. 'I want him to think –'

Darby jumped to her feet and grabbed the phone.

39

+05.50

The gunman's robotic voice echoed over the speakerphone: 'Is this line being recorded?' he asked.

'You bet your ass it is, you son of a bitch,' Darby replied.

'Dr McCormick. Good, you're there. I want to go on record as saying I did not – I repeat, I did not – kill Trey Warren. And Danny 'Mr Murder' Hill was an accident. He wasn't supposed to be home today.'

A part of Darby felt vindicated. Her theory on Hill had been correct.

She was about to speak when Big Red said, 'Go to five-forty-eight Greenview Street in Dorchester. The woman who lives there, Clara Lacy – I want you to move her and her family someplace safe. BPD, Donnelly, the FBI – they're not to know her location. They're not to be trusted. Don't send anyone else, she'll only speak to you.'

'I'm not your errand bitch,' Darby said. All eyes were on her, the men wondering what she was doing. She didn't look at them, only at the speakerphone. 'I gave you a chance back there – I told you what would happen if you killed that woman, what I –'

'The second IED is located at one-fifteen River Street in Hyde Park, a place called C & J Automotive Repair.'

'How do we disarm it?'

'You only have nine minutes left. Your people won't make it there in time.'

'How do we disarm it?'

Big Red didn't answer. Darby thought he had hung up when he said, 'It's a seven-digit code. Enter it into the keypad and the bomb is rendered safe.'

Rendered safe was another cop term, which again strengthened her feeling that the gunman had been law enforcement or had some law enforcement background.

'The garage is closed up and boarded, you'll have to break down the front door,' Big Red said. 'The bomb is to the right, inside the office.'

'The code?'

Big Red rattled off a series of numbers. Everyone wrote on notepads.

Darby had a pen but no paper; she wrote the code on her palm. She saw the sequence of numbers and felt her stomach turn.

Gelfand was out the door, and Coop stole a glance at her from across the table when Big Red said, 'Call me when Clara Lacy and her family are safe.'

'Not until I speak to the hostage.'

'Are you a fan of Fitzgerald?'

The question took her completely by surprise. Darby was stunned into silence.

'F. Scott Fitzgerald, the writer,' Big Red said.

'Make your point.'

'He said a line that has always stuck with me: "Show me a hero and I'll write you a tragic story." After you've secured Clara and her family, when I know they're safe, then you're free to leave and go back to your life.'

'I want –'

Click.

Big Red had hung up.

40

+05.53

Within short order, Gelfand had coordinated the bomb location and the code needed to disarm it with the bomb commander, Ted Scott. They were rushing against time, and the bomb squad did not like to rush, not when their lives were at stake, not when they feared they could possibly be walking into a trap.

Scott placed the call to evacuate the area. Fortunately, a Boston Fire Department station, the Ladder Company 28 and Engine Company 48, was directly across the street from the Hyde Park address the gunman had given them.

Darby had another thought about the address and shared it with the group. 'The mayor's home is in Hyde Park. How far is it from this auto garage?'

'About five miles,' Gelfand replied. 'You know anything about the garage, does it hold some special significance for you?'

Darby shook her head.

Gelfand quickly gave out their assignments. Grove was going to set up in conference room B. He quickly stressed the importance of not allowing the gunman to engage with Clara Lacy until they were told the fate of the hostage. And if the gunman was watching the news on his satellite phone, it might prove useful to have the media there, showing the Bureau delivering the Lacy woman and her family to a waiting car.

Coop was to remain behind here, inside the MCP, and set up in the third and only other spare room and wait there for the evidence, which was, coincidentally, coming from the BPD storage facility in Hyde Park. Darby wondered if there was a connection there as she threaded her way through the trailer – walking, not running. She was sick of running from place to place, trying to put out fires, trying to figure out what was going on and then trying to piece everything together when the gunman pulled the puppet strings again and got them all to dance.

She felt she had cut the strings, but she still didn't like this coming and going. She needed to be still and think. Needed to cut out all the sirens and shouting and just *be* so she could think. This second wind she was experiencing right now wouldn't last long.

Darby was taking the APV to Dorchester; she saw the same driver from earlier sitting behind the wheel. Gelfand wanted experienced bomb personnel there in the event there was a problem. You couldn't be too careful.

Coop caught up with her and asked for a quick word. She knew what she wanted to talk to him about and immediately felt her stomach turn.

The air was loud with sirens and shouting and the

throbbing of big diesel engines, the entire parking lot lit up by a carnival of flashing blue and white and red lights. There was nowhere to speak privately, and it was snowing.

They stood by the APV's back door, away from the wind but not the snow. He leaned in close to her so she could hear him, and she saw he had a folder tucked underneath his arm.

'Those numbers to disarm he bomb,' he began.

'I know,' Darby said. The numbers were the month, day and year of her birthday.

'What is this guy's fascination with you?'

'He's read my press clippings and believes he can trust me to help him bring the truth to light. I think he included me in this because he knows I'll keep digging even if they kill him.'

'Or you. If this guy is, in fact, working alone, and if he isn't responsible for killing Trey Warren –'

'I know what it means.'

'Either Howie or I will call you with instructions on where to take Lacy and her family,' Coop said, opening the back door for her. 'Stay safe and keep your eyes open.'

And here she was, back in Dorchester, at not yet three o'clock, and the sky pitch black. The snow had picked up, and the flashing lights bounced off the windows of mismatched and sad-looking homes crowded together, and off the windshields of the cars parked bumper to bumper against the sidewalks. The narrow street was already clogged with unmarked Bureau cars, the grill lights flashing. All the lights inside Clara Lacy's house were turned on, and as Darby made her way across the street she saw more lights peeking out at her from behind the curtains of falling snow – the lights belonging to TV cameras.

Someone must have tipped off the media. Again. Was it one of the federal agents inside the MCP? Or had one of the news helicopters followed the APV here?

The commotion had drawn the attention of the neighbours, who had put on their winter gear and come out of their homes to see what all the fuss was about, why state troopers and BPD patrolmen were trying to move families off their porches and out of their homes and bring them down the street in the unlikely but still possible event an IED had been left here by the gunman, if the man had decided to lead them into a trap.

Clara Lacy lived in a small Cape home with chipped green paint and overgrown hedges. There were no outside lights but she could see footprints everywhere, heard one or two bomb-sniffing dogs barking somewhere behind the chain-link fence for the backyard.

Darby was moving across the walkway and looking to her left, at a German shepherd wearing a tactical vest and sniffing at something inside the hedges, when a mountain moved in front of her and blocked her path.

41

+06.02

Detective Murphy was grinning like a Cheshire cat. His hair was wet from the snow and he had a lit cigarette pinched between his stubby fingers.

'Law enforcement personnel only,' he said to Darby. 'Please turn around and leave.'

'SAC Gelfand instructed me –'

'Murder isn't a federal crime and you're not law enforcement, which earns you a one-way ticket to "get the fuck out of here".'

Murder. Darby felt her entire midsection disappear. 'What happened?'

'None of your business, that's what happened.' He moved closer to her, grinning. The dark light worming its way into her eyes, reminding her of certain men who got off on verbally abusing women. 'Time for you to leave.'

Darby didn't move. Murphy screwed the cigarette into the corner of his mouth, and when he grabbed her roughly by the arm she pivoted on her foot and used the heel of her palm to shatter his nose.

Murphy howled and clawed at his face as he staggered to his knees, blood spurting between his fingers.

Darby grabbed him by the shirt collar and leaned forward, near his ear.

'Try and arrest me and I'll say you groped me and you'll get hit with a sexual assault change. It'll go into your jacket, and you'll be riding a desk until retirement.'

Murphy couldn't answer, even if he had been so inclined; he was too busy choking on the blood pouring into his throat.

'Keep your fat ass right here, away from the crime scene, or you'll contaminate it. Now put some ice on that nose,' Darby said, and then threw him face-forward into the snow.

A handful of law enforcement officers had heard Murphy's plaintive howl and emerged from the curtains of snow to stare at her with a mix of wonderment and admiration and disgust.

'Any of you Feds?'

Two men stepped forward.

'Follow me,' Darby said, and moved up the front steps.

She tried the front door. It was unlocked.

'SAC Gelfand wants this crime scene secured,' she told the agents. 'That means no one is to go in there. You can't handle that, call for backup, but under no circumstances are you to let anyone in here.'

Then she stepped inside a small foyer that opened up to a living room holding old and mismatched and hand-me-down furniture and decorations. The air was warm and smelled faintly of fried bacon, and the pale walls were decorated with cheap frames holding family photographs and pictures of Jesus and his mother Mary and the Pope.

Not having any forensic equipment and not wanting to contaminate the crime scene, she slipped out of her boots and placed them on the mat by the front door. Then she took the stairs, sticking close to the side, away from any potential footwear evidence. She was halfway up the stairs when the odour of cordite mixed with blood and feces assaulted her.

Breathing through her mouth, she carefully navigated her way to the doorway at the end of the hall. From there, she studied the murder scene.

Slumped in the corner, near a rickety-looking TV cabinet holding a flat screen, were the bodies of a man and woman, both African American, both in their early to mid thirties and dressed in sleepwear: bathrobes and pyjamas. The man was barefoot, and the woman wore a single pink slipper. Both had been shot in the forehead, and the exit wounds in the back of their skulls suggested they had been shot with a hollow point round – like Trey Warren. The blood spray patterns on the wall behind them clearly stated they had been shot while standing.

A single bed in here, a queen, and the African American woman lying underneath the quilt and a mound of blankets had a pillow over her head. She had bony arms and arthritic hands, and when Darby pinched the edge of the pillowcase and lifted, she saw grey hair and a gaunt face ravaged by time and disease. No gunshot wounds or blood. The woman had been smothered to death.

Darby replaced the pillow back across the woman's face, for the crime scene investigators, and then touched the woman's wrist with her bare hand. The skin felt relatively warm. She lifted the arm and felt no resistance; rigor mortis hadn't set in, which meant the murder had occurred in a three-hour timeframe, proof that the gunman couldn't have done this.

Someone else had killed Clara Lacy and her family.

Someone else had killed Trey Warren.

Someone else was killing people who were connected to the gunman's agenda, silencing them.

42

+06.06

The media had gotten wind of something going down in Dorchester. When Darby left the house, she saw half a dozen or so camera crews set up on the sidewalks, behind walls of patrolmen and state troopers working hard to keep them at bay.

Shit. If the gunman was watching live coverage on his satellite phone . . .

Darby got on the horn to Gelfand. She spoke to him from inside the back of the APV so no one could overhear her.

Gelfand was quiet after she told him about what she'd discovered inside Clara Lacy's home. Darby imagined Gelfand slipping a Rolaid on his tongue – probably the entire roll.

'A couple of your agents have secured the house,' she said dourly. 'If I were you, I'd send reinforcements. Boston PD isn't going to let this slide without a fight.'

'I'm already on it.'

'One other thing,' she said. 'The press is already here.'

'I know. I'm watching the horror show right now. Someone must have tipped them off.'

'It's too late to try for a media blackout, so I suggest this: hold off on the pathologist and the Evidence Response Team in case he's watching. Knowing Lacy and her family are dead might push him over the edge.'

'Suicide?'

'Maybe. The satellite jammers Ted Scott was trying to procure from the military bases, what's their status?'

'They arrived in Boston. He's setting them up now.'

'Tell him to hurry up. Howie, before I let you go, we need to get all BPD personnel out of here. Have your people do it, have them appear on TV wearing anything that says FBI on it. I want the gunman to see your people. If the news about Lacy and her family doesn't get out, we can sell the gunman on that: the Bureau is protecting them inside the house.'

'And when he demands to talk to her?'

'One problem at a time.'

'Where are you?'

'Inside the back of the APV.'

'Stay there. I'll call you back in five.'

Darby placed the phone on the counter. Then she propped her elbows on it and dropped her face into her hands and sat alone in the cooling dark, massaging her forehead and wishing she could find a way to slow if not completely stop the roller coaster she was on. There was no case to investigate, just pieces to find and put together. Just jumping from one crisis to another.

Her phone vibrated against the counter. Gelfand.

'Scott says the jammers are in place and working.'

'Finally, some good news.'

'I've got some not-so-great news. First is Rosemary Shapiro. I think she leaked something to the media, 'cause they're saying that she's on her way to see us, that she may have a connection to Big Red – you name it, they're speculating. It's all over the TV. Second thing is the IED in the garage. Gunman was telling us the truth – it was in there – but the bomb squad guys couldn't get the robot in there in time to take a look at it so they decided to let the thing blow. No casualties, though, which is a relief.'

'I've got to find the guy who drove me here and then I'll be on my way back.'

'Listen, I've got to tell you this now.'

'Tell me what?'

'Donnelly has been working the phone – along with the mayor and governor – calling people above me, and Above is telling me I've failed to establish a nexus of terror – God I love that phrase – and that means the ball bounces back into BPD's court.'

Darby had been worried about this. 'You just served a federal subpoena to the BPD on the basis of corruption and possibly a criminal enterprise,' she said. 'They can't just decide to shut it down now.'

'Oh, they can – and they will. The Bureau can deal with the police corruption/criminal enterprise shit later. Right now the FBI wants Donnelly to spearhead this abortion, which is *exactly* where this thing is heading. Tell me I'm wrong.'

He wasn't. The Bureau was going to dump the

gunman on Donnelly's lap and watch from the sidelines. When this op turned to shit – and it probably would – then the blame game of musical chairs would start, with Donnelly as the ringleader, saying that the op wouldn't have gone south if he and BPD had been given the reins earlier, when they requested operational control over the incident. The Bureau wanted to back off now and then use the corruption and criminal enterprise charges, if anything came of them, if and when Donnelly decided to go on the attack. Pure politics. As usual.

Darby squeezed her phone. 'How much time?'

'Who knows? And, frankly, who cares? I'm about ready to go tie one on and then go home and jump in the sack with my wife, provided my prostate is still up for the job, see if I can convince her to try this new position called a "reverse cowgirl". Maybe you can give me a few pointers on how to introduce the subject. Then I'm going to call it a day and wake up tomorrow and go see my kids, maybe take them to that indoor waterslide up north. You want to come? My son's thirteen. He'd love to see you in a bikini.'

'What about the case files and materials for Sean Ellis?'

'They're on their way here, along with Rosemary Shapiro. Is it true you hired her to sue the city?'

'I met with her but I didn't hire her.'

'Why not?'

'You know how these things go, Howie. How the case drags on for years and years, the city's attorneys always stalling and hoping you give up or, even better, die from all the waiting. Then, if they actually *do* decide to settle, they make you sign documents that prevent the entire truth from coming out.'

'Can I give you a piece of advice, Doc?'

'No.'

'Sue the city. Then go and settle down with Cooper or another guy, adopt a kid or a puppy. Get off this merry-go-round of bullshit and go and enjoy your life – I mean, suck the *marrow* out of it. Eat, drink and be merry, and go to bed every night next to someone who makes you laugh and has your back. That's it, that's the meaning of life. You're welcome.'

'Where's Coop?'

'Here, waiting for the files to be delivered.'

'Tell him I'm on my way.'

'Go home. Go back to your life.'

This is my life, she wanted to say. 'I need to see this through to the end, Howie.'

'It always ends the same way, Doc, with someone's blood painted all over the walls.'

43

+06.20

It was psychologically jarring to go from the adrenaline-fuelled and life-jeopardizing moments compromising almost every minute of the last few hours to being asked to sit inside a small, cramped room and sort through paper. Darby also felt a distinct physical shift inside herself. Now that she knew she'd have to sit still, her body instinctively wanted to crash. It told her to shut off all the lights and curl up on top of the table and go to sleep. Better yet, head back to the hotel and slide into a warm, soft bed.

Instead, she took off her jacket, draped it over the back of a chair, and chugged the Coke she'd grabbed from the galley.

Coop wasn't wearing his suit jacket. His tie was undone, and he had rolled up his shirtsleeves. 'It's too damn hot in here,' he snapped, pulling off the top of an evidence box.

He was right about the heat. There were no windows to open and no separate thermostat, and with the piles of boxes, almost all of them pitted with water stains, not much room to move.

Coop pinched his temples and then massaged his

eyebrows with his fingers as his gaze bounced over the room, at the staggering amount of boxes holding files and evidence for Sean Ellis and Anita Barnes's grandson, and the pair of retired cops murdered last year, Frank Ventura and Ethan Owen.

'I don't know even where to start.'

'With Sean Ellis,' Darby said. 'I'll do the paper. You can –'

'This is bullshit.' His jaw muscles bunched, his eyes watery and heated. 'This asshole says jump and we drop whatever we're doing and go running off to the next thing. We're not investigating anything, we're just jumping from one thing to the next.'

'No argument there. But I genuinely feel he's –'

'Let's just get to work,' Coop said, and handed her a thick black three-ring binder.

She had known him for a long time, knew his rhythms and facial expressions and tics. She knew something else was eating at him – something that was at the moment caged but wanted to get out and start tearing down walls, knock over buildings. She also knew pressing him to talk when he was in this place was useless; he'd just shut down. Retreat.

'We have access to BPD computers?' she asked.

Coop ran a finger down the inventory list of evidence. 'Last time I checked,' he said. 'The Ellis case, though, wasn't in the system.'

It *should* have been logged into the computer system. But a lot of the old cases – and this was one of them – hadn't been entered when BPD switched over to computers because of cutbacks and lack of personnel.

'If Donnelly takes over, BPD access disappears,' Coop said with distaste. 'Better hurry.'

Eyes dry and burning with fatigue, Darby flipped open the binder, the spine cracking from age, and dived into the typewritten pages yellowed by time.

At six p.m. on September 30, 1992, Boston Patrolman Stephen Fitzpatrick spotted what he wrote up as a 'suspicious black male' looking at a pre-teen girl sitting alone on a stoop near a bus stop on Dixwell Street in Dorchester. Something in the way the man was looking at the girl made Fitzpatrick wary, and the patrolman decided to make an approach.

The suspect immediately began to walk away. Fitzpatrick followed him through Egleston Square, where it quickly turned into a chase.

Fitzpatrick pursued the man through a park on Columbus Avenue and down Cleaves Street, which ended in a fifteen-foot drop to the street below it, Boynton Avenue. By the time Fitzpatrick reached Boynton, he had lost sight of the suspect. There, an unidentified bystander told Fitzpatrick the suspect had fled into a fenced yard on the other side of the road, at 7 Boynton.

Fitzpatrick approached the fence and, peering through the slats, saw the suspect.

Fitzpatrick testified that after he climbed the fence, the suspect attacked him. During the struggle, which lasted almost two minutes according to the patrolman's testimony, the suspect managed to pull Fitzgerald's service weapon, a semi-automatic nine-millimetre Glock, from the holster and fired it three times. One shot hit Fitzpatrick in the right buttock. The other two hit him in the lower back. The suspect fired at least two other times, Fitzpatrick stated, before jumping the fence.

BPD's response was swift. Cops were already swarming the area while EMTs treated Fitzpatrick, who had suffered from a single GSW to the buttock. His bulletproof vest absorbed the two shots fired at his lower back.

A two-hour search of the neighbourhood failed to find the shooter. The man seemed to have made an amazing getaway.

But a little over half an hour after the shooting, a group of patrolmen led by Detective Daniel Hill knocked at the door of the house abutting the fenced-in yard. Other officers, the police report noted, had previously knocked on the door and gotten no response.

Hill had better luck. The door opened and the owner of the house, a forty-two-year-old African American woman named Clara Lacy, informed them that the shooter had forced his way inside her house and then held her and her eight-year-old son Raymond at gunpoint for roughly ten minutes before leaving the house.

Clara Lacy told police she didn't recognize the black man – had never seen him before or around the neighbourhood. He carried a nine-millimetre handgun and she described him as 'thin and tall, a couple of inches shy of six foot, and had dark brown eyes'. He wore jeans and Nike high-top basketball sneakers and a black knit hat and a black coat. The man took off his hat at one point and wiped at a cut on his face. Lacy described him as having a close-cropped haircut. She told Hill the shooter stuffed his hat in his coat pocket then helped himself to a can of Coke sitting on a coaster on the table. Hill confiscated the can and logged it into evidence.

Darby now knew the particulars of the incident. And she already knew the outcome: Sean Ellis was convicted of the shooting and served nearly twelve years of a fifteen-year prison sentence before being exonerated on October 3, 2004 after the fingerprint evidence used to convict him was proven to be wrong. He was twenty-eight when he went to prison, almost forty-one when he left. Eight months later, in 2005, someone entered his house, beat him to death with a baseball bat, and then, as he lay dying from massive internal injuries, tied a plastic shopping bag around his head.

The cops who were murdered last year, Ventura and Owen, had been tied down to a chair with duct tape and worked over by a blunt object and then suffocated to death by a plastic shopping bag.

'The evidence for the Sean Ellis homicide,' Darby began.

'Right behind you.'

Darby found the box. Opened it and found the plastic garbage bag sealed inside a clear evidence bag. The garbage bag was white, no writing on it. A generic bag that could have come from anywhere.

The evidence boxes for the Ventura and Owen homicides were stacked in the corner behind Coop, who was busy at work examining the fingerprint evidence used to convict Sean Ellis. Darby pulled the boxes, opened the tops.

The shopping bags used in the homicides were gone.

44

+06.35

Darby grabbed the laptop Coop had brought with him. She tapped a key and the screen came out of sleep mode, Darby relieved to discover the connection to the BPD's computer network was still live.

She had the case numbers for the Ventura and Owen homicides, which gave her access to all the case evidence. A few keystrokes and mouse clicks and she found out why the shopping bags were missing: they had been submitted to the FBI lab for analysis. The BPD crime lab didn't have the ability to run down the manufacturer of the bags, but the Bureau could.

According to the file, the bags were still with the FBI lab. No big surprise there. The federal lab was, and would always be, backed up. Take a number and then wait weeks, sometimes months, for your answer. Typical.

The crime scene pictures of the shopping bags used to kill the two retired cops and the pictures of the same bags taken at the BPD crime lab, where they were measured and photographed under bright light, were included in the file. The bags were white and contained no writing, logos or any printing – just like the one tied around Sean Ellis's head. The bags had been fumed for fingerprints, all of which had been submitted to the federal database, IAFIS. No matches to any known offenders were found, no matches to any other cases.

Something was nagging at her about the Ventura and Owen homicides.

She spent twenty minutes bouncing between the two case files until she found it.

Her mouth was dry, her voice tight when she said, 'Coop.'

He looked at her. Waited.

'The date Frank Ventura was murdered,' she said. 'It's the same month and day of my father's birthday.'

Coop waved it away. 'Coincidence,' he said. 'Don't read into –'

'Ethan Owen was killed on the exact same day my father was shot.'

Coop sunk back in his chair. Darby stared at the floor.

No doubt Lopez had been grilled as to why she had asked Darby to consult on the two case files. Darby didn't know why specifically – she thought she was doing a favour to a friend and colleague – but if the reason why Lopez wanted her to look was because she knew the dates of the two homicides matched Big Red's birthday and death, then it stood to reason Lopez had passed along this information to a Boston detective, maybe even the commissioner himself.

'Do those cases have any significance to you?' the governor had asked her. And she had said no, because it was true – they didn't have any significance to her at that

point because she hadn't read the case files, hadn't seen the dates. The governor, Donnelly – any of them could now spin it to say that she had deliberately lied to them, had withheld information. They would step on her like a roach.

'The evidence for the Sean Ellis homicide is still on the BPD system,' Coop said. He was looking at the computer screen now. 'The bag tied around his head had also been fumed for fingerprints. Nothing on IAFIS.'

'The plastic shopping bag used to kill Ellis looks an awful lot like the ones used to kill Ventura and Owens.'

'I saw that. The prints came up empty.'

'Right, but we should see if any of the prints from the Ellis bag match the prints found on the bags used to suffocate Ventura and Owens. Judging from what I'm reading there, the prints on all three bags haven't been compared. If there's a match –'

'Already spoke to the boys working in the mobile lab. They're on it, getting the info from the federal lab.'

'Then why didn't you just tell me that before I started on this?'

'I look like I'm taking a vacation here? You didn't ask. Now you did, and I answered the question.'

Her face felt hot, the back of her white shirt damp, stuck to her skin. She was tired and angry and she wanted to dump it all on Coop. Instead, she pinched the bridge of her nose and took in a deep breath.

'When I brought out Anita Barnes, she still had duct tape on her mouth. We should see –'

'The guys in the mobile lab are already doing a comparison,' Coop said. He was studying the fingerprint chart shown to the Sean Ellis jury. 'They're in touch with the people in our duct tape library. When I know, you'll know.'

You could have told me that in the beginning and saved me some goddamn time, Darby thought. The words were on her lips, ready to launch, when she swallowed them and sat back in her seat, angry. She didn't try to breathe it away. Anger was underrated; it made a great partner, lit a fire under your ass and cleared away the other bullshit. Darby was wide-awake and laser-focused as she tore through the remaining documents on Sean Ellis's conviction, seeing the holes in the defence and the prosecution.

When she finished, she leaned back in her seat, rubbed her eyes and checked her watch. Almost an hour had passed.

'BPD's radio communications don't add up,' she said.

'I noticed that too.'

'Well, it looks like you've already got the whole thing figured out, so why don't you tell me what I'm missing and we can call it a day.'

Coop's face softened a bit. Just a bit. His face and his eyes were still coiled tightly, like a fist, when he looked up from the fingerprint chart and placed it aside, giving her his full attention.

'The case materials arrived before the evidence did, so I had a chance to dig into the Ellis case a little before you got here,' he said. 'Tell me what you've found, your thoughts. Let's talk it out.'

She stared at him for a beat. Then she said, 'Fitzpatrick radioed that he was going to climb the fence and go after the suspect, but he doesn't mention he's in trouble, that he suspects he's in any trouble. Four seconds later he radioes in a shots fired, then eight seconds later there's a call for an officer shot. Fitzpatrick testified that he had – and I'm quoting here – "a lengthy struggle with the suspect."'

'Said it lasted almost two minutes.'

Darby nodded. 'If that's true, the radio times negate that. And then there's the witness testimony on the evening of the shooting. One witness said there wasn't a struggle, that Fitzpatrick kicked open the gate and went in with his gun drawn. Another witness said he saw the shooter crouched behind the fence, that the guy had his *own* gun drawn, and fired it when Fitzpatrick entered the yard. What's ballistics say?'

'Haven't double-checked the evidence yet, but the report says the shots all came from the same gun – Fitzpatrick's. Thing that's bothering me is Fitzpatrick's testimony regarding the shooter.'

Coop leaned back in his seat, crossed his legs. 'Not long after he's shot, Fitzpatrick starts telling people he knows the shooter – has seen him before, had a few encounters with him, but doesn't know the guy's name. So he's shown an eight-person photo array. Ellis's picture is in it, and Fitzpatrick says Ellis "most resembles" the person who shot him.'

'But he's not positive,' Darby said. 'Those were his exact words.'

'Right. Not positive. So, Fitzpatrick asks for a live lineup because he wants to be sure. That's where it gets real hinky.'

'The lineup comes two *weeks* after the shooting.'

'And by that time, Ellis's name and face are all over the papers and on TV as the main suspect. Everyone in Boston knows him.' Coop shook his head. 'Two *weeks*? That doesn't add up. Fitzpatrick was out of the hospital in two days, they could've arranged it when he was discharged, but two weeks? Nobody does that.'

'And don't forget the grand jury specifically asked for the lineup from Fitzpatrick because Clara Lacy was shown the exact same eight-man photo array and failed to identify Sean Ellis. Lacy and her eight-year-old son – who are now dead.'

'Fitzpatrick goes in, picks Ellis out of eight men, and the next day Ellis is indicted.'

'And the same day Fitzpatrick does the lineup, Clara Lacy is brought in and she fingers Ellis. What's that suggest to you?'

'Possible collusion,' Coop said. 'But as you and I both know, you need evidence to get a conviction, and that's where this comes in.' He tapped the fingerprint chart. 'This is what got Ellis a fifteen-year sentence, this fingerprint evidence doctored by Trey Warren.'

'Doctored,' Darby said.

Coop nodded, kept nodding, Darby feeling as

though some part of him had checked out of the room, was off searching for something, maybe hiding.

'We know Warren didn't have any fingerprint training,' she said.

'True. Here's the thing, though. The chart? The print on the left was taken from the soda can. The print on the right came directly from Sean Ellis, the inked print they took when they booked him. Two things immediately jumped out, the first of which is it says right here on the chart – and in the testimony given by Warren – that he found *sixteen* points of identification. It's unheard of.'

'And the second thing?'

'The print lifted from the soda can? That print doesn't match the one displayed on the chart used on the jury. Warren – or maybe Warren and Hill – maybe a whole group of people wanted to put Ellis away for some reason, and they did it by selling the jury on this bullshit fingerprint testimony back in 'ninety-two.

'What I can't figure out,' Coop said, 'is why.'

45

+07.57

They were quiet for a moment. Through the walls they could hear the chatter of people talking. She wondered how the bomb at the garage in Hyde Park played into the gunman's agenda.

'Ellis was exonerated on DNA evidence,' Coop said. 'DNA from the soda, DNA from the crime scene in the yard – not one single sample matched Sean Ellis. But Ellis doesn't find that out until twelve years into his sentence, when his attorney, Shapiro, and the Innocence Project out of New York pressed for the DNA to be tested *because* BPD never tested it.'

'Judge gets the DNA results back, decides to exonerate Ellis.'

'And the AG at the time, Reilly, says he's going to retry Ellis and never does. My guess is it's because of the fingerprint evidence. He found out there wasn't any fingerprint evidence, maybe even found out it was doctored, and let the thing go.'

'The same year Ellis was convicted was the same year BPD shut down its fingerprint unit, started over from scratch.'

'You read the background material on Ellis?'

Darby nodded. 'Guy wasn't an angel – he was pinched a few times for shoplifting, mainly luxury clothing – but he wasn't a gang-banger, and according to everyone who knew him he hated guns.'

'Was scared of them, according to friends,' Coop added.

'He didn't live in that neighbourhood – lived on the other side of Dorchester. Time of the shooting, Ellis had an old outstanding warrant for a failure to appear in court on a shoplifting-related charge. Why put him in the photo array?'

'Not that unusual, putting in someone different to mix things up.'

'But Hill had already fingered Ellis as a lead suspect when Fitzpatrick was shown the photos two days after the shooting.' Darby flipped open the binder, thumbed through the pages, stopped. 'Here,' she said. 'The day after the shooting, Ellis was arrested on an outstanding warrant and handed over to the lead detectives on the case, Hill and . . . Christ.'

'What?'

'Ventura was one of the lead detectives on the case. Him and Ethan Owen and Hill.' Darby kept reading. Hunting. 'They brought in Ellis to question him about the shooting, told him that they found his prints at the crime scene, as well as DNA and fibre evidence.' Only none of that was true; the detectives didn't have one shred of evidence on Ellis or anyone else. Lying to a suspect was a commonly used interrogation technique to try to elicit a confession, make the suspect feel as though he was cornered, the walls about to fall down on him.

'Who arrested Ellis?' Coop asked.

'That's what I'm looking for.'

It took five minutes of flipping pages and checking a second binder to find it. Darby saw the name and her stomach clenched.

'Robert Murphy,' she said, getting to her feet. 'Son of a bitch was there.'

'Where?'

'At Clara Lacy's house. If I had known this, I could've taken him in then.' Darby had her hand on the doorknob, was thinking about something more sinister: what was Murphy doing at the Lacy house? Could he have been responsible for shooting Clara and her family? Warren? What was Murphy doing inside the lobby this morning?

Coop said, 'He made me clean up after the parties.'

She let go of the doorknob and turned around, feeling thrown off-kilter by his random statement, like she was standing on a boat plunging down the other side of a wave.

'I'm not talking about Murphy,' he said.

Darby waited. Coop stared hard at the fingerprint chart resting on his lap, like he was waiting for a hole to open up so he could disappear through it.

'I'm talking about ghosts now,' he said, his voice raw. 'I'm talking about Frank Sullivan.'

Now Darby swallowed. She wasn't the only one

whose life had been affected by Frank Sullivan. In some ways, Coop had suffered the worst, having grown up in Charlestown.

She wanted to go sit next to him but for some reason was afraid to move, as though the act would cause Coop to shut down. She rested her forearms on the top box of one of the stacks and looked across the table at him.

He wouldn't look at her. 'That garage in Hyde Park? Sullivan owned it, back in the day,' he said. 'I don't mean legally, I'm saying it *belonged* to him. He was there a lot, especially at night, late at night, well after the place shut down. There was this room in the back, a good size one. Sullivan hosted some private . . . get-togethers there.'

Darby said nothing. She knew Sullivan had held private parties all over Boston, featuring every kind of drug imaginable and scores of underage girls, all locals, who were forced into sex to pay off drug and financial debts. He held the parties at hotels and people's homes and all sorts of other places, and a lot of times he secretly recorded what went on and sold the videotapes to porno distributors overseas. A lot of the men wore masks so they couldn't be identified. A lot of the men were law enforcement – BPD, Staties, Feds – who were on Sullivan's payroll.

'Murphy?' she asked.

'Can't say for sure. I never picked him up.'

'Picked him up?'

Coop shifted in his chair. He still wouldn't look at her.

From outside the door, and past the chatter, Darby thought she heard the distinctive ring of the hostage phone and wondered how many times the gunman had called, if he was just calling now for the first time.

They both jumped when the desk phone on the table suddenly rang.

46

+08.06

Darby was the closest to the phone. She reached over a box and scooped up the receiver.

It was Gelfand. 'Why aren't you answering your cell?' he asked.

'It's in my jacket pocket. Why are you calling? Why not just –'

'I'm with Grove. Big Red has called twice. Wants to speak to you about Clara Lacy.'

'What did Grove tell him?'

'Big Red keeps hanging up. Says he'll only speak to you.'

'Is Clara Lacy on the news?'

'Not yet, so he doesn't know anything. It's been an hour and a half, Doc. Where do we stand?'

'I've got some info. Listen, I need your people to quietly find a Boston cop named Robert Murphy and bring him in.'

'The guy you cut off at the knees in the lobby this morning?'

'That's him. He works out of Kenmore. I think he's tied into this thing with the gunman. I'm not sure how yet.' Then she told him about meeting Murphy standing outside Lacy's house when she arrived, leaving out the part about rearranging his nose.

'Shapiro's here,' Gelfand said. 'She's waiting in the conference room with Donnelly and Nappa.'

'The attorney general?'

'Yep. They're here to take over. You got anything to blow them out of the water?'

'Give me five. Actually, make it ten. We still have to check ballistics.' Darby hung up.

Coop stood and grabbed the ballistics stuff. He seemed glad for the distraction.

She didn't have to prod him to speak. Coop knew they had limited time. 'Everyone who lived in Charlestown knew what Sullivan was doing, the drugs and murders, the extortion, but you never went to the police,' he said. 'If you did, you were killed or you disappeared. If you were lucky, maybe he'd only burn down your house. You kept your distance from him, but if he wanted to find you – if he wanted something from you . . .'

Darby knew all of this, was all too familiar with Charlestown's Code of Silence, the fierce tribal street mentality where all matters were settled in the neighbourhood, not by the police. And Coop knew she knew this already. But she didn't say anything because she could feel him circling around whatever it was he wanted to tell her.

'Sullivan saw me witness him killing that guy and he knew he had me – knew I was terrified of him because everyone was, because this guy had the power to make you disappear and no one could stop it,' Coop said. 'So, when he told me to get my ass over to C & J garage, I went. When he handed me keys to one of the cars and told me go pick up so-and-so, I went. I didn't ask any questions.'

'You pick up cops?'

Coop shook his head. 'He had me pick up girls. Locals, mostly. I did, I dunno, maybe a dozen or so trips. I don't remember the faces.' He was quiet for what seemed like an hour, then his voice cracked slightly when said, 'What I remember mostly was them crying. There was a lot of crying.'

Darby said nothing. He had never shared this particular piece of history with her, but one night three years ago when he was drunk, when they were still with BPD and working a case of a skeletal set of remains buried for nearly two decades in the dirt basement of a home in Charlestown, he had told her how an FBI agent picked him up and brought him to the basement where Frank Sullivan was cracking peanut shells as he sat next to a girl around his own age tied down to a chair and gagged with duct tape. Coop had made the fatal mistake of going to a priest and, under the seal of confession, said he couldn't live with the guilt of not telling the police about the man Sullivan murdered. The priest told Sullivan.

And then came the part that changed Coop's life: Sullivan putting a gun to Coop's head and Coop gaping in wide-eyed horror at the girl whose fingers were caked in dirt and bloody from having been forced to dig her own grave with her bare hands, Sullivan saying to him, *One of you is going in that hole. I'll let you make the decision.*

Darby blinked the image away as Coop said, 'A lot of ghosts are in that garage. I don't know any of the cops who were there, don't know how it connects into what's happening with the gunman, his agenda.'

'But Boston cops were definitely there.'

'Yeah. Definitely. I remember seeing a handful there back when I was doing, you know, errands for Sullivan. But those guys are all dead now. I checked.'

'You tell Gelfand about the garage?'

He shook his head.

You should, Darby wanted to say. That would help keep the ball in Gelfand's court, keep the case from turning over to BPD. But she knew why he hadn't said anything.

'You worried Murphy might tie you back to the garage?'

'Of course I am,' he said sombrely. 'What I'm more worried is . . .' He swallowed, steadied himself. 'I killed that woman, Darby. Nothing's going to change that.'

'Sullivan didn't give you a choice.'

'I was the one who put that bag over her head and suffocated her.'

Coop had tied a plastic bag over the woman's head. The two cops from last year had died the same way. Darby wondered if there was a connection between the two, one that led all the way back in time to Frank Sullivan.

'Coop . . . there's nothing from that time that can come and bite us in the ass,' Darby said. 'We destroyed the evidence tying you to that body.'

'I know.'

'What are you worried about, then?'

'Karma,' he said.

47

+08.16

Darby opened the door to the conference room and saw Gelfand standing to her right with his back against the wall and his arms crossed over his chest, his face filled with a sour contempt and directed to a person sitting at the corner of the table: a striking olive-skinned woman with full lips and thick, long black hair that spilled across the shoulders of her ruffled white button shirt.

'I'll say it again, Howie, but this time I'm going to say it extra slow,' Rosemary Shapiro said, her voice thick with sarcasm – her de facto mode of communication. 'I cannot – I repeat, I can*not* discuss the particulars of the Ellis case because of the protective orders that are in place. Now, a protective order is –'

'I know what it is,' Gelfand said, looking relieved to see Darby and Coop, the case materials in their hands.

'Nice to see you again, Darby,' Shapiro said, rising to her feet. She wore big silver loop earrings and a grey pinstriped pencil skirt that hugged her wide and curvy hips. Her gaze landed on Coop, and she smiled brightly. 'Always nice to see *you*, Agent Cooper.'

Two other people were in attendance, both of them

stone-faced, eyes bright with anger, both seated at the opposite end of the table: Commissioner Donnelly and a thin pixie woman with blonde hair worn in a bob – Massachusetts attorney general Tina Nappa.

Shapiro saw the case materials and, rubbing her hands together, said, '*Ooooh*, I love show and tell.'

AG Nappa said to Gelfand, 'Dr McCormick is no longer a law enforcement officer. She can't be present if we discuss sensitive or confidential information.'

Shapiro was grinning from ear to ear. 'I was just telling Howie that I can't speak to that unless Commissioner Shitbird and Mayor Hankey waive the protection order.'

Darby couldn't resist. 'Mayor Hankey?'

'You a fan of the cartoon *South Park*?'

'I've heard of it. Why?'

'There's a character in it named Mr Hankey. He's a piece of shit who lives in the sewer and wears a Santa hat and looks a lot like Mayor Finch, minus the sense of humour – and I'm not saying that because he's black – or African American, or whatever the politically correct term is. What I'm trying to say is they're both pieces of shit.'

Shapiro had been a public defender before becoming one of the most successful attorneys in the city of Boston. At thirty-two, she was involved in a car accident that left her in a medically induced coma for nearly a week. She emerged from it a force of nature and, some liked to say, certifiably insane. The truth was she had never liked to operate within the bounds of propriety or political correctness. She enjoyed making people uncomfortable – especially men – and she spoke a mile a minute, barely let anyone speak and had absolutely no filter.

Gelfand said, 'Big Red has already shared confidential information with Dr McCormick. The cat's out of the bag, Ms Nappa, and Dr McCormick needs to be briefed on all information for when she has to go in and speak to the gunman.'

'Agent Gelfand, this is a waste of time. We're not here for show and tell, as Ms Shapiro so eloquently put it. We're here because Commissioner Donnelly and his people are taking over the situation. Now if –'

'That hasn't been decided yet. I've called my boss, who has bumped the matter up to a federal level. We've got someone from Justice en route, and I think he's going to be very interested in the stuff we're about to show you. Grab a seat everyone.'

'I've always wanted to do this,' Shapiro said, then propped her feet on the corner of the table, not far from Gelfand – a stunning pair of high-heeled black leather boots that came up past her knees. 'They're Givenchy,' she told Gelfand. 'Try not to lick them.'

Coop took the lead. He went over the fingerprint chart shown to the jury and shared his findings. Donnelly, Darby could tell, was itching to get this over with so he could take over the reins. The attorney general listened passively to Coop, Darby knowing the woman was using the time to line up her artillery, aim it at the FBI's vulnerable areas to sink the ship.

'This is the most important part,' Coop said. 'Warren

testified the prints contained sixteen points of identification, making what he called a "strong match".'

Shapiro chimed in. '*Identical* was the word he used in court.' Then she rolled her head to the AG and Donnelly and added, 'Sixteen points of identification, that's far higher than necessary even under the most rigorous standards for a match. Isn't that right, Agent Cooper?'

'It is,' Coop replied. 'The prints recovered from the soda can, they all belonged to Lacy and her son. Sean Ellis's prints weren't anywhere on it.'

Shapiro slapped a hand on her meaty thigh. 'The independent forensic team I hired came to the *exact* same conclusion. Imagine that.'

The AG said, 'The prints were mislabelled. It was an unfortunate mistake –'

'*Unfortunate mistake*?' Shapiro swung her feet off the table and turned in her chair. 'Unfortunate is when you get in a car accident or your bratty kid throws a baseball through your neighbour's window. That, you skinny bitch, is an unfortunate mistake.'

'Ms Shapiro, if you're going to resort to name-calling, this meeting is –'

'Sean Ellis went to prison for twelve years because Boston police officer Trey Warren, a well-known drunk and addict and all around shit of a human being – deliberately falsified evidence. That isn't *unfortunate*, Ms Nappa, it's illegal. It's *criminal*.'

'Miss Shapiro, you're dangerously close to violating the terms of the protective order.'

'The *only* reason Mr Ellis was exonerated was because

I finally managed to convince a judge to get the DNA from that soda can *we* tested. BPD did nothing with it. You people dumped the evidence in a box and forgot about it.'

'Let's not forget that both Ms Lacy and Officer Fitzpatrick were shown photo arrays of eight potential suspects, and Mr Fitzpatrick picked Mr Ellis – and he also identified Mr Ellis in a live lineup.'

'And *that* occurred two weeks later, when the grand jury considering a case against Ellis specifically requested it. By that time Ellis was all over the news.' Shapiro straightened. 'If Fitzpatrick were alive, I'd bet he'd be singing a different tune. Do you know what happened to him?'

The AG stiffened.

'He blew his brains out six months after Ellis went to jail,' Shapiro said. 'Gee, I wonder why he'd do such a thing.'

'Officer Fitzpatrick had a history of depression –'

'Which he *coincidentally* developed shortly after Sean Ellis was arrested.'

AG Nappa ignored Shapiro; she looked directly at Coop. 'Mr Ellis was, in fact, exonerated of the shooting by DNA evidence,' she said primly. 'As for the fingerprint evidence, we're not at liberty to discuss that matter because Mr Ellis, represented by Ms Shapiro, engaged in civil litigation against the city – and won. The terms and conditions of that suit were negotiated and filed under a protective order.'

'Ellis is dead,' Coop said.

'But the protective order is still in place unless it's waved by the mayor, which he has no intention of doing,' Nappa said to Coop. 'The Sean Ellis case has no bearing on the siege; frankly speaking, we've wasted enough time. All of you are dismissed.'

'The Ellis case is directly tied into what's happening, which means –'

'You can't prove that.'

'I don't need to,' Coop said. 'The fingerprint evidence in the criminal case against Ellis was falsified. No, don't say anything, Ms Nappa, because you don't have a leg to stand on – *especially* concerning the ballistics evidence. BPD officer Mark Noonan was head of ballistics when Ellis was indicted, am I correct?'

The AG folded her hands on her lap – a defensive move people used when they wanted to wall themselves off from the truth. The woman must have caught herself, because she immediately pushed herself up against the table and leaned slightly forward, as if she appeared interested in listening.

'Am I correct?' Coop prompted.

'You are. However, I –'

'In the evidence file – again, we're speaking strictly the criminal case – Officer Noonan stated he collected, stored and examined bullets and shell casings from the crime scene. Later, he testified in court the shots fired at Officer Fitzpatrick all came from his service weapon, a nine-millimetre Glock. Do I have that right?'

A curt nod from the AG.

'Then explain to me why Noonan didn't examine

the bullets that actually hit Officer Fitzpatrick,' Coop said.

'I'm not following.'

Yes you are, Darby thought. *I can see it in your eyes.*

'When EMTs treated Fitzpatrick at the scene, they didn't find an exit wound, which meant the bullet was still inside Fitzpatrick when he was brought to the hospital. That bullet should have been retrieved by doctors and given to BPD. That's standard practice in a shooting, wouldn't you agree?'

'This isn't a courtroom, Agent Cooper, and I would appreciate it if you –'

'A cop shooting is a high-priority case,' Coop said. 'I should know because, unfortunately, I worked several of them when I was at BPD's crime lab. And, for the life of me, I can't understand why the bullet lodged inside Fitzpatrick was never handed over to one of the lead detectives on the case.'

'It was an oversight.'

Darby said, 'Or something worse.'

Coop nodded in agreement. Said, 'According to Noonan's testimony *and* his own notes and reports, he said he examined all three bullets – the one collected from Fitzpatrick, which we know was never collected, and the two bullets lodged inside Fitzpatrick's bulletproof vest. Those last two bullets are still inside the vest. They've never been removed and tested, yet Noonan said all three came from Fitzpatrick's gun.'

AG Nappa said nothing, her face impassive, as though Coop had been discussing a weather forecast.

Shapiro was barely containing her glee, chomping at the bit, waiting to talk. Donnelly, though, looked as still as a dog that was about to lurch and bite.

'Here's what I think,' Coop said heatedly. 'Actually, let me rephrase that. Here's what I *know*. The criminal case against Sean Ellis was . . . I don't know what to call it other than atrocious. Every single piece of crucial evidence was either deliberately misrepresented or missing or never examined. I've never seen anything like this.'

AG Nappa held up her hands in surrender. 'Clerical errors and mistakes were made,' she began.

'No. That shit won't fly with me – and once Justice sees this, forget it. To call what happened to Ellis a miscarriage of justice – the words haven't been invented to describe the massive screwing you people gave him, a guy who was innocent.'

'Amen, brother,' Shapiro added.

Darby, leaning close to the door, thought she heard the hostage phone ring.

'And the thing is, what makes me sick to my stomach, is this protective order bullshit,' Coop said. 'Ellis sues the city, turns it into a civil case, and while you guys go back and forth with appeals so you don't have to pay him off, you use the protective order to keep BPD's dirty laundry from becoming public knowledge. Because if BPD screwed up this badly on Ellis? Then you can bet your ass there's a trail of others before him.'

Shapiro, her eyes closed, was swaying her arms high

above her head like she was attending a gospel church service when the door opened and Grove popped his head in and asked for Howie and Darby.

Donnelly and Nappa got to their feet.

Darby said, 'Put your asses back in those chairs. We're not done yet.'

48

+08.24

Darby and Gelfand followed Grove back to his tiny room. Grove didn't speak until he had shut the door.

'Big Red has called five times in the past two hours to talk to Dr McCormick,' Grove said. 'The first four times I tried to engage in conversation, each time he hung up. The fifth call, he was more open to negotiation.

'When he calls back – and he will – the agreement is for him to give over the location of the third bomb *before* I put Darby on the line.'

Gelfand said, 'What about making him wait until we have verification about the bomb? He might send us to a false location, have us run around in circles.'

'That's an excellent point – and I've thought about it. He's going to want to speak to Clara Lacy, obviously, so we'll consider it after we have confirmed the bomb's location *and* after he's released a hostage. How's she doing, by the way? Lacy and her family?'

Shit, Darby thought. *He doesn't know.*

She told him. Grove's mouth parted slightly, just for a moment; then he blinked and whatever he was feeling got kicked aside, swept back under his cool and confident mask.

Gelfand said, 'He won't find out about Lacy and her family. There's nothing about it on the news, for one thing, and we're jamming the satellite signals in that area so if he's using a sat-phone to keep updated, that's cut off.'

'That probably explains his repeated calls to me using the hostage phone. He's now officially cut off from all outside communication. Are you positive the news about Lacy didn't play anywhere before you shut down his satellite access?'

'I checked the internet on my phone,' Gelfand replied. 'Still nothing.'

'Dr McCormick, if the gunman finds out Lacy and her son and daughter-in-law have been murdered, it might push him over the edge. To suicide.'

'You want me to lie to him,' Darby said flatly.

'I want you to dance around the truth as much as you can.'

The phone inside Grove's unit began to ring.

Grove held up a hand, signalling Darby to wait. He let it ring once, twice, three times before picking up the receiver.

And then Darby heard the gunman's robotic voice on the speakerphone: 'Dr McCormick, is she back from Dorchester?'

'She's standing right next to me,' Grove replied. Gelfand had his pad and pen ready. 'You remember what we spoke about during our last conversation?'

'Yes.'

'Okay, Big Red, we're ready.'

'Go to Quincy, 239 Bare Hill Road. Big modern Colonial, white. The bomb is inside the garage on the left, underneath a John Deere riding mower.'

'Who lives there?'

'A man named Robert Murphy. He's a detective with the Boston Police.' Darby and Gelfand glanced at each other as Big Red said, 'The code to disarm it is the same.'

Darby felt her skin crawl as the gunman rattled off the numbers for her birthday. Gelfand finished writing and darted out of the room, forgetting to shut the door behind him. Darby did it for him.

'I'll put Dr McCormick on,' Grove said, pointing to the second receiver.

Darby scooped it up from the table. The phone felt damp and greasy against her palm.

'I'm here,' she said.

'Did you speak with Clara Lacy?'

'I want to speak to Laura. I want to know she's safe.'

The gunman didn't answer.

Darby wasn't about to speak when she heard the woman named Laura's voice on the other end of the line: 'I'm fine. Me and the other woman.'

'What did you say?'

'The other woman with me,' Laura said. 'He didn't kill her.'

'She's alive?'

'Yes. I'm looking at her right now.'

'Put her on.'

A brief silence followed.

Then Darby heard a woman say, 'I'm alive, Dr McCormick.'

Darby felt a sweet relief flooding through her, as bright and as warm as the sun.

'Clara Lacy,' Big Red prompted.

Darby mentally checked out, and then she was back inside the dark, cool lobby, the gunshots going off, *pow-pow-pow*. Saw herself dropping to the floor and clawing her way across the cold marble covered with rock salt and grit and small puddles from the snow that had dropped from her boots and melted – the gunshots were random, no target. Shots made in anger and frustration.

'Clara Lacy,' Big Red said again, his voice forcing her attention back inside the room. Darby became aware of the beads of sweat crawling across her scalp and down the small of her back. 'Did you speak to her?'

'I tried to,' Darby replied.

'What does that mean?'

'She's frightened. They all are.'

'Where are they?'

'Home.' Darby closed her eyes for a moment and saw them in the bedroom, all dead. 'They're all together inside her home.'

'I asked you to move them someplace safe.'

'When I arrived, members of the Boston Police were already there. If I moved Lacy and her family, they might have followed us.'

Big Red said nothing.

Darby spoke into the silence. 'I had to make a decision, and I had to make it fast, and I decided the best thing was to keep everyone inside the house. The FBI is guarding them.'

'I want to talk to Clara.'

'You realize she's not in the best of health. She's in no shape to travel.'

'Then bring her son.'

'I reviewed the case and evidence material from the Sean Ellis case,' Darby said. 'I know what happened.'

'Not all of it.'

'So tell me what I'm missing.'

'That's why I sent you to Clara. To fill in the missing pieces.'

The spike that travelled through her midsection and impaled her heart felt nearly identical to the moment when she was twelve and feeling certain that her father was going to come out of his coma, only to arrive at the hospital room suddenly and unexpectedly, to see her mother standing next to the bed and weeping, the life support already disconnected and Big Red no longer breathing, his brain slowly dying. There was no turning back. It was over. Done.

The silence on the phone was getting longer. Darby rushed to fill it, not wanting the gunman to hang up, and said only things she believed were true.

'I know you're hurting, and I know that no matter what I say I can't take away your pain or carry it for you. I don't know who you are or how the former mayor and Hill and Warren and whoever else hurt you. The one thing – the only thing I know for sure right now – is that you and I are both hanging by a thread.'

Darby felt the weight of Grove's attention. She felt the weight of everything.

'In the next room the Boston police commissioner and the attorney general for the state of Massachusetts are arguing with the FBI for control of this situation. Chances are Boston is going to take over, because what happened to Sean Ellis, how Trey Warren and Hill and God only knows who else framed him and how it affected you – all that stuff is in the past, and it's taking a backseat to the main priority, which is making sure the remaining hostages are safe and locating and disarming the remaining explosive devices. That's it. That's all these people care about. If the city takes over, I get pushed aside. They don't want me involved in this – they're going to pull out every stop they can and call in every favour and pull every legal manoeuvre they have to get me as far away from you as possible. But if you let me help you, I will. If you let me speak for you, I will. That's the only promise I can make. But we're running out of time.'

Big Red didn't reply. She wanted to keep speaking but told herself to let the silence hang for a moment, give a chance for her words to cook.

Grove spoke for her – *to* her.

'He's gone,' he said.

49

+08.28

'He hung up,' Grove said. 'Right after you said, "That's all these people care about."'

'I didn't hear him hang up,' Darby said.

'You wouldn't, not on your line.'

Darby replaced the receiver back on the table and then rubbed her damp palms on her jeans.

'That was a good shot, that speech at the end,' Grove said. 'Don't go anywhere. He'll call back.'

'You sound pretty confident.'

'Well, I *have* had a tad bit of experience in these situations.' Grove grinned wryly as he took a seat.

'How'd they go, your past experiences?'

'Like every situation in life, some better than others.'

'How incredibly Zen of you.'

Grove chuckled. Smiled. He had tiny baby teeth. 'How are you holding up?'

'Tired. Pissed off. Mainly tired.'

Darby started to pace. There wasn't a lot of room, and she suddenly felt claustrophobic. Boxed in. Grove clasped his hands behind his head and leaned back in his chair, turning his attention to the wall-mounted TV, which was tuned to Channel 5 and soundlessly playing news coverage of the hostage crisis. The air inside here felt as hot as an oven, yet Grove's forehead was dry, the underarms of his shirt free of perspiration stains. She envied the man's enormous calm, wished she could bottle it. Use it. Like now.

'How do you do it?'

'Do what?'

'Not care,' Darby said. Then she stopped pacing. 'That came out wrong. I meant –'

'I know what you meant. And to answer your question, yes, I do care about what's happening – care deeply, as a matter of fact. But the depth of my caring, the intensity of it, has absolutely no impact on the outcome. What's happening is largely beyond my control – *our* control. The other part – and I don't mean to sound callous – but what's happening right now? This is my job. No matter what happens, good or bad, I go back to my life, which I keep completely separate from all of . . . this.'

Darby nodded, kept nodding, as she paced.

'If you don't mind me saying,' Grove began.

'That's what someone always says before they insult you.'

'Or share an observation, which is that you invest yourself too emotionally. That's your biggest mistake. It also happens to be your biggest asset. I don't have that, Doctor. Why? Because I don't care about people the same way you do. I love my wife and my two grown children and my new grandson who, God willing, I'll see long enough to grow up into a fine young man.'

'You talk like a character from *Downton Abbey*. Anyone ever tell you that?'

'What I'm saying is, at the end of the day, you need someone to care about and someone who cares about you.'

'You're the second person today who has said that to me.'

'Maybe God, the universe, whatever your personal belief system, is trying to tell you something. Do your job, but don't sacrifice yourself for these people. They're not worth it.'

Darby didn't know if he meant people like the gunman or the people who worked for the BPD and FBI.

Then she saw Grove lean forward in his chair, his gaze fixed on the TV. She turned around and saw the 'BREAKING NEWS' banner on the bottom of the screen, along with live video showing one of the hostages, the woman with the curly white hair, running away from the police station, nearby SWAT agents swarming around her.

The door was thrown open. Gelfand came in, his face flushed. 'He released a hostage,' he said.

'We're watching it now,' Darby said. 'Any news on Murphy?'

'In the wind at the moment, but not for long. He's on duty, using his unmarked car. It's got a GPS.'

All the city, state and federal vehicles did, the GPS pinging its location every five or so minutes to a central system that could be accessed by any law enforcement agency. The federal-sponsored system was implemented a few years ago to keep track of where everyone travelled and locate an officer in trouble. Mainly, though, Darby thought it was yet another micromanagement offer from Big Brother, kept cops and agents in a perpetual surveillance state while they were on the job.

'Where is he now?'

'Travelling south on ninety-five. Looks like he's heading towards Quincy. I've got people on the way. Speaking of which, Briggs made it out in time. He should be in Boston within the hour.'

The hostage phone rang.

Rang again before Grove could answer it.

'I released a hostage, as a show of good faith,' Big Red said, his robotic voice echoing over the speakerphone. 'I would like something in exchange.'

Of course you do, Darby thought, and braced herself for what she knew he was going to ask, to talk to Clara Lacy or her son.

'It's a simple request,' Big Red said.

'I'm listening,' Grove said.

'I want to speak with Rosemary Shapiro.'

50

+08.31

'I know she's there, somewhere on your compound,' Big Red said.

'What makes you think that?' Grove asked.

'Please don't lie. We're way past lying. I just . . .' The gunman didn't finish his thought.

'You just what?' Grove prompted.

'Put Dr McCormick on.'

Grove handed the phone to her.

'I'm here,' Darby said.

'I'm tired. I want this to be over,' Big Red said. 'Let me talk to Ms Shapiro.'

Gelfand, Darby knew, had no intention of putting Shapiro on the phone; Gelfand wouldn't be able to control her in any way, and that could prove to be dangerous.

'If you want a lawyer, I can provide you with one,' Darby said.

'I want to speak to Rosemary.'

Rosemary, Darby thought. Did he know her? Was he a client?

'Why Ms Shapiro?' Darby asked.

'Put her on the line and you'll find out.'

'If I do that, we need to trade.'

'We've already traded, and I released a hostage.'

'Former mayor Briggs is on a helicopter to Boston. He'll be here within an hour. If you want to speak to him, he'll need assurances of his safety.'

'I'm not the danger.'

'I don't understand.'

'Put Rosemary on the line.'

Gelfand was shaking his head.

'Ms Shapiro isn't with us at the moment,' Darby said. 'I can promise you I'll get in contact with her, but I can't guarantee that she'll want to talk with you.'

'She will.'

'What message should I give her?'

'My first name is Karl. That's Karl spelled with a "K". I'll tell the rest to Rosemary.'

Big Red hung up. As Darby returned the receiver to its cradle, Gelfand said, 'This is still a federal investigation, and as long as it remains as such I can't allow a lawyer – a criminal lawyer with a history of suing the city, no less – to get on the phone with the gunman, for a whole host of legal reasons I'm too tired to explain.'

'I understand,' Darby said.

'And, frankly, I've had about enough of this guy jerking my crank.'

Grove said, 'I couldn't agree more. It's possible his need to speak to Shapiro may have something to do with his need to surrender.'

'You think he actually might do it?' Gelfand asked.

'I think he's considering the possibility – and it's one we should explore.'

'Using Shapiro.'

'Yes. What would you like to do?'

Grove was very good, Darby thought. Grove was being outwardly manipulative, trying to get Gelfand over to his way of thinking – much like a patient father dealing with a particularly stubborn child: *I agree with everything you've said, but the question is, what do* you *want to do about it?*

'Tell her to get her fat ass in here,' Gelfand said reluctantly.

51

+08.33

Coop brought her; Shapiro smiling like someone who had just discovered a winning lottery ticket. Her perfume quickly overpowered the room, like an insecticide.

'Little cramped in here – and hot,' Shapiro said. 'Why is it so hot?'

'Temperature gague is broken,' Gelfand replied, scratching an eyebrow with his thumb.

'That's what I love about the federal government. You guys buy nothing but the best.'

'Rosemary –'

'Ooh, it's Rosemary now. This sounds serious.'

'It is serious. The gunman has asked to speak with you.'

'He wants me to represent him?'

'I don't know. He says his name is Karl with a "K". You have a client by that name?'

'Howie, you know I can't break attorney–client privilege. That's legal one-o-one. 'Course, I might be willing to drop my ethics if Cooper here agrees to strip down to his skivvies. Or are you one of those boring middle-age boxer guys now, Coop?'

Coop stared up at the ceiling, suddenly fascinated at the patterns in the acoustic tiles. Grove stared at Shapiro as though she had grown a third eye. Gelfand, appalled and livid, said, 'Hey, Rosemary, in case you forgot, we're dealing with a terrorist –'

'Cut the shit, Howie. I've heard the way you talk. Why can't a woman joke around and bust balls? I'm sorry, Cooper. The accident I had, it did something to the part of my brain responsible for judgement. Just unbutton your shirt and show me your eight-pack and we'll call it even.'

Darby pinched her temples between her thumb and forefinger and squeezed, feeling like she had just stumbled inside a Tourette's support group.

Gelfand said, 'Attorney–client communications do not extend to statements pertaining to a crime or fraud committed in the future. If you have, or had, a client who told you he was going to hijack the BPD headquarters and then plant bombs all over the city and you failed to report it, we're talking a serious ethics violation. We're taking disbarment.'

'Thank you for explaining the law to me, Howie.'

'Good. So I don't have to explain to you how the government can compel a defence lawyer to reveal information about a client in an emergency or life-threatening situation. What I'm saying to you is, if you screw me, Rosemary, I will make it my life's mission to destroy you.'

'Noted. And for the record, my ovaries are officially quivering. Also, for the record, I would like to state I have no knowledge, nor was I ever in possession of such knowledge, of a client or person who shared with me his thoughts about blowing up the BPD headquarters or killing cops or doing any other revenge-related activity.'

'What about a client named Karl?'

'Sorry, baby, that's confidential.'

'What about a woman named Clara Lacy?'

The sarcasm bled away from her face, and her eyes clouded with thought.

'Is she a client of yours?'

'No,' Rosemary said. 'She was going to be a witness at the Sean Ellis civil case against the city.'

'Was?'

'Ellis was killed by a person or people unknown, and the case never went forward – which, I'm sure, gave our former mayor a big chubby.' Shapiro smiled brightly, the biting sarcasm and cockiness having returned. 'Nothing gets that man more excited than saving a dollar, even if the dollar isn't his.'

'What was her testimony going to be?'

'That Sean Ellis was not the man who entered her home on the evening of the Fitzpatrick shooting.'

'So, why did she pick him out of the lineup?'

'So glad you asked, Howie. Here's the thing: Clara, before she found God, was a drug addict and a prostitute. This was a long, long time ago, you understand, before you and I were even in diapers. The time of the Fitzpatrick shooting, Clara had been clean and sober for several years, was working as a secretary for a shipping company while raising her son. She –'

'You haven't answered my question.'

'I was trying to, before you opened your fat yap and interrupted. Now, as I was saying, Clara found God, Jesus, Mary and everyone else and was living the good life when the shooter entered her home. And the shooter was – you ready for this? – a white man. Not black or brown or yellow, but *white*. Now ask the next question. Go ahead, don't be shy.'

'All the reports said the shooter was a black man.'

'And that's because – brace yourself, people – Danny "Mr Murder" Hill *made* her say that. Threatened there'd be all sorts of legal repercussions if she didn't go along – not jail, necessarily, I'm talking about minor stuff. Stuff where she'd have to pay fines and fees that she couldn't afford, that whole death by a thousand paper cuts you law enforcement types are so *good* at. Danny Boy also threatened to put her son into foster care by creating all of these problems that would make her look like an unfit mother. So what did you think an uneducated, poor and frightened black woman did, Howie?'

'Everything we've read about Fitzpatrick and Sean Ellis was a lie. That's what you're saying.'

'Look at you connecting all the dots by yourself like a big boy. I'm so proud of you.' Shapiro clapped.

'If what Lacy says is true –' Gelfand began.

'Oh, it is.'

'– then why didn't she turn around and sue the city?'

'Because, as you may recall, after Sean Ellis was released from prison, someone killed him. Lacy said she wanted to drop the whole thing and live out her life, didn't want to be involved with BPD – or the Feds, when I suggested we persue this on a criminal level. Don't give me that look, Howie. Back then, BPD was a cesspool of Irish inbreeding and ineptitude that rivalled, well, the Boston FBI office. Did you hear what that US congressman said not that long ago on the report that came out on the Frank Sullivan case.'

'I read it. Now –'

'He called it one of *the* single greatest failures in the history of federal law enforcement. Congratulations, by the way.'

'If Ellis wasn't the shooter, who was?'

'That, Super Special Agent Gelfand, is a great question – the ten-million-dollar question.'

'Was the Fitzpatrick shooter, this white guy, was his name Karl?'

'I don't know the shooter's name, Howie.'

'But if you did –'

'If I did, I wouldn't have to tell you, technically speaking. But since you've been nice to me, the answer is no, I don't know who this gentleman is. I might know more about the gunman if you put me on the phone and let me speak to him. What's it gonna be, Sweet Cheeks? I'm not talking to you, Cooper, I'm talking to Howie now.'

52

+08.37

Coop looked visibly relieved when his phone rang.

'Howie, I've got to take this.'

Gelfand nodded, looking tired and weary. Shapiro studied Coop's backside as he left, whistled after the door was shut. 'That boy is sexual napalm,' she said to no one in particular. Then, to Darby: 'What's wrong with you, not tapping that?'

Shapiro sat while everyone else remained standing, everyone but her on pins-and-needles as they talked strategy. She picked up the second receiver and, as Grove placed the call to the gunman, Rosemary admired her manicure, her face undisturbed, as though she was waiting on the line to make a dentist appointment or to get her oil changed.

Darby leaned her back up against the far wall and crossed her arms over her chest, staring at the speaker, listening to the phone ringing . . . ringing . . .

Big Red picked up and said, 'Do you have Rosemary on the line?'

Shapiro perked up, perplexed by the deep, modulated voice.

'She's sitting next to me,' Grove said.

'Who else is there?' Big Red asked.

'Dr McCormick and SAC Gelfand.'

'Can they hear me?'

'They can.'

'And is this line still being recorded?'

'It is.'

'I want to retain her services. Put her on.'

Shapiro got on the line. 'This is Rosemary. We're on an unsecured line, which means –'

'I know what it means,' Big Red said.

'Don't say anything, okay? Just listen for me for a moment. This line is being recorded, and people are listening, so it would be in your best interest not to talk because anything you say could be used against you. Do you understand?'

'I understand. I have a question about the Justice Initiative.'

Shapiro straightened a bit, her eyes narrowing in thought.

'You know the one I'm referring to?' Big Red asked. 'The document created after the Boston Police Department underwent a series of internal investigations that resulted –'

'I'm familiar with it. Why?'

'Please explain it to our guests. It's a public document, available to anyone, so there are no legal ramifications in speaking about its contents. Tell them.'

Shapiro, confused and trying to follow the logic in the man's thinking, spoke in a dry monotone: 'The document is the result of a series of two internal investigations – the first conducted by a state attorney general was a criminal investigation that was presented to a grand jury; the second a comprehensive review by the Suffolk County District Attorney. The Boston Police Department also conducted its own independent audit.'

'And the result of these investigations?'

'The report concluded that the wrongful convictions in cases like Sean Ellis and several others did not – and this is a direct quote – "did not result in a system failure". The report laid most of the blame on false or erroneous eyewitness identifications.'

'And your legal opinion?'

'It's all horseshit,' Shapiro said.

'And what do you base that on?'

'Evidence. My firm has represented, to date, fifteen wrongful conviction cases with the Boston Police.'

'And when did these cases take place?'

'Between 1993 and 2004.'

'And 2004 was the same year the Boston Police's fingerprint and ballistics units were shut down and then restarted with qualified personnel.'

'Yes.'

'And the officers involved, Trey Warren and Mark Vickers, were any criminal charges ever brought forth?'

'No.'

'And what about Detectives Daniel Hill, Frank Ventura, Robert Murphy and Ethan Owen?'

'They were never charged.'

'Disciplinary actions?'

'Not that I'm aware of. How can I help you, Karl? You're name is Karl, right? That's what they told me.'

'Yes. I'd like to retain your services.'

'Smart move. As your attorney, I suggest that you and I meet and discuss –'

'I don't want you to represent me,' Big Red said. 'I want you to represent Clara Lacy. Dr McCormick will take you to her – and only Dr McCormick. I want Clara and her family to be moved to a safe location.'

Darby felt her stomach lurch as a greasy sweat broke out across her hairline.

'I can take care of that,' Shapiro said, watching Darby now.

'I sent a Priority Mail envelope to your office,' Big Red said, Darby thinking he had, like her, planned to use Shapiro from the very beginning. 'Inside you'll find a bank cheque for $250,000. Is that a sufficient retainer?'

'As long as the cheque clears,' Shapiro said.

'If you should need more money, follow the wiring instructions I sent in along with the payment. The envelope should arrive no later than tomorrow.'

'I get a lot of mail. What name should I be looking for?'

'I put my name in the return address. Walter Karl Torres. That's my legal name. But everyone calls me Karl.'

Shapiro's jaw went slack. She stared down at the table, as though a crevasse had just opened in front of her.

'I want to speak to Clara before you send her away,'

Big Red said. 'Once I do, I'll call and give the location of the fourth bomb. Goodbye.'

Darby spoke first. 'Do you know who Walter Torres is?'

'Yes,' Shapiro replied. She placed the phone carefully on the counter, as though it was fragile, and then quickly recovered, looking heatedly at Gelfand as she said, 'Yes, we do.'

53

+08.00

Gelfand didn't want to talk about it inside the small command room. Truth be told, he didn't want to talk about it at all, Darby could tell, but since Rosemary Shapiro definitely could not ethically talk about Walter Karl Torres because Torres was a client, it was up to Gelfand to supply the details, which he most definitely did not want to do. It was written all over his face.

He's scared, too, Darby thought. *Scared and sick*. Gelfand, as far as she had been able to tell in their handful of past encounters, hid his true emotions behind sarcasm and barbs and anger. Or maybe now that he was dying, he felt he didn't have to work as hard to hide anything any more.

'Rosemary,' he said, his voice hoarse, 'would you excuse us, please?'

'Sure thing,' Shapiro replied, the woman barely able to contain her excitement at her luck at now having a ringside seat to what would turn out to be the single biggest case of her career. Shapiro had just been granted her ultimate wish: to be a media fixture, maybe even a local media icon, for months if not years. 'Darby, call me when you're ready to go to Dorchester. Here's my card, cell number's written on the back.'

Walter Torres has to be either former FBI or a current agent, Darby thought as Shapiro left the room. There was also a third possibility: federal informant. Pick any one of the three and it would explain why Gelfand looked like he was moments away from experiencing a heart attack, a real chest-burster.

Darby and Grove stared at Gelfand, waiting. Gelfand stared at the tops of his shoes, hands deep in his pockets, thinking.

When he didn't speak, Darby said, 'We can't tell her about Lacy and her family. If she finds out, and the gunman asks, legally she has to tell him the truth. She can't willingly deceive him.'

Grove nodded. Added, 'Walter Torres obviously cares about Ms Lacy and her family's safety. If he finds out –'

'I get it,' Gelfand said quietly. 'I get it.'

Gelfand's gaze bounced around the room, looking like a man who had been handed a gun loaded with only one round and asked to fend off an enemy invasion.

'I'm going outside for some fresh air,' Gelfand said. 'And a cigarette.'

Darby didn't wait for an invitation. After slipping inside the galley and chugging down a bottle of water, she grabbed a PayDay candy bar and then went outside, the cold winter air amazing after being slowly roasted inside the heated trailer.

She found Gelfand smoking furiously and pacing underneath the awning of the side of the trailer. The wind had stopped – had tired, really – and the snow fell softly and quietly around them, the air still packed with the same sounds, the same throbbing engines and chatter and now, the low drone of the helicopters which were mercifully further away.

A fireman swung around the other side to grab a smoke under the awning. He saw the expression on Gelfand's face, turned around and left.

Darby joined him. 'We going to play twenty questions or are you going to tell me about this Torres guy?' she asked, taking a big bite from her candy bar.

'Never met him.'

'So why do you look like you just dropped a loaf in your drawers?'

'Said I never met him. Didn't say I didn't know him.' Gelfand sucked deeply from his cigarette and watched the falling snow. 'This is gonna be one for the history books.'

Darby chewed, wondering if he was talking about Torres or the upcoming nor'easter which, if the weathermen were to be believed, would dump up to five feet of snow by tomorrow afternoon, the time when the storm would start to lose its power, begin to fade.

She waited for him to get to it. Finally, he did.

'Torres was a federal informant.'

'How important?'

'TEI status.'

Top Echelon Informant was the code given to the

FBI's most valuable informants. Darby knew this because Frank Sullivan had been one such informant. The TEI status gave the FBI a lot of leeway and discretion – or it least it had until a couple of years ago, when the truth about Sullivan and the law enforcement corruption came out; Congress enacting a massive investigation and overhaul into how such informants were handled.

'Frank Sullivan was TEI,' Gelfand said as she drew closer.

'He was also an undercover federal agent.'

'You think I forgot that fact?' Gelfand glared at her for a moment. 'Every family's got a scumbag or two. Doesn't mean we're all scumbags, Doc.'

'Never said you were.'

'But you were thinking it. Your old man was an upstanding guy, righteous, tried to do the right thing, what have you. So naturally people assume you're the same way, right, because what else would you be? But if your old man was a notorious thieving serial killer, then it's guilt by association. People think the apple doesn't fall far from the tree because it's in the blood.'

'I thought we were talking about the Bureau.'

'What I'm saying is, we're not alike. Feds, cops. Families. We don't share, you know, the same mind.'

Gelfand then rested his arms on top of the fence and looked out at the traffic. 'You take the job as SAC of a field office, you inherit the good and the bad, all its dirty secrets. Your job is to keep the old secrets guarded and keep the news ones from getting out. It's like being the owner of a storage facility, only you get to wear a suit every day and carry a gun. Thing is, if something happened a long time ago, something you had nothing to do with, you've got to pay for it because that's the job. You get stuck with it.'

Darby sighed, her patience wearing thin. She was about to press him to get to it when he said, 'I didn't handle him. Walter-Call-Me-Karl-Torres.'

'Okay.'

'This went down before I was here. Back in the late eighties and early nineties.'

'The Sullivan era.'

'Right. Before Karl became an informant, he was working with Sullivan, moving in large quantities of heroin; made it popular and cheap here in Bean Town.'

None of this surprised her. Confidential informants were key to solving cases and preventing new ones, and the best informants were high up the food chain, the truly awful and ruthless. The shaky alliance was constantly fraught with risk and danger.

'So, Karl. Guy was a real nasty piece of work. Smart, though. Savvy. The drugs and murders – nobody can pin anything on him, not even us. He gets it in his head to supply information on Sullivan to the FBI so he can take out Sullivan, become the new king of the hill. What Karl doesn't know is that Sullivan is an undercover Fed who's supplying information on Cosa Nostra, the Italian mob, which everyone here had a major hard-on for at the time. It was all about dismantling the Italian mafia's stronghold here in New England, which meant corners could be cut, things overlooked, sins forgiven. Problem is, shortly after Karl made contact with the Feds, he finds out that it's Sullivan who's been doing the snitching.'

'And Karl doesn't need anyone to connect the dots for him, knows that the Feds will leave him high and dry, so he decides to contact Rosemary Shapiro.'

Gelfand nodded and picked a piece of stray tobacco from his lips, studying it. 'Nothing came of it. I mean, Rosemary, from what I heard, made some meetings, but then she cancelled and kept cancelling and the thing just sort of, I dunno, disappeared.'

'And now we're to believe that, what, twenty years later, Walter Karl Torres is back for revenge?'

Gelfand seemed to be considering how he was going to answer the question when his phone rang. He saw the number on the screen and his face momentarily brightened.

'Stay here, it's about Murphy,' he said and answered the call.

Darby listened to Gelfand utter 'Okay' and 'What else?' as she thought about why Walter Karl Torres, a drug dealer and murderer, would wait decades to stage a coup at Boston Police headquarters when the real enemy seemed to be the FBI's Boston field office. Maybe the federal players were dead. Maybe Hill, Warren, Murphy and the others were involved. But what did the Sean Ellis case and the former mayor have to do with this? And why did Torres suddenly develop a conscience? Did the man have some Come to Jesus moment and decide to air all the dirty laundry – and why do it in such a gigantic public display?

Gelfand said, 'Murphy didn't go home.'

'Where is he?'

'At a Lowe's in Quincy. He just parked his car and went inside. I'm guessing you and Cooper can get there in about ten minutes.'

'Why us?'

'Because I trust you and Cooper, and because I want you guys to question Murphy on the way back, have him tell you about Karl Torres.'

'Murphy knows him?'

'Not saying he does. I'm hoping he can enlighten me on something.'

'What's that?'

'What Torres is doing alive,' Gelfand said. 'Son of a bitch is supposed to be dead.'

54

+08.45

Because new helicopters were watching and practically tracking every single car that left the campus, Gelfand didn't want to take a chance on having Darby and Coop followed and quickly arranged for them to be driven to a nearby parking garage belonging to a hotel where, once inside the garage, they would be given the keys to an ordinary vehicle and, God willing, not be followed to Quincy.

Face cold and her hands tucked deep in her jacket pockets, Darby made her way across the parking lot, heading for the gated entrance where a Bureau car would take her and Coop to the garage, Darby wishing she could have spoken to Rosemary Shapiro about Walter Karl Torres, see if the woman would share some information on her client, hand over the details of how and where he'd died. The only thing Gelfand could tell her, and it wasn't much because he didn't have access to any of the Torres information, all of the files sealed and stored in the vaults on the impenetrable fifth-floor rooms at FBI headquarters, was that Torres was shot to death somewhere in Texas and buried there in 1995, maybe later.

People rising from the dead didn't contain the same shock value any more. The FBI and WITSEC did it all the time, make one person die on paper, resurrect him or her with a brand-new life on new paper. Happened all the time, and when you worked in law enforcement, you heard a lot of these stories.

What she was having a hard time wrapping her head around was the timeframe. If 'Walter Karl Torres' died on paper in 1995, why did he wait twenty-one years for revenge?

'Darby.'

Darby stopped and saw Rosemary Shapiro standing underneath an umbrella, the woman navigating her way through the snow and clearly unhappy that she had chosen to wear a pair of three-thousand-dollar Givenchy boots. She held a cigarette, a Virginia Slim.

'Talk to you for a moment?' Shapiro asked.

'Just a moment.'

The revolving lights from a nearby fire truck washed red across the woman's face, Shapiro's beauty reminding Darby of the opera singer Maria Callas.

Shapiro inhaled deeply from her cigarette. 'What did Howie tell you about Karl Torres?'

'Not much in terms of detail. I know he was a federal informant and that he's supposed to be dead.'

'Both true.'

'He enter Witness Protection?'

'No. No, definitely not. He wasn't the government-trusting type. He'd have lived as a fugitive – and could have, successfully, too. He made a lot of money in drugs.'

'Are you trying to tell me that your client, Karl Torres, was the real shooter in the Sean Ellis case?'

'You know I can't say anything to implicate my client.'

'But you know why he's here, don't you? Torres?'

'Look, you know how the game is played. You know –'

'*Game?* This look like a game to you?' Darby threw her hand over her shoulder at all the law enforcement and emergency personnel, Shapiro giving her that dead expression all lawyers had, like either they didn't care or give a shit. 'You've got something to say, Rosemary, say it now.'

'I can't speak too much about him other than that he is a client, that I haven't heard from him in decades.' Shapiro's brow furrowed, as if she was having trouble comprehending the number. '*But* I can tell you a couple of things. Number one, he's not a good guy. A psychopath. Number two, I was told he did die by someone in-the-know. Died in Texas.'

'Who killed him? Feds or BPD?'

'I can't say.'

'You hear about the parking garage in Hyde Park?'

Shapiro nodded.

'That mean anything to you?'

Shapiro licked her plump lips. 'Hill and Murphy, and the two cops who got murdered last year, they were all involved in as many as forty homicides that are now being reviewed, based on witness intimidation and faulty and manufactured evidence. BPD knew what these guys were doing. Feds, too, I'm sure, because some of these cases overlapped with Frank Sullivan's . . . goals. My point is, they closed a lot of cases back then and homicide rates declined, and Briggs had these great numbers that made Boston look like a safe city to live in and to visit, you know, spend a lot of dollars.'

'You're saying this is about *tourism*? That Briggs, what, went along to get more people to ride the duck boats and visit the Bull & Finch *Cheers* restaurant?'

'That restaurant closed. Ever been there? Had great steak tips.'

'I've got to go, Rosemary. Good seeing you.'

'You should have sued. It's a different Boston now. Donnelly, the mayor and governor – even Briggs knows all about the past problem with the BPD. Hill was the only one left from that time, and now he's dead. The DA is probably doing an Irish jig right now because Hill was so toxic.'

'Why?' Darby asked.

'The DA recently filed a request with the judge asking that the opposition be barred from telling jurors about their past – that's reserved for a criminal with a record, not a cop.'

'You've got something to say, Rosemary, say it now.'

'What's going on with Clara Lacy?'

'I'll deal with that later, when I come back.'

'She's dead, isn't she? They got to her.'

'They?'

'Just tell me the truth. I need to make plans. Protect myself.'

'She's inside her house with her family. Bureau's watching them.'

'You need to protect yourself, too, Darby. They'll kill you or they'll drive you to suicide, like Fitzpatrick. You know how scared that guy was? His daughter came into his bedroom and saw him with the gun in his mouth and he *still* pulled the trigger. What's that say to you?'

'Fitzpatrick's family,' Darby said. 'They still native or did they move?'

'Wife packed the daughter up and left town.' Shapiro shook her head then inhaled deeply from her cigarette. 'Laura was never the same.'

Laura.

The same name as the pregnant woman, the last hostage.

Darby kept the surprise from reaching her face. 'Laura?'

'Fitzpatrick's daughter.'

'She still here?'

Shapiro shrugged. Then her instincts kicked in. 'Why are you so interested in a dead cop?' she asked.

'Because I want to talk to Fitzpatrick's wife and daughter. They can help us build a case, get the truth out about what's happening. What's the wife's name?'

'Toni or Tori, I forget which.'

'Last name?'

'Levine.'

The gunman's voice: *Ask Briggs about Levine.*

Darby felt the realization rip through her and said, 'Okay. Thanks.'

'Torres is pulling all of these strings to get to Briggs so he can kill him,' Shapiro said. 'If you're in there when the bomb goes off or the shooting starts, trust me, he'll kill you too. He's just waiting for the right moment.'

Darby left. She glanced once over her shoulder and saw Shapiro smoking her cigarette, looking like a woman who was waiting for a train to come and take her someplace far away.

55

+08.49

Coop didn't speak during the ride to the hotel's parking garage, which was less than a mile away. There, he was given the keys to a black BMW, a 7 series with tinted windows.

Darby didn't tell him about her conversation with Rosemary Shapiro.

An advance team consisting of three other vehicles would leave one by one to get the helicopters or anyone else that had followed her off the scent. Hopefully. They wanted everything to go down nice and quiet at Lowe's.

It was a clutch, and since Coop didn't know how to drive one, Darby got behind the wheel. The car handled well in the snow. About three inches had fallen, according to the radio.

Coop spent a good amount of time on the phone, coordinating with the agents at the Lowe's parking lot. Murphy's car was still there, and he was still inside the store, shopping. His shift had officially ended two hours ago.

'Murphy got in some sort of accident,' Coop said after he hung up.

'You mean like a car accident?'

'Don't know.' He pressed the heels of his palms to his eyes and made circular motions. 'Agents shadowing him said his nose is all busted up. Splintered. Also want to talk to you about the autopsy reports for Owen and Ventura. May mean something or it could be nothing, but they both had late-stage cancer. Pathologist said the two of them only had months to live. I'm wondering if the gunman somehow found they were sick and decided to kill them, use them as a calling card but also because they wouldn't be alive right now to see what's going on.'

'Maybe. It's a thought. You find anything on Torres listed on NCIC?'

'Yeah.' He seemed confused for a moment, then he reached behind him and grabbed a file from the backseat. He clicked on the map light above the console and flipped through the pages. 'Walter Karl Torres, born in Lynn, Massachusetts, was twenty-eight when he was shot to death by two unnamed gunmen while coming out of a liquor store in El Paso, Texas on February 11, 1995.'

'That's four-and-a-half months after Fitzpatrick was shot.'

'And a month after Sean Ellis was sentenced for it.'

'And now we're supposed to believe Torres, who would now be fifty-eight or -nine, is the one inside that lobby. That his death was, what, faked?'

'I checked Torres's stats. Guy was five-eight, which is the same height as the gunman, give or take an inch.'

'What about eye colour?'

'Blue.'

'Same as the gunman. You got a picture in there of Torres?'

'No. Nothing listed on NCIC, and didn't have time to Google. I don't think Torres is dead. I think he's inside the station.'

'What makes you say that?'

'Anita Barnes,' Coop said, Darby hearing the woman's name for the first time in a while but feeling as though what had occurred this morning happened in another lifetime. 'The duct tape we recovered from her had prints on it, and they all belonged to Walter Karl Torres.'

56

+09.01

Darby had never stepped foot inside a Lowe's. The big box do-it-yourself home improvement chain hadn't been around when she was a kid, and by the time they were popping up in pretty much every city and town across America, she was already living in a condo in Beacon Hill, where a contractor serviced all maintenance and home-improvement issues.

The first thing she noticed was the ceiling, how it seemed as far away as the moon. The place felt like it should have its own zip code it was so big, aisles everywhere, all of them numbered and labelled, everything placed neatly on shelves, everything you could possible need to fix, repair, replace or make something right at your fingertips. It was dizzying, all the options.

Darby stomped her boots against the wide floor mat beyond the automatic front doors and quickly shook the snow out of her hair as a big, rumbling heater blasted hot air down on her. Bags of rock salt and Ice Melt and shovels that promised to save your lower back surrounded her and in the centre directly in front of her, a handful of leftover snow blowers for people who were either too stupid or too absent-minded not to have prepared for the winter, which was already shaping up to be one for the record books. The storm was hitting hard but just gathering its breath, and the smart play was to get inside your house and wait it out – which was why it surprised her how busy the store was, a lot of the customers were women and children wearing sour expressions at having been dragged along on Mom or Dad's errands.

Murphy, they had been told, was standing in aisle six, on the far left-hand side of the store. The four agents in here watching him all wore plain winter jackets so they could blend in with the other shoppers. They didn't want Murphy to spot the agents and panic.

They didn't have to talk about what to do; the plan had already been discussed. Darby and Coop took the centre aisle to the left, the two agents with them taking the main aisle in the centre of the store. They all wore earpieces and wrist mikes so they could talk to one another. The entrance and emergency exits were all covered.

Darby passed light bulbs and light fixtures and then aisles for paint and for every type of screw, nail, nut and bolt known to mankind, Darby thinking how much her father would have loved a place like this; Big Red was the type of guy who knew his way around tools, could fix or build anything.

'Remember,' Coop said in a low voice, 'we spot him and we go up to him all nice and friendly, say we couldn't get him on his cell. We tell him the gunman has targeted him and we need to bring him to safety, then get him out here nice and easy.'

'Something I should tell you,' said Darby.

'What's that?'

'He was at Clara Lacy's place.'

'And?'

'We had sort of an altercation and I sort of broke his nose.'

Coop slowed his pace, looked at her for a moment. 'And you're sharing this with me now?'

'It slipped my mind.'

'How convenient.'

'It wasn't that big of a deal. He might not be in the best of moods, is what I'm saying.'

'He's not the only one,' Coop replied, and shot her a look that clearly let her know he was pissed – and she didn't blame him. After all, she'd kept the whole thing quiet because she wanted to be in on this, wanted a chance to take Murphy down herself, rip the truth out of him.

They were nearing the end of the store, the place where all the lumber was kept; she could smell pine and sawdust in the cool air, someone on the overhead speakers calling for Jacob Fisher, telling him to come to the customer service desk.

Coop subtly brought up the wrist mike to his mouth and said, 'I'll make the approach. Everyone standby.'

Then, to Darby: 'Hang back. Don't argue with me.'

She didn't argue with him. She veered off to the shelving at the end of the aisle and sidled up next to it, angling her head and looking through the gaps until she could see Murphy.

And then she saw him in profile, saw the steel bridge placed across his nose and held down by tape, his eyes swollen with fluid. He had cleaned his face but not his clothes; she could see bloodstains on the back of his shirt and jacket collar and wondered why he had come here dressed like this, looking like this. Maybe he just didn't care. Murphy was gripping the shoulder of another man and leaning in close like a baseball coach giving a quick pep talking to a player. Darby crept towards the corner leading into the aisle to get a better look and then saw the man's wool tweed patchwork cap and his gaunt face and moustache. Detective Danny 'Mr Murder' Hill's head was tilted down and he was listening solemnly, as though a grave secret had just been whispered to him.

57

+09.05

Whether it was simply curiosity or instinct or the fact that she wanted to make sure she had Coop's back in case the shit hit the fan, Darby moved around the corner and into the aisle, the Sig tucked in the back of the waistband of her jeans. A part of her relaxed, told her she was just imagining things because Danny Hill was dead, that Murphy had bumped into someone who *looked* like Hill and, no, that was wrong, it was all wrong because the man *was* Danny Hill, there was no question. The height was right and although he had lost a ton of weight and looked gaunt and sickly and scared – oh yes, there was no question he was scared right now – he had the same black moustache and dark brown eyes and worm-shaped scar that started just below his lip and ended an inch or so below his chin, a scar, Hill had told her long ago, at a retirement party, that he had got at eight when he was playing street hockey and got clipped by someone's stick.

You're supposed to be dead, Darby wanted to say. Her feet felt welded to the floor. *Your house was blown up and you were in it because they found your leg on top of a car and why didn't you call and tell anyone you were alive?*

It was Hill who saw her first, Hill backing away from Murphy like the man had suddenly burst into flames. Hill stared at her in cold fear and Darby felt that slow-motion terror creeping through her as Hill shifted his gaze to Coop, who had also recognized him, Coop's momentary confusion and uncertainty – *This can't be Danny, Danny's dead* – snapping into a larger confusion on how to proceed because Hill wasn't dead and now he was here having some clandestine meeting in the lumber section of Lowe's with Murphy.

Danny Hill had his hands tucked in his coat pockets. They stayed in there even when his back bumped up against the tower of lumber behind him, Hill developing the awful stillness of a mongrel dog that was about to strike, rip flesh from limbs.

But not Murphy; he was shocked to see Coop – and at the moment he only saw Coop. He didn't see the agents who were crowding the other end of the aisle, and Murphy, strangely, looked relieved and grateful, like he had been marooned on a desert island and had given up all hope of ever being rescued.

'He killed Warren and the old black lady and her family,' Murphy said, his voice loud, his words drawing the attention of the customers in the aisle, a good handful who weren't moving yet, Darby wanting to tell them to leave their shopping carts or whatever it was they were holding in their hands and to leave now. She was standing well behind Coop and Murphy was moving to him and she lost sight of Hill as Murphy said, 'Let's keep this in the family, okay? He gave himself up. Let me bring him in and –'

A gunshot went off and Darby saw Murphy's forehead explode like a watermelon before she dropped to the floor, people screaming and running. Coop had his sidearm out and he didn't have a clear shot and the agents swarming in the aisle didn't have a clear shot because everyone was running and screaming, Coop shouting at Hill to drop his weapon when Hill tore a woman away from her shopping carriage and yanked a kid twelve or eighteen months old from the seat.

Darby left her Sig tucked in the waistband of her jeans as she scrambled to her feet, Hill clutching the kid close to his chest, using him like a shield the way the gunman had used the pregnant woman. The boy, dressed in a bright red parka, was frightened and trying to squirm away and he jumped when Hill screamed at the top of his lungs: '*Back away, back the fuck away right now, you lying sons of bitches, or I'll pull the trigger!*'

Coop's face, Darby saw, and the front of his jacket and clothes were splattered with blood and pieces of Murphy. The agents were looking to him for direction; he was the senior man, the one in charge. He nodded and as they retreated to give him some room, Coop said, 'Danny, I'm gonna put my gun away, okay?'

'Put it on that shelf next to you.' Hill was looking at Darby now, too, Darby standing in the aisle with them, not about to leave Coop. 'Then both of you, do it.'

Coop said, 'No problem. Look, I'm putting my gun down.'

Coop placed it on the shelf to his left. Darby's jacket was unzipped; she pulled the leather aside and said, 'I'm not armed, Danny. We didn't come here for you. We came here to speak to Murphy.'

'Goddamn liar is what he is.'

'I know that,' Darby said, keeping her tone calm, using it to get Hill to calm down, too, hopefully. Hill had his back pressed up against a stack of two-by-fours and he had dug the muzzle of his nine-millimetre against the boy's stomach, the boy crying now, calling 'mama'. Darby could hear the woman screeching from somewhere behind her, in another aisle, the agents doing everything they could to calm her down, get her to be quiet.

'Goddamn liar,' Hill said again, and this time his gaze dropped to Murphy, who lay against the floor, motionless, the wreck that was his face mercifully pressed against the floor, out of view. 'Bunch of goddamn liars, all of them.'

It was then that Darby noticed he was drunk. He was slurring his words and he was having trouble standing up straight, his eyes rheumy, threaded with tiny pink veins.

Darby showed Hill her empty hands, kept them near her sides. 'We came here for Murphy,' she said, fighting the trembling feeling sliding up and down her arms and legs. 'We just came here to talk to him.'

'Talk,' Hill snorted. 'Like talking ever solved anything. Nobody listens when you talk. I don't want FBI boy here.' He nodded with his chin to Coop. 'Go back to the rest of the liars and thieves, FBI boy.'

Darby said, 'We didn't know you were alive, Danny. Why didn't you call us? Why didn't you let us help you?'

His eyes, bright with alcohol (and she could smell it now, too), kept bouncing from her and Coop and the end of the aisles where the agents had taken strategic positions, waiting for orders. No doubt SWAT had been called, emergency vehicles. She prayed to God it wouldn't come to that.

'I'm not going to jail,' he screamed. *'You people aren't gonna pin any more shit on me.'*

The kid was bawling in the way only a one-year-old could: piercing shrieks that felt like glass being ground into the eardrums. Hill shook him. 'Shut up.' Shook him again. *'Shut up.'*

'We didn't come for you, Danny, we came for Murphy,' Darby said again. 'We thought you were dead.'

'I'm supposed to be, right?' Hill snorted again. Swallowed. 'Took the day off to help my brother with some stuff and then he calls.' Hill nodded with his chin to Murphy. 'Calls and tells me to drop what I'm doing 'cause he needs my help, shit's about to go down today.'

'So Murphy was purposely waiting in the lobby today?'

'Yeah. Yeah, that's right. He was there to talk to a ghost.' Hill giggled drunkenly.

'Walter Karl Torres,' Darby said.

She saw the name hit home, Hill tightening his grip on the kid.

'Son of a bitch was in my house,' Hill said. 'Put a bomb in there and then blew it up.'

'I know.'

'Raised my kids there – my wife, God rest her soul, she died there. In our bed.'

'Heart attack, right? Went peacefully.'

The kid was squirming in his arms and Hill was using all of his energy to keep standing up straight. 'My *house*,' he said again.

'I know. Someone was in there today, someone we thought might've been you – a guy with a Marine tattoo.'

'My brother. We had the same tattoos, on the same leg. Got them together when we went into the Marines.' Hill paused for a moment, fixed on a private memory. His eyes were bright and his voice was tight with emotion when he said, 'He's dead, isn't he?'

Darby nodded. 'Yeah,' she said solemnly. 'Yeah, he is. I'm sorry.'

Hill nodded, wiped his nose on the kid's jacket. 'Been staying with me. My brother. Wife finally left him. They always do, you know. Women. You use us and then spit us out. We're never good enough. I've gotta sit.'

Hill slid awkwardly to the floor and then crossed his legs, trying to keep the kid close to his chest, the kid squirming and trying to claw free and not giving a shit if it pissed off Hill because the kid had no idea what a gun was. All he wanted was his mother. All he wanted was for the steel tube digging into his stomach to go away.

'I'm going to sit with you, Danny.' She didn't want to be looming over him. 'I'm going to sit right across from you and Coop's going to leave, right, Coop?'

'Yeah,' he said, numb with adrenaline. 'Yeah, sure thing.'

Blood was pooling all over the floor around Murphy. She stepped over the blood and, with her hands raised near her shoulders, carefully made her way to the shelving across from Hill.

58

+09.08

'I'm going to sit down now,' Darby said.

Hill said nothing, lost inside his thoughts. She lowered herself to the floor and then sat with her left leg bent and her arm propped on her knee, the Sig digging into her back, the kid's screams piercing her skull like nails, hammering into the meat of her brain. 'You and I need to work this shit out.'

'Goddamn right we will.'

'I can't hear you over the screaming. Let him go so you and I can talk. Just put him on the floor and let him crawl away, and then you and I can sit here for as long as you want, until we figure out what we need to do.'

Hill put his pinkie finger in the kid's mouth. The boy stopped wailing, traded it for chewing.

Hill winced. 'That's what I thought,' he said, his head swaying a bit. 'Little guy's teething.'

'You got kids, right? A girl and a boy?'

'Two girls. Grown. Claire just had a kid. A boy. Parker.' Hill snorted. Shook his head. 'Jesus, what an awful name. That's her husband's doing, his choice. Watched too many soap operas, I think. But he's the breadwinner, and when you're the person with all the money, you get to make all the rules.'

Then Hill's gaze jumped to Murphy. Coop, Darby saw, was no longer standing in the aisle, no doubt coordinating the resources with Gelfand.

'Murph was a good kid,' Hill said.

Then why did you kill him? Darby wanted to say.

'Known him since he was a patrolman,' Hill said, wiggling his finger inside the kid's mouth as he bounced him up and down, trying to soothe him. 'Didn't know about the other stuff until much later, until it was too late.'

'What other stuff?'

'I tried. I really did. I tried to do the right thing.'

Darby waited, her gaze locked on Hill.

'But sometimes people take that power away from you when you're not looking,' Hill said. 'Like Murphy. I didn't tell him to kill Warren and Lacy and whoever else. He did that all on his own. Came here to give me the gun, asked me to get rid of it for him.'

'You called him?'

'No. No, he called me.'

'Where have you been all day?'

'His house. Couldn't go back to mine. Hanging out there while we tried to figure out what was happening.'

'Walk me through it so I can understand.'

Hill looked down at the kid, who was greedily gnawing on his finger, the kid no longer crying but his eyes still bright with tears, his nose running. A ghost of a smile flickered on Hill's face then vanished.

'Murph called me early this morning. Said there was a gunman inside the police lobby and he took three hostages. Said we had a problem.'

'What kind of problem?' Darby asked.

'Murph got a call early this morning from someone, this guy with a bad cold, he said. Guy said he wanted to meet Murph inside the station this morning, to talk about a few important matters.' Hill kept widening his eyes. His mouth was dry, spittle dotting his lips. 'Said he had information on who killed Sean Ellis after he got out of prison.'

Darby weighed the next question, debating whether she should ask it or just let Hill keep talking.

It didn't matter. Hill wanted to talk. He said, 'I didn't kill Ellis. That was him.'

'Murphy?'

Hill nodded. 'And Ventura and Owen. The Three Amigos, we called them. Did everything together when they were patrolmen. When they were coming up.'

'Why did they kill Sean Ellis?'

'Because Ellis was going to go ahead with a civil trial, bring certain things to light – things that wouldn't be good for Murphy and the others. For any of us.'

'You talking about BPD?'

'I'm talking about the Feds. They're the ones who can make people disappear with a snap of their fingers, wave a magic wand and give anyone they want a real name – or sell them down the river.'

'Send people to jail based on faulty or made-up evidence.'

'Exactly.' Hill looking at her like she really understood him. 'Warren, the fingerprint guy? Deep down, he wasn't a bad guy, but he had some vices, like we all do. And they exploited that. They made him do shit with fingerprints to close cases. And the guy who was running ballistics back in the day, this guy Vickers – it was the same thing. Fudge the ballistics report, make some evidence disappear or asked to look the other way. Same thing with me, same thing with . . . No, not Murphy. He got off on it. He liked being in control.'

'Who gave the orders, Danny? Who inside BPD?'

Hill looked at her as though she had dropped a hundred IQ points. 'You can only make deals on a federal level,' he said. 'I mean, look at the mortgage crisis from a few years back. Investment bankers caused it. Stockbrokers and mortgage companies – they all preyed on people, and they lost their homes and their life savings. Then the federal government bails them out and the guys who did it? They still get their fifty-million-dollar-a-year bonus. Not a single one of them went to jail. Shit, not a single one of them was even arrested.'

Darby wasn't sure where he was going, if his alcohol-fuelled brain was making a connection back to what was happening at the police station or if he was simply babbling. She decided to let him continue, feigned listening, all the while watching for Hill to move the kid away just far enough so she could get a shot, just a clean shot. One was all it would take.

'What I'm saying is, the people who are really responsible don't get punished. They're too high up, protected by paper. You play chess, who's the most valuable piece? The king. You protect the king or the game's over, right? That's why you sacrifice the pawns. Same thing with wars. Generals don't go rushing into enemy fire. You sacrifice your infantrymen. And no matter who you are, you think you're smart enough to avoid that trap. But anyone can put you into that spot any time they want. No one protects you in this life. You've got to do that yourself.'

Then a thought wormed its way through his drunken haze and his eyes brightened. 'I want to make a deal,' he said. 'Give me immunity and I'll tell you what you people want to know. Briggs and the garage, everything.'

'You can talk to a lawyer. We can –'

'Don't want a lawyer, I want someone in charge. Tell the district attorney to come here.'

'DA's not coming here, Danny, not with you holding a gun, not with you holding a gun on a kid.'

'I'm not gonna hurt him.'

'I know that.'

'But I've gotta hold on to him 'cause they were going to kill me. Second I let him go, someone here will kill me.' He swallowed, his eyes bright with tears. 'Our thing isn't nine to five. You don't check out at the end of the day and put what you do behind you, go back to your family. You carry what you do and the stuff you see. It's there when you hit the pillow. You don't get any break from it. You have to carry this shit, learn to live with it, you know?'

'I know.'

‘They don’t teach you how to do that. How to carry the stuff. How to lock it in a box and learn to . . . not forget, but how to make room for it. How to live with it. And when you *do* reach out for help, the people who are supposed to help you don’t. So where’s that leave you? Purgatory. You stay there and it’s like you’re living every moment with a held breath, waiting for your number to come up. And now it’s my turn.’

He wasn’t making much sense. Darby was trying to get him to a point when she said, ‘Tell me what you’re holding, Danny. Tell me so I can help.’

‘Don’t run that psych bullshit on me, okay? Just don’t. Things I’ve seen and had to live with? I . . . ’ Hill shook his head. ‘Gave up my life for this city. Those cases I worked on? They were righteous. Then the Feds come in and screw everything ’cause they’ve got to protect their confidential informants – make us take the freight. “Put that evidence over here,” they say. “Make this guy the suspect,” they say. And I get swept up in the tide. I didn’t know the guys who said they had my back were working deals with the Feds to protect Sullivan and the others. I mean, what other choice did I have?’

It’s all about choices, Darby wanted to say. ‘You’ve got a choice now, Danny. You and I can go and make a deal with the DA. I can . . . What’s so funny?’

‘I was thinking about something your old man used to say, how “it’s all about choices”. Big Red said that all the time.’ Then a dreamy, boozy smile tugged the corner of his mouth. ‘He was a good man.’

‘The best.’

'He didn't deserve to go out like that. But you know what I admired about him the most? He always tried to do the right thing. Stuck to his guns and never turned his back on anyone. Went out with respect.'

'Do you know Big Red, Danny?'

'No idea.'

'Murph didn't tell you anything.'

Hill shook his head. 'He just said not to worry, that he'd take care of everything, the way he always did. Now look at him. At us.'

'Walter Karl Torres,' Darby said.

For a moment, Hill turned as still as a statue.

'We know he was a federal informant,' Darby said.

'He's dead.'

Darby shook her head. 'We have some evidence that shows Torres is alive – that he's the gunman.'

'Bullshit.'

'No. No bullshit. I just found out myself. He –'

Hill suddenly let go of the kid. Darby's attention wasn't on the child; it was on Hill, who was bringing the gun up towards his chin, taking the coward's way out. *Let him do it*, a part of her said – and she would have too, if she didn't need him as a witness. Her hand was already gripping the Sig when she brought it up and fired.

59

+09.11

Darby walked numbly out of the aisle, dimly aware of the agents and mix of SWAT and emergency personnel flooding past her and crashing into her, asking her questions she could barely hear behind the ringing in her ears from the gunshot. The mother of the kid was crying somewhere behind her and men were shouting in front of her and all the sounds seemed distant and garbled, as though she was listening to them from somewhere deep underwater. She brushed off an EMT who wanted to help her and stepped across the centre aisle and entered an open-space area of waist-high shelving and counters holding an array of power saws and blades that could cut through concrete and steel.

Coop was standing in the aisle, near Hill. She could see his head and shoulders above the others. His face had been cleaned up a bit, but most of his clothes were still covered in Murphy's blood. Coop was looking at the mother holding her son. The kid was fine, maybe a little rattled by the gunshot, probably needed a new diaper; but chances were he'd never remember what had happened when his mother or someone else brought it up, because the only people inside the store were cops, not a single asshole holding up his or her phone to capture the moment to post on YouTube.

Coop's head turned to Darby, and their eyes locked for a moment, the two of them so close now they shared their own language.

I'm giving you some space but I want you to know I'm here, his expression said.

She nodded and something inside him seemed to relax, and he returned his attention to Hill, who was sitting up on the floor with his hands cuffed behind his back and hissing back pain from the gunshot wound and ignoring the EMTs working on him. Darby had shot him in the top-right part of his collarbone and the round exited cleanly, or as cleanly as being shot could. There was no need to shoot again, as much as she wanted to: Hill had dropped his weapon and, by the time his addled and pickled brain had registered what had just happened, she was already on him. When she pinned him on the floor he decided to projectile vomit – away from her, fortunately.

Hill, Darby saw, had started to cry. Not just a few stray tears but actually bawling. She didn't like it when men cried. A sexist thing to admit, sure, but there you go. Men, she believed, should always be the strong and silent Clint Eastwood types, men like her father, men of few words but plenty of action. Men who could size up a situation and know how to handle it. And if a situation turned to shit, or if they got hurt, they'd suck down their pain and get back to the business of life, because they knew that life didn't care about anyone or anything. Or maybe it bothered her because of the *way* men cried, reduced them to little boys who just had something vital and critical torn from them, something they needed to hold on to the face they presented to the world. Hill was crying that way now, his body wracked with sobs; and maybe because of the weight loss and the angle of light inside the store, the distance she now had from him, she thought Hill looked incredibly old and frail, a man who no longer had any command over his physical body and mental faculties and was terrified of having to deal with the knowledge trapped inside his head.

Darby's phone vibrated inside her pocket. When she reached into her pocket, she looked down and saw that her shirt and jacket were sprayed with blood. She touched her face with her free hand and her fingertips came back with faint traces of red.

Gelfand was calling. 'Coop gave me the rundown,' he said.

Darby could barely hear him. She increased the phone's volume to its maximum. 'Say that again?'

'Coop told me what happened. You okay?'

'Fantastic.' She filled in Gelfand on what Hill had told her.

'Good,' he said after she finished. 'That's great.'

'You don't sound too excited about it, Howie. Does that have anything to do with the fact that everything, as usual, points back to the Bureau being a bunch of –'

'You're not going to get any argument from me,' Gelfand said wearily. Something about his tone took the fight out of her. 'I don't know the players involved, probably never will; they're either dead or so buried in documents that were more likely than not shredded.' He sighed. 'There are times that I feel like I've got these invisible strings on me and someone's pulling them and I'm either too blind or stupid to see it. Anyway, it doesn't matter. I'm off this.'

'BPD took over?'

'No. Hostage Rescue. The HRT is about to touch down. I've got orders to step aside.'

'They're going to take him out,' Darby said.

'Yep. The pregnant woman and the building will be written off as collateral damage. Feds will pick up the tab.'

'All because they don't want Torres to testify to what he did for you guys.'

'That about sums it up, yeah.'

'Why are you telling me this?'

'Just wanted to give you the lay of the land. Of course, if there was some indication that Torres was ready to surrender . . .'

Darby said nothing, watched the flurry of activity around her.

'Briggs is here, boasting that he would've gone in there to talk to him.'

'He said that to you?'

'To me and to the press,' Gelfand said. 'He issued a statement. Now HRT is taking over and he gets to look like the good guy. You will too when this is all over and done with. Come back to the campus and you can talk to the hostage he just released, Linda Amos. She said she was there to meet a colleague – she's a trooper – and they were both heading up for a job in Vermont, financial crime.'

'No tie to Torres or Ellis?'

'Not according to her. But I didn't talk to her that much. You can take a run at her, if you want. Or you can go home. Either way, the United States would like to thank you for your very valiant and courageous service, et cetera, et cetera.'

Then he was gone and then Darby found herself walking towards the front door.

The automatic doors slid open, the front area blocked off by the same carnival of flashing vehicles, and behind them cops keeping back people, almost every single one of them with their phones out, talking to someone or snapping pictures or recording video. And Darby just wanted to find a quiet corner to sit, someplace where no one would talk to her or take pictures or video. She was so sick and tired of it all.

She found what she was looking for; a patrol car with the engine already running. She opened the door and the young cop behind the wheel flinched slightly when he saw her face.

'They need you in there,' she said.

He nodded. Got out of the car carefully, like she was preparing to shoot him.

'Something wrong?' Darby asked.

'You might want to get cleaned up. You've got pieces of brains in your hair.'

'You mind leaving the keys in your car? I need to warm up and to, you know, be alone for a bit. Sort my head around what just happened.'

'Sure. Sure, no problem.'

When the young cop disappeared through the store's front doors, Darby slid behind the wheel.

60

+09.16

Darby had been in plenty of patrol cars, but she had never driven one of the new models, the Ford Inceptor, and ten minutes after driving out of the parking lot she had to pull over to figure out the switches for the sirens and lights, how to shut off the police radio.

As the traffic parted in front of her and the wails pounded through the glass and against her ears, the wipers cranked to their maximum setting and working furiously to clear the windshield of the snow, Darby had an odd and completely irrelevant thought: this was the first time she had ever stolen something. Her father, when he was alive, told her how much he detested liars and thieves, and he had exploded in a rage – the only time he had ever gotten angry at her – when, at seven, she took a pen with a pink flamingo, of all things, and stuck it inside her pocket just because she thought it was pretty. She didn't know why she was thinking of this now as she drove, didn't have the time or the inclination to analyse it. She needed to focus on the road.

It also occurred to her that, technically speaking, she wasn't law enforcement, which meant she had zero legal authority. A private investigator had more leeway and rights than she did. And, legally speaking, she had technically stolen not just a car but a police car, and now she was going to break at least a dozen more laws, state and federal.

Let the good times roll, Darby thought, killing the lights and sirens as she hooked on to Tremont. She realized she was not herself. And why should she be? She had just shot a man who had used a kid – a baby – as a human shield. And not just some nameless scumbag, either, but someone who she'd respected and thought was stand-up. She knew she was physically and emotionally exhausted, maybe not of sound mind or body, a lawyer would say, but the root of her numbness had to do with the plain and simple fact that she'd had enough of being the victim of people who cared only about their base desires and personal agendas and sacrificed people's lives and families like they were nothing more than pawns on a chessboard. And the thing was, if she didn't stop it – if she didn't take a stand – then who would? If she didn't stop it or take a stand, she couldn't live with herself.

A mile and a half later, she saw a pair of cruisers parked at a sideways angle in the middle of the street. Beyond them, in her headlights and through the curtains of falling snow, she saw the bright reflective orange paint of sawhorses parked in the street and along sidewalks, the entire area deathly quiet. If this were a movie, she'd slam her foot on the gas and rocket forward, turning the sawhorses into splintered wood. But this was real life, and when she sped up a bit, the tyres slipping, trying to seek purchase through the snow, and casually drove through the space between the cruisers. She navigated her way around the saw-horses and then she was driving to the station, no one shouting at her to stop, no one following. The snow continued to fall, the streetlights continued to glow, everything quiet and soft, like something captured in a tranquil postcard or nature picture.

Darby pulled up to the front doors and put the car in park, then left the engine running. She went in feeling stronger and more confident than she had to. She stepped up to the marble column, the ferns in the planter rubbing up against her shirt that was splattered with blood. Darby knew he was watching her through his NV scope and seeing the blood-coloured black against her clothes and face and shirt.

She spoke into the cold darkness. Her voice didn't waver and she didn't feel afraid, or maybe her brain had simply gone numb from shock.

'Briggs landed in Boston.'

'And you came all the way here to tell me in person. How thoughtful.'

'No, I came to tell you Bob Murphy is dead.'

'Did you kill him?'

'No. I'm just wearing his blood.' Darby moved up to the edge of the marble planter. 'Danny Hill blew his brains out in aisle six at the Lowe's in Quincy. It appears Danny wasn't inside his house this morning after all, when the bomb went off. It'll be all over the six o'clock news, I'm sure.'

‘He’s alive? Detective Hill.’

‘Yes. We have him. And I talked to him. He told me about Sean Ellis, the FBI, all of it. But not about the agents involved in the cover-up.’

Again the gunman’s robotic tone: ‘They’re all dead. And Detective Hill will make some sweetheart deal, request immunity in exchange for a reduced sentence. I’ve seen it happen before, too many times.’

‘The FBI told me Walter Karl Torres is dead.’

‘Did they now?’

‘Said he was shot in El Paso, Texas, and buried there.’

‘The wonderful thing about money is that it allows you to purchase all sorts of promises and lies. My new life came at a hefty price. Have you ever been shot?’

‘No.’

‘But you’ve been close to death, I know, I’ve read about the things that happened to you. It’s ugly, that moment. You’re praying. Begging. I turned to God and said if He let me live I’d make restitution.’

‘That’s what this is all about? Restitution?’

‘I accepted Jesus as my personal lord and saviour. He has forgiven me for the things I’ve done, and I swore to Him I would make things right. Did the FBI tell you it was my bullet that killed Anita Barnes’s grandson?’

‘No.’

‘It was an accident, of course. I’m not a monster. I was protecting myself.’

‘From what?’

‘I was supposed to meet my FBI handlers when Detectives Murphy and Ventura appeared and suddenly started shooting. I survived and ran, and my handlers made arrangements with certain Boston police officers so I wouldn't be found. I was too valuable an informant.'

'And Officer Fitzpatrick?'

'I shot him. Tried to kill him, but he survived.'

'And now you have his daughter. Laura Levine.'

Big Red – Torres – said nothing.

'Why now?' Darby asked. 'Why wait two decades?'

'It took me all that time to gather my courage. Pathetic, isn't it?'

'Briggs isn't coming here.'

'I told you he wouldn't.'

'That's why you called the political reporter, Dave Carlson, isn't it? To make sure the public knew about your demand about wanting to talk to Briggs so no one could twist it. No matter how this ends, you know Carlson will keep digging. Only he's not going to find anything.'

'Mr Carlson is very resourceful.'

'The FBI's Hostage Rescue Team landed in Boston,' Darby said. 'Do you know what HRT does?'

'They're assassins. Did they send you here?'

'No, I came on my own. I wanted you to know what you're up against now. I wanted you to know the truth – especially about Clara Lacy and her family. They're dead. Bob Murphy killed them, if Danny Hill is to be believed. We'll have to wait and see how it shakes out.'

The gunman didn't respond. In the silence that followed, Darby heard the pregnant woman, Laura Levine, whimpering.

'It's over,' Darby said. 'They've won.'

'I'll blow the bombs and kill –'

'*They don't care.* Don't you get it? They're going to sacrifice you, the hostage and this building. Me. They'll write the story any way they want to. I'm breaking all sorts of laws by telling you this, by being here – I stole a police car to get here. When I leave, they'll arrest me. It's over.'

'Why are you telling me this?'

'To let you know the score.'

'I could kill you right now.'

'You could. You can do anything you want. It's not going to change the outcome. But you've got one final play.'

'What?'

'Dave Carlson.'

'They won't let him come in here.'

'You're right; they won't. They won't let you speak to him. But they may let *me* speak to him.'

'In exchange for what? What do you want?'

'For Briggs to come here, for the truth to come out. And you're making me do it. That's what I'm going to tell them. You've taken me as a hostage.' Darby nodded with her chin to the throw-phone. 'May I?'

61

+09.35

'Make the call,' Torres said.

The phone was connected to the unit by a long wire. Darby grabbed it and pulled the receiver to her.

Grove answered on the third ring, and she immediately asked to speak to Gelfand.

Gelfand didn't hide his contempt. '*What* are you doing in there?'

'I need to speak with Dave Carlson.'

'Are you out of your mind?'

'We can still resolve this peacefully.'

'That's not going to happen.'

'Resolving this peacefully or talking to Carlson?'

'Darby, you –'

'I have a gun to my head,' Darby lied. It wasn't a lie, per se; the man *did* have a gun, that was a fact, and he could very well be pointing it at her head, she had no way of knowing. 'If you don't patch Carlson through and put him on the line, he's going to kill me.'

Gelfand said he'd call her back.

Darby waited in the cold silence, sweating beneath her jacket and telling herself that she had made the right play. The line for the hostage phone was being recorded. Everything she said would become part of the record.

When the phone rang, Dave Carlson was on the other end of the line.

'Mr Carlson, can you hear me?'

'Yes.'

'Did they inform you this line is being recorded?'

'They did. And I should inform you that I'm not alone. I have three federal agents with me right now. One of 'em is listening in on this conversation.'

'The gunman's name is Walter Karl Torres. He's a former federal informant. He has assured me he will surrender his suicide vest and the remaining bombs right now provided you accompany the former mayor Briggs inside the lobby and conduct the TV interview. Will you do that?'

His response was swift, but he was nervous, too: 'Yes,' he said. 'Yes, I will.'

'Mr Torres wants to speak to the former mayor Briggs about his possible involvement with the Sean Ellis case. After the interview is finished, he will surrender himself. He wants you to publish that now on your Twitter feed to make sure the public knows that he wants to resolve this peacefully, without bloodshed.

'Howie, call building management and tell them to turn on the lights for the lobby. Once the devices have been disarmed, I'll contact you.'

Darby hung up.

'It's done,' she told the gunman. 'The rest is up to you.'

Karl Torres didn't reply.

She could hear movement in the darkness. Whimpering.

Now she heard footsteps.

The lobby lights came on, her eyes burning from the sudden brightness. When they finally adjusted, she didn't see Torres or Laura Levine anywhere.

'The vest and backpack are on the conveyor belt,' Torres said, still using the voice modulator. 'They've been disarmed.'

'And your jamming unit?'

'Turned off. It's in the backpack.'

'The bomb robot will have –'

'No. You take them out. I don't want anyone else in here.'

'They're made with TATP. It's –'

'I know what it is. They have a stabilizer in them. The bombs won't blow unless you throw them in the air. Carry them and place them gently on the ground and you'll be fine. Don't come back in here until Briggs arrives, please. I need some time to prepare.'

'For what?'

Karl Torres refused to answer.

62

+09.50

They brought Briggs in the APV, of course, not because the former mayor was in any danger but because the vehicle looked good on TV – a big, menacing, futuristic tank that could protect anyone or anything tucked inside its steel bulletproof and bombproof womb.

That or Briggs had insisted on being driven here in it because he was a pussy, Darby thought.

A Channel 5 news van came up the rear and parked behind the APV, snow dancing in the headlights, the power back on inside the lobby, lights everywhere except inside the patrol car she'd driven here. She sat behind the wheel and watched the APV and the van. She didn't have to turn on the wipers because the patrol car was parked underneath a glass roof. She could see everything clearly.

Darby wasn't worried about a bomb going off. She had spoken to the bomb commander, Ted Scott, over the police radio, the only frequency that wasn't being jammed in the area. He'd told her that during the day his men, with help from the BPD and state police bomb squads, had conducted a thoroughly exhaustive and painstaking search, block by block, checking every parked car and city trash can. They'd even checked the nearby buildings, looking for some IED that might've come in today's mail, dropped off by a mailman or someone from UPS or FedEx.

Using the radio, she'd asked to speak to Gelfand but was told he was unavailable. Same deal with Coop. She was sure they had already been pushed aside to make way for the big boys who were going to come in and clean up.

She needed to stretch. Get the blood flowing through her limbs, breathe in the cold air to clear her head and keep her awake and alert. She opened the door and stepped outside. She had already cleaned her face and her hair and got most of the blood off her jacket using a shirt she found in the small gym bag on the passenger's seat.

In less than a minute her eyes were no longer dry and she didn't feel exhausted, the cold air filling her lungs invigorating her, making her thoughts and everything in her vision feel sharp, laser-focused.

The APV and van still had their headlights on, their diesel engines chugging. No one had stepped out yet but, behind them, she spotted pinpoints of light, tiny beacons from TV cameras now situated in the small park directly across the street, landing on the APV, waiting for Briggs to emerge. Now that all the explosive devices had been removed, the media had gotten the all-clear to get closer to the station. When the storm took a moment to breathe, she could see blue uniforms working crowd control.

Darby didn't want to be on TV, didn't want to be seen pacing back and forth like she was nervous, even though she was. She pressed her back up against one of the squared marble columns holding up the roof and, hands deep in her jacket pockets, stared at the bevelled glass in front of her, wondering if Torres was going to try to kill Briggs on live TV.

The question kept bouncing through her head, searching for an answer.

She thought – okay – believed that Torres wouldn't kill Briggs. Better to embarrass Briggs on TV and let him die a slow and painful death afterwards than to kill him. Better to let him go and try and live with his sins that he would have to make public.

But the thing Torres didn't understand about politics was that politicians, by and large, didn't care about what people thought of them. People were simply voters. You couldn't care what people thought of you or you couldn't be a politician, and every successful mayor, governor and president shared that psychopathic trait. Other people were nothing more than tools, a means to an end, animals manipulated through words and emotion. It didn't mean he or she was a psychopath; it meant that they had the ability to shut off feelings, to be so self-absorbed that how he or she felt was the only thing that mattered. Guilt, shame and regret – those were crippling emotions. Feel them and you couldn't get anything done, couldn't make the hard decisions. Deep down, some of them believed they were above the law, but the real secret of their success was that they were hard to embarrass and had proved, time and time again, that they could explain away their actions through the sheer force of their charisma. Briggs fell squarely into that camp; a bona fide Bill Clinton type who would always rise above the fray and be forgiven.

Charisma and sincerity, whether it was real or manufactured: the two critical ingredients of a successful politician or CEO.

Or a psychopath.

Would Briggs deliver the goods, or would he choke and flame out on national TV?

Time to find out. The APV's back doors opened, and when Darby turned around she saw Briggs step outside and bathed in the glow of TV lights.

63

+10.00

Edward Briggs seemed taller than Darby remembered. Younger and even more confident and sure of himself and his ability to bend people to his will. He wore a camelhair overcoat and a plaid scarf, and his presidential hair – thick and still a dark brown, unmovable in the wind – hadn't receded at all since the last time she'd seen him.

Briggs had an aide with him, a well-dressed woman standing off to the side underneath a golf umbrella. She kept casting nervous glances at the front door. No one had left the news van.

Briggs turned to the nervous woman and said, 'Give us a few minutes, Christine.'

Christine. Briggs's personal assistant, the woman Darby had heard on the phone.

'Sir,' Christine said, 'I think –'

'I'll be fine.' Briggs flashed the woman his full-wattage smile, the same one he had used on TV thousands of times as mayor, to let the people of the city of Boston know that everything was under control, no reason to worry, trust me. 'Five minutes. That's all I'll need. Thank you, Christine.'

The woman trotted away, trying to make a call on her smartphone when she remembered that all the signals here were being jammed.

Darby's eyes were still on the woman when Briggs said, 'So, the man inside.'

'Karl Torres.'

'I'm told he's some sort of drug dealer and murderer.'

'And federal informant. What can you tell me about him?'

'Nothing. I don't know the man.'

'But you recognize the name.'

'Not beyond what the FBI told me. From my understanding, he seems to know you very well.'

'I don't know him.'

'What does he want?'

'To talk to you.'

'I already know that. I want to know what he wants – what he *really* wants, what this whole affair is about.'

'I'm guessing it has something to do with the Sean Ellis case.'

Briggs said nothing. Waited.

'You familiar with the case?' Darby asked.

'I was briefed back at the campus. I didn't have anything to do with that.'

'But Sean Ellis was released from jail while you were mayor. You put protective orders in place.'

'Absolutely. My job was to protect the city.'

'And now?'

'Darby, you got your wish. I'm here. I'm here because I want to resolve this peacefully. What do *you* want?'

'The FBI's Boston office, along with the BPD, used Ellis as their scapegoat. Set him up to take the fall for Torres.'

'What else?'

'Torres confessed to me in there that he accidentally killed a four-year-old boy from Dorchester. His name was –'

'Right, right, the Anita Barnes thing, they told me. But what does he want, what's his purpose?'

'Retribution.'

'For what? What did I do to this guy?'

Darby shrugged. 'I think it has something to do with that garage in Hyde Park. The one that's practically down the street from the mayor's home, where you once lived.'

'Honestly, I'm as in the dark as you are.'

'In my experience, people who start off a sentence saying *honestly* or *quite honestly* are usually lying.'

Briggs shot her a withering look. Then he turned to his right, to the doors leading into the station, and studied them for a moment, his eyes flickering with nervous thought.

'I feel like I'm about to step inside a confessional, only I'm about to be judged by a lunatic,' Briggs said. Then he sighed. 'The public doesn't understand what people like you and I do, Darby, the sacrifices we have to make. Take Jackson Cooper, for example. You have a legal obligation to tell the authorities that he suffocated that woman.'

Darby felt the skin of her face stretch tightly across the bone.

'We both know Frank Sullivan forced him into it,' Briggs said, looking back at her. 'A judge and a jury would see it that way, probably. His FBI career would be over, of course, but the silver lining is that he most likely wouldn't go to prison. But the fact of the matter is that he never told anyone what he did, and neither did you, when you found out. You're in possession of information on a crime. How do you think that woman's poor family feels, not knowing what their daughter's last moment of life was like?'

Darby felt like her entire midsection had been scooped away. Like a blade had entered through her temple and sliced its way through her brain. She was the only person who knew what had happened to Coop. But now Briggs knew, and the only way he knew was because . . . How? How did he know?

Briggs said, 'You never know when someone could be listening in on your conversation. If you're recording me now, you might want to shut off the tape.'

'What do you want?' Her heart was racing, trapped in her throat.

'Are you recording me?'

'Nope.'

'Do you mind if I pat you down?'

'Do it and you'll go inside the lobby with all your fingers broken.'

'People make all sorts of sacrifices for love. You love Cooper – everyone knows that – and you chose to protect him. I love this city. More than my wife, more than my kids. Not a good thing to admit, but there you go.

That's who I am. And neither I nor Commissioner Donnelly want to see any harm come to Agent Cooper, which is why you're going to be a good girl and accompany me inside the police lobby and protect me – at all costs. If something happens to me, then, well, I don't have to spell out the rest for you.

'Don't look at me like that, Doctor. I take no joy from this. But I have to protect myself from angry and irrational people who wish to do me harm, and the city I love. Be nice and play along and keep that poisoned mouth of yours shut and maybe, just maybe, the conversation you had with Cooper in the trailer will remain private. Do you think you can do that?'

Darby gritted her teeth.

Said nothing.

'Say it,' Briggs said.

'Say what?'

'That you promise to be a good little girl.' His voice was neutral, as if the two of them had been discussing what font to use on a spreadsheet. 'Can you do that, Doctor? Can you be a good little girl?'

Darby made fists inside her jacket pockets, thinking of the satisfying crunch she heard and felt when she broke Murphy's nose. How great would it be for Briggs to go on TV looking bloodied.

'No one has to know Cooper is a murderer,' Briggs said.

'I promise.'

'Then say it.'

'I just did.'

'No, I asked you to say you'll be a *good little girl.*' Briggs leaned in closer. 'You want to make Daddy proud, don't you?'

The back doors of the TV van opened. In the light she saw Dave Carlson, stocky and bald, heading their way.

'Showtime,' Darby said, and slapped Briggs so hard on the shoulder the man teetered and nearly fell.

64

+10.04

Dave Carlson, Darby thought, looked like a kid who had come down Christmas morning and discovered he had been given the present of his dreams – in his case, a shot at another Pulitzer. He was clearly anxious, though, his large brow shiny with sweat, and his voice trembled a bit when he spoke. The two cameramen, both in their early to mid-thirties, both black, wore heavy parkas and baseball caps with 'Team Center 5 News' on the brims and the back of their coats. The one with the wide shoulders, kneading a wad of gum between his front teeth, carried a small flat screen TV.

'So Mr Torres can see himself on live TV,' Briggs explained to her.

'Everything in there's being jammed.'

'They're going to cut that off. Don't worry, we're living up to our end of the bargain. I'm sure you will, too.'

Inside the station, Karl Torres was sitting in a rolling chair behind the pregnant woman who, Darby thought, had entered into that stage of shock she had seen in so many victims of violent crime; a complete and total detachment from self. Karl Torres, still wearing his mask, whispered something in Laura Levine's ear, and when she didn't move he whispered something again and dug the barrel of his handgun deeper into her stomach. Laura Levine still didn't move or respond, so he lifted her up by the neck, the woman staring off into space, wondering where she was, praying to God for him to produce some magical escape hatch for her and the unborn baby she was carrying to disappear through, to put this nightmare behind them.

Walter Karl Torres moved the gun to Laura Levine's head and looked only at Darby while the cameramen set up their equipment. The TV went on top of the reception desk. A cable was fed into one of the cameras. Torres didn't ask any questions. Dave Carlson didn't ask any questions. Only the big-shouldered cameraman spoke, explaining what he was doing, him and his partner moving with exaggerated slowness, not wanting to alarm the gunman.

Darby stood in the background, sitting on the end of the conveyor belt while the cameramen went about testing their equipment. Something about the absence of the bombs had taken away the stress of the past several hours and made her feel . . . it wasn't that she didn't care any more. Far from it. She didn't have anything left. She felt hollowed to the core. Empty. A part of Darby wished she could close her eyes and go to sleep, wake up tomorrow and see it for the terrible but temporary dream it was.

Then she thought of Briggs and what she felt in that moment was a cold and blinding hatred.

Briggs remained outside with his assistant or aide or

whatever she was. The jamming units must have been shut down because she could see and hear Briggs talking on his cell phone. His aide was using a makeup sponge to apply some cover-up to his eyes.

Big Shoulders said, 'We're ready.'

Darby looked to Torres and said, 'The gun.'

'Not until after the interview is over.'

Torres's robotic voice made Carlson and the cameramen flinch in surprise.

'We can't let you on TV holding a loaded gun to a hostage's head,' Darby said.

'If I don't have the gun, you'll try to trick me.'

'And if you have the gun, you may decide to kill all of us.'

'Impossible,' he said. 'There's only one round chambered. Tell them.'

At first Darby thought he was speaking to her. Then Laura Levine said, 'It's true. He only chambered one round. I saw him do it.'

Her voice was just as robotic as his. *She's checked out*, Darby thought. *Gone.*

'I only have one round,' the gunman said. 'To shoot her in case any of you try to deceive me. If you don't like it, back up and leave, and I'll take my chances with Mr Carlson finding out the truth. You will find out the truth, won't you, Mr Carlson?'

'Yes,' Carlson replied. 'You have my word.'

'It's fine,' Briggs said.

Darby hadn't even heard the door open.

'We agree to your terms, Mr Torres,' Briggs said. 'Dr

McCormick, your job here is done. Thank you. The city of Boston owes you a great debt.'

The gunman said, 'I want Dr McCormick on TV, standing next to me.'

'I don't think that's wise,' Briggs said. 'She has blood on her.'

'I want the public to see her.'

'Fine. We'll get her cleaned up.' Briggs motioned Darby with his hand.

Torres said, 'No. I like her just the way she is. The viewers will too.'

Briggs looked like he was about to counter. Then he smiled tightly and said, 'As you wish. Let us know when you're ready.'

'Mr Carlson, I'll let you ask your questions after I've spoken with the former mayor,' Torres said. 'Do you understand?'

Carlson nodded. Said, 'May I ask one question now?'

'Please.'

'May I record this to augment my notes?'

'Yes, by all means.' Then, to Big Shoulders: 'I'm ready.'

Torres ordered where everyone was to stand: Darby next to him, followed by Briggs.

The cameramen took their positions. Big Shoulders said, 'Excuse me, but the . . . gun. Could you maybe put it somewhere else? Broadcasting regulations forbid me to show it.'

Darby didn't know of any such regulation. But she said nothing.

Surprisingly, Torres complied. Moved the gun behind the woman's back and pointed it at her heart.

'We're live in three . . . two . . . one,' Big Shoulders said.

Torres glanced quickly to his left, to the TV set up on the reception counter. They were, in fact, live.

The gunman removed his balaclava.

Not Walter Karl Torres.

A woman.

65

+10.09

Get rid of the mannish haircut and take away the men's suit and put her in a pair of jeans and a sweatshirt and she would be one of those women Darby saw at a Boston Bruins' hockey game, those rough *don't you dare fuck with me townies* who had long, fancy fingernails and smoked cigarettes and had absolutely no problem getting into a fistfight with another woman or man. They liked to throw down, these kind of women, and they liked to party and they all completed a semester or two at Bunker Hill Community College, the total sum of their ambition getting a state job or just one that would cover the bills because, like the old Loverboy song, they were simply working for the weekend.

The eyes were her most feminine feature. That and her voice – her natural speaking voice, which was soft and free of a Boston accent; and she didn't seem or act nervous in the slightest way when she said, 'Thank you for coming, Mr Briggs.'

Darby saw it clearly now: the reason why the voice had been disguised, the black hat that fully covered the gunman's – gun*woman's* – head and ears.

Would the male-dominated BPD and FBI have

taken the threats and demands seriously if they knew they were dealing with a woman and not a man? Darby already knew the answer, saw it in the cameramen and in Carlson, how they were standing a little taller, more confident, the three of them now thinking they had the upper hand because they were dealing with a woman now, the gunman no longer a clever and powerful threat but someone who could be reasoned with and manipulated, managed and controlled.

That's why she's using that voice-altering device, Darby thought. Why she disguised her voice earlier when talking to Anita Barnes over the phone and then the taxi driver. But they bought her off as a man recovering from a bad cold or suffering from laryngitis, Darby knowing the way a woman could train herself to change her voice, make it deeper and more monotone, the way men usually speak. Transgendered females did it all the time.

The gunman – *gunwoman* – said, 'I just want to talk, I don't want to hurt anyone. That was never my intention.'

Briggs, like Darby, like everyone else, seemed flummoxed. But Darby couldn't tell if his reaction was because, like her, he'd been expecting to see Walter Karl Torres, or if he knew this woman and was shocked to see her.

Whatever it was, Briggs, knowing he was on live TV, quickly pushed it aside and said, 'I'm here to listen. How can I help you?'

'First I want to apologize to Anita Barnes and Linda Amos and Laura Levine for the trauma I've put them through. I also want to apologize to everyone in the city of Boston for what happened today. And to anyone I may have hurt today, you have my deepest apologies and sympathies. I'm not asking you for your forgiveness. I made this decision of sound mind and body. But this was never about hurting any of you, the good and honest people that make up this great city, the place where I was born and, even though I moved with my mother to El Paso, Texas, still consider my home.'

The woman spoke confidently. Smoothly. She didn't stumble over any of her words. She reminded Darby, ironically, of a politician who had to address people after a tragedy. Darby guessed the woman, whoever she was, had rehearsed this speech for a long time.

Darby's attention flicked briefly to the pregnant woman, who was still clearly in shock, still holding on to the arm clamped around her neck for balance; then she looked to the reception desk where she saw a close-up of the hostage's face on the TV screen, the scroll underneath it reading: 'LIVE FROM BPD HEADQUARTERS.'

'My name is Grace Castonguay.' The woman paused, looking directly at Briggs to see if the name registered. If it did, Darby thought, he didn't show it.

'I took my mother's maiden name,' the woman said. 'Maybe you know my father, Walter Karl Torres?'

'Tell me about him, Miss Castonguay.'

Smooth, Darby thought. He completely avoided the question. Grace Castonguay, though, had picked up on that, too. Darby saw a spark of anger fly through the woman's eyes.

'My father told me he was shot and killed by a Boston Police detective named Robert Murphy,' Grace Castonguay said. 'He didn't die right away, my father. He lingered until he died from his wounds. During that time, he decided to make amends for his sins. My father was raised a God-fearing man and wanted absolution. He asked a priest to forgive him, and was forgiven.

'But my father also wanted our forgiveness – mine and my mother's. He told me about how he, along with a man named Francis Sullivan, the FBI undercover agent who was a serial killer and the head of Boston's Irish mob, had been instrumental in introducing heroin to Boston, especially South Boston, Charlestown, and Dorchester. He was also a murderer, my father, and he told me about several people he had killed – men, women, and one child, a four-year-old boy from Dorchester named Tae Jonah Fallows, the grandson of a woman named Anita Barnes. He did all this while he was a federal informant. The FBI didn't arrest him. They protected him.'

Briggs nodded, kept nodding. Then it became clear Grace Castonguay wanted him to speak, so he said, 'If what you're saying is true, then I can promise you we'll –'

'My father also told me he had tried to kill Boston Police Officer Stephen Fitzpatrick on the evening of September 30, 1992. My father escaped with the help of his FBI handlers, whose names I don't know, and with the help of officers from the Boston Police Department.'

'Miss Castonguay, if I may just interrupt you for a moment and say that –'

'The names of the Boston police officers are Robert Murphy, Daniel Hill, Frank Ventura and Ethan Owen. I am responsible for the deaths of former detectives Ventura and Owen, whom I killed last year. They were already dying of cancer, and because they wouldn't live long enough to see this moment, I decided to kill them.

'But I did not – I repeat, I did *not* kill Trey Warren or Clara Lacy and her family. Dr Darby McCormick, who is standing to my right, said that Detective Hill told her that Detective Murphy was responsible for that. Isn't that correct, Doctor?'

Darby felt beads of sweat dripping down the small of her back. Her shirt felt plastered against her damp skin. 'That is what Detective Hill told me,' she said.

'Detective Hill said that after he shot and killed Detective Murphy this afternoon.'

'Yes.'

'And he's alive.'

'He is.'

'Mr Briggs,' Grace Castonguay said, 'you were aware that a Dorchester man named Sean Ellis was convicted for the crime of shooting Officer Fitzpatrick and spent nearly twelve years in jail based on false witness testimony and doctored evidence.'

'I was recently made aware of these allegations.'

'That's a lie,' Castonguay said calmly. 'You've been aware of these allegations for years but you chose not to deal with them. You know how I know this? I wrote to you.'

Briggs shifted his stance. 'I got a lot of letters while I was mayor. Still do, as a matter of fact. Too many to count.'

'But I wrote to you one hundred and twenty-six times. That's a letter every quarter for twenty years, plus a few extras.'

The words hit Briggs somewhere, Darby could tell, like someone had suddenly driven a needle into his spine. He quickly recovered. He always did.

'Mr Briggs, I've written you about Sean Ellis and everything that my father confessed to, and asked you to look into the matter. Everything my father said, I put in writing and sent to you. One hundred and twenty-six times. One hundred and twenty-six chances to make things right, and what did you do?'

'You didn't put your name on those letters, did you?' Briggs asked.

'No, of course not.'

'We get a lot of letters that are from cranks, see, and we –'

'My father told me not to use my name because you sent Detectives Owen and Ventura down to El Paso to kill him.'

'All due respect, Miss Castonguay, I –'

Grace Castonguay moved the gun up to the hostage's head.

66

+10.13

It felt like the air crackled with an electric current, Darby feeling every muscle fibre tightening and flexing, her attention locked on the muzzle smashed into the side of the hostage's head, the pregnant woman staring into space and gripping her belly with both hands and silently weeping through a prayer as Grace Castonguay said, 'You promised you would tell the truth.'

'Of course I will. Of course,' Briggs replied. 'You have my word.'

'I don't want your word, I want the truth. Lie to me again and I'll pull this trigger, and the death of Laura Levine, the daughter of Boston Police Officer Fitzpatrick, will be on your hands, sir. I don't want to do it, but I will to make a point. Because violence and blood are the only way to get the attention of people like you, Mr Briggs.'

'I want to help you, and I want to make things right,' Briggs said. 'Please tell me what I can do to help you correct this massive injustice.'

Grace Castonguay stared at Briggs like she wanted to kill him – and Darby hoped she would try. If the woman did, she'd have to move the gun away from the hostage's head. If she did, Darby would be ready. Darby knew it was a small window; she'd have just a second or two to disarm the weapon.

'Since you're not going to talk about Sean Ellis and my father,' Grace Castonguay said, 'let's turn to a subject you *do* know a lot about: the auto garage in Hyde Park.'

And then Darby felt it creeping through her blood and across her skin, that awful sensation of a situation about to become unhinged. Only this situation was unfolding on live TV, every action, breath and facial expression being recorded in high definition and being played on TV and the worldwide web for people to view and pick apart, forever and ever, amen.

'Tell us so I can help you,' Briggs said, only he wasn't looking at Castonguay any more; no one was, Darby included, everyone was staring at the wet spot spreading across the hostage's crotch and moving down her legs.

Grace Castonguay, though, was apparently oblivious that the woman's water had broken, the amniotic fluid splashing across the hostage's legs and on to the floor. The cameramen didn't pan down because Darby glanced to the TV screen and saw a tight shot of Castonguay, her face crumpled in rage and contempt; and the woman wouldn't look away from Briggs, saw only Briggs. Castonguay's eyes were bright with tears and burning with the kind of bottomless hatred that could never be satiated.

'You're obviously in possession of information,' Briggs said, using his ingratiating Bill Clinton-like charisma. 'Let's hear what –'

'Tell the people of Boston how you ingored my letters? The truth! Tell everyone what happened in the garage!'

'Okay. Okay.' Briggs was nervous, yes, but he wasn't acting like someone who was about to go down in flames. His empathy was manufactured and so far he hadn't admitted to anything that could be used against him later. And if Briggs did agree with something Castonguay said, admitted to something, anything, he could turn around later and say, yes, he had admitted to such-and-such because he wanted to go along with the woman's agenda to save the hostage's life. And if the Castonguay woman decided to kill the hostage, well, Briggs could still turn around and say he did everything in his power to save the woman. No matter what Briggs said or did, he'd win. He'd come out of this looking like a hero. He'd run for governor and win by a landslide.

But it was the way he kept casting nervous glances at Big Shoulders, as if the man was going to intervene, that made Darby know this whole thing had been manufactured, a show. This wasn't running on live TV, and Big Shoulders and his partner weren't cameramen but either SWAT or HRT, both men looking for the right moment to take down the gunwoman.

'The city of Boston is watching you – God is watching you,' Castonguay hissed, spittle flying from her trembling lips. 'Tell us the truth or so help me, God, I'll –'

Castonguay cut herself off, clearly having decided she was wasting her breath, and tightened her grip on the Glock; her finger looked like it was about to pull the trigger when she swung the nine away from the hostage's head.

Darby saw her chance and lunged, grabbed Castonguay's wrist with both hands and shoved the handgun up towards the ceiling. Castonguay fired but she knew it was too late and she howled in either defeat or pain, or both. One quick movement and Darby snapped the woman's wrist and the pregnant woman stumbled forward and the two cameramen had compact nines in their hands.

The men both fired, a pair of double-taps that hit Castonguay in the chest. Big Shoulders slammed into Darby and pushed her to the floor to protect her while his partner moved to Castonguay, who was splayed against the floor, her limbs crooked, limp.

Briggs had grabbed the pregnant woman, who was still crying, and wrapped her arms around him. He was escorting her across the lobby, moving around the planters, heading for the exit, the woman leaking amniotic fluid along the way and clutching the precious cargo inside her stomach.

Big Shoulders was trying to move off her when Darby roughly pushed him aside and scrambled to her feet. Briggs was moving towards the front doors because he wanted to go outside so all the TV people across the street could capture this heroic moment, turn him into Boston's version of former New York mayor and 9/11 icon Rudolph 'Rudy' Giuliani.

Darby was running now, past the security checkpoint, Briggs on the other side of the raised marble planters and talking to Laura Levine, saying, 'Just a few more steps and we'll get you to the ambulance, you're doing great.'

The door opened, and the cold blast of air that hit Darby felt like a fist. She hopped over the column but Briggs was already outside.

She followed. When she stepped outside, she saw the woman doubled over in pain. Briggs saw Darby and he scooped the woman up in his arms, carrying her like she was his bride and they were about to cross over the threshold into their new life together. The cameras across the street were capturing the moment, and Darby heard cheering, a roar of approval. What they didn't see was Briggs's smug look of satisfaction at having won. His back was to the media and they didn't see what only Darby could see: the handgun in the woman's hands, which she pressed underneath the former mayor's chin and pulled the trigger.

You read what it's like to die and you watch all these TV shows and you see it in movies but nothing prepares you for the actual moment. I know I'm dying and I . . . peaceful is the wrong word. Right now, I'm strapped to a gurney inside an ambulance and I can see faces hovering above me and I can hear voices shouting and I can feel needles and IVs being stuck into my skin, flooding my veins with saline and what I'm guessing is morphine or some other narcotic to help fight the pain. And it's working. I can't feel anything.

And that's a gift. When I imagined this moment I saw myself sprawled out on the floor, bleeding out. I imagined hearing a gunshot go off and then it entered my brain and I'd feel nothing. But I'm alive at the moment, and I can see and feel and hear, and I can think, and I'm not thinking about dying. I'm thinking about how you get one life, how that's the only thing we know for sure. You get one life and you get to decide how you want to use it.

And I decided to use mine to tell the truth.

Some people can let things go, turn their back, move on, whatever. I wanted to be one of those people who left a mark. I wanted to leave making sure the world – or at least the people of Boston – knew the truth about my father. He wasn't a good man. As he lay dying, he told me his secrets. His sins. He revealed to me the man who lived behind his eyes.

And the world needs to know that. Because we only have one chance to make a mark in this life, and I chose how to make mine. I want people to know that I cared about the truth. That it mattered.

The truth of our lives is what matters most.

67

The next day

Darby woke up the next morning to a fire alarm.

No, not a fire alarm or even the blaring alarm of the hotel's clock radio, but the angry and deafening bleating of the hotel phone, the ringer so loud she was sure it had woken up everyone sleeping on the first floor.

Coop was on the other end of the line. 'I tried your cell,' he said, his voice thick with exhaustion. 'I called three or four times.'

Darby sat up in bed and saw the red numbers on the clock: 1:14. Not a.m. but p.m. She knew that because, after her deposition, she had been dropped off at the hotel at 1:34 a.m.

She picked up her smartphone. It didn't turn on.

'Battery's dead,' she told Coop. 'I forgot to charge it.'

'Laura Levine hasn't asked for a lawyer, and she refuses to speak to anyone but you.'

'She's definitely Fitzpatrick's daughter?'

'Yeah. There's no question.'

'She from Boston?'

'She was born here, then she left after her father died. Lived with her mother in Arizona until her mother died.'

'The fingerprints on the duct tape, you said they belonged to Torres.'

'They do.'

'How did they get on there?'

'I don't know. How quickly can you get here?'

'Where are you?'

'Government Center. I'll have someone pick you up.'

'I can walk.' The FBI's Boston field office was less than a twenty-minute walk.

'Most of the sidewalks haven't been cleared yet,' Coop said. 'It'll be easier and quicker if I sent a car to pick you up.'

'Give me ten.'

Darby showered in less than five; her father, a former Marine, a big believer in efficient bathing. As a kid, if she spent any longer than five minutes in the shower, Big Red would enter the bathroom, pull back the shower curtain and shut off the water.

She used the blow drier, not wanting wet hair clinging to her shoulders, not in the winter, and put on her spare pair of jeans and a collared shirt, this one white. The rest of her clothes went into the garbage. She'd buy another spare set of clothes somewhere down the road, wherever the road took her.

Eight minutes later, she was standing outside, underneath the heated roof over the hotel's main doors, hands in her pockets as she looked out at the people, mostly business owners, shovelling and snow-blowing the sidewalks in front of their businesses and creating tall white mountains on the edges of the street which was, at least at the moment, free of traffic.

Within the relative quiet of the morning – okay, afternoon – she reflected on last night.

After the Levine woman shot Briggs, she dropped the gun, a .32, a six cylinder, and then dropped to her knees and put her hands behind her back. Darby didn't have any authority to arrest her – didn't have handcuffs. The cameras captured everything, and while Darby stood next to the woman, the patrolmen from across the street hearing the gunshot and running their way, Levine closed her eyes and tilted her head up to the falling snow, as if it was going to wash her clean.

Darby didn't feel guilt over her decision not to warn Briggs. She wondered what that said about her and decided she didn't care. She wondered about a lot of things these days. She was four years shy of fifty, and in spite of everything she had seen and witnessed not just last night, but over the course of her life, she didn't feel any wiser.

What she did feel was content. Comfortable in her own skin.

Maybe that was all that mattered in life.

It was certainly all that mattered to her.

Darby looked through the two-way mirror, into the federal interrogation room. It was much nicer than the ones at the BPD stations: Starbucks coffee and folding chairs with padded seats and backs. Laura Levine, dressed in an orange inmate jumpsuit with her hands cuffed together and secured to the chains around her waist, folded her hands on the table's smooth top and stared at the two-way mirror like she was a college student listening to a particularly interesting lecture. The tips of her fingers were stained black from ink, and the skin under her eyes was bruised and puffy, but she didn't look like a woman who was facing a murder charge along with several other federal charges that would prevent her from ever turning her face into the snow again.

If anything, Darby thought, the woman looked lighter. Like some tremendous burden had been lifted off her shoulders.

Coop and Gelfand were in the room with Darby. They both wore the same clothes they had had on yesterday, only they were rumpled, and they both looked like they wanted nothing more than to shut their eyes and go to sleep, wake up when this had all disappeared.

Gelfand held up a big clear evidence bag that contained the Levine woman's prosthetic pregnancy stomach. 'Definitely a homemade thing,' he said. 'There's a side compartment right here where she hid the gun. These dangling tubes? She had them taped to her crotch and legs, and all she had to do was press the lever right here and the bag of water would release, make it look like her water broke. Clever shit.'

'Psych. eval.?'

'Yeah. Guy who smelled like Burger King with dandruff on his shoulders came in and tried to talk to her. She said she was completely sane and said she would only speak to you. Guy tries to evaluate her and she starts singing Céline Dion songs. At the end of every verse she asks for you. So, how about it?'

'Has she been read her rights?' Darby asked.

'No, we decided to bypass them, go for something different. Come on, Doc, what kind of question is that?'

'Does she understand her rights? If she's mentally incapacitated in any way –'

'She constructed this,' Gelfand said, shaking the evidence bag. 'This look like someone who's mentally incapacitated?'

'I'll speak to her only if she knows she can have an attorney at any time.'

'Rosemary's on standby, drooling for a chance to represent her. You talk to Rosemary? She stayed in town overnight. Boston Harbor Hotel. Had a press conference there this morning, saying she's available. You want to go in there or not?'

'What about the charges against me?' Darby asked.

'We're not going to pursue them.'

'Can I get that in writing?'

'In that folder next to you,' Gelfand replied. 'I'll give you whatever you want, okay? You want a pony, I'll get you a pony.'

'I want to talk to Commissioner Donnelly first.'

'No need to. That thing you're talking about? It's all wrapped up. Right, Cooper?'

'Right.' Although Coop was clearly ashamed and embarrassed. Sick.

'Wasn't recorded and, besides, it wouldn't hold up,'

Gelfand said. 'Donnelly acted on the instructions of the governor and mayor, placed a listening device in there so they could see what we were up to. Donnelly doesn't want to have to admit that in court. Now, how about we wrap this shit up so I can go home and see my kids?'

68

Darby opened the door to the interrogation room.

Laura Levine saw her and brightened. Sat up in her chair, smiling.

'Hello.'

'Afternoon,' Darby said, pulling out the chair across from her. 'Have you been read your rights?'

'Oh yes. Several times.'

The woman had a surprisingly deep voice, the kind created from too many years of smoking or drinking, or both. Or maybe it was genetic. Laura Levine didn't have the face of a smoker or drinker. She didn't have much in the way of wrinkles or laughter lines, either.

'Do you want an attorney?' Darby asked.

'I have a few things I want to say.'

'Anything you say can and will –'

'Can be used against me, yes, I know all about it.' She looked over Darby's shoulder. 'Are they listening to us?'

'They are.'

'Recording?'

'Yes.'

'Excellent. First, I want to say that I'm of sound mind and body. Meaning, I'm not insane. Second, I willingly killed the former mayor Briggs. You saw me do it.'

Darby didn't reply, a part of her wondering if Laura Levine was going to say something along the lines of: *You saw me holding that gun and you could have warned Briggs and didn't. We both know that. Maybe he would have lived, maybe he wouldn't, but you didn't say anything and so I shot him. And by the way, I saw your face after. You looked relieved.*

'I don't have any regrets about what I did,' the woman said. 'What I've done.'

'Is Laura Levine your real name?'

The woman nodded. 'Levine is my mother's name. I've been living in Seattle, Washington, but flew back here for Grace.'

'Grace Castonguay.'

'Yes.'

'And you're Officer Fitzpatrick's daughter.'

Another nod. 'Grace and I followed your career for years. We know all about what happened to your father, and the two of us decided that if anyone would understand us, what we went through, it would be you.'

'Because of what happened to my father,' Darby said.

Laura Levine nodded, kept nodding. 'We wanted someone we could trust – a reliable witness. Someone who would stand up and tell the truth which, as you know, is easier said than done.'

'What do you want from me?'

'Now? Nothing, except to thank you and to also apologize for what Grace and I put you through. That was unfair of us to do, I know, but again we needed someone who had, well, character.'

'How do you know Grace Castonguay?'

'We met in a grief support group back in . . . Gosh, we were both so young. Both in our late teens. It was a support group for kids who had lost a parent or parents to violence. It was one of those total coincidence things. As the years passed, we kept in touch and then we began to trust one another – trust, as you know, is difficult for people like us, Darby – and we became like sisters, and eventually Grace told me about her father, and I told her about mine and, well, you can imagine our surprise when we realized how much we had in common. It was like fate had brought us together. Fate or God. It brought us incredibly close. Loss.'

'And the two of you, what, decided to join forces and come back here to Boston for revenge?'

'We wanted the truth to come out and, as you know, sometimes the truth requires sacrifice.'

Darby said nothing.

Waited.

'Grace wanted the world to know what her father had done, what a bad person he was,' Laura Levine said. 'He wasn't like your father, Darby. He wasn't an honest man, he was a coward. I'm not speaking ill of the dead; Grace would have told you the same thing, had she lived, which she knew wasn't going to happen.'

'We found Walter Torres's fingerprints on the duct tape retrieved from Anita Barnes.'

'That roll of tape belonged to Grace's father. Grace made sure her father's prints were on the tape. We wanted you to find them.'

Darby smiled wanly. 'You thought of everything, didn't you?'

'You're Catholic, right?'

'Sometimes,' Darby said.

'Then you know the importance of confession. How good it is for the soul.'

'Only they weren't your sins.'

'Grace and I knew what our fathers did. We couldn't just sit back any more and keep our mouths shut any longer.' The woman seemed disappointed, maybe even disgusted, at the suggestion of doing such a thing. 'It's so liberating to go out on your own terms, isn't it? Make your own mark instead of having someone take it from you?' She smiled brightly. 'But I don't have to tell you that. I can tell you know exactly what I'm talking about.'

'I don't understand,' Darby said. 'What did your father have to do with this?'

'He lied about what happened. He knew Sean Ellis didn't shoot him.'

'Why did he lie?'

'You'd have to ask him. But it ate him up, keeping that secret. At any point he could have done the right thing and he took the – not the easy way out, that's not fair. He tried to do good, but in the end that choice was taken away from him.'

'By whom?'

'Everyone. First by Murphy, and then by the others. They forced my father to lie. And he did. He did. But he had a conscience. He wanted to make things right. He went up the flagpole, told everyone in the BPD brass that Sean Ellis didn't shoot him, it was that evil bastard Karl Torres. And when my father refused to keep his mouth shut? They disciplined him. That's when he decided to go straight to the top, to speak to Mayor Briggs. But Briggs kept ignoring him, and then they took my father.'

'Took him? Took him where?'

'To the garage,' Laura Levine said. 'That's where Murphy and the others had their little parties – drugs, prostitutes and gambling. My father went there once, beforehand, thought it was just a place where guys hung out and played cars. You know who used to work there?'

'Clara Lacy,' Darby said, remembering Shapiro telling her that Lacy was a prostitute.

'My father only wanted to do the right thing. He complained to the people in charge, all the way up to Mayor Briggs. And when that happened, the police, his so-called friends, picked up my father and brought him to the garage. They beat him unconscious. Karl Torres was there, too. Told him that if he didn't shut up and let the matter go away, he'd wake up one day and find out I disappeared.'

'So your father let Sean Ellis take the fall.'

'And it ate him alive!'

It took almost a full minute for the woman to collect herself.

Then she said, 'My father was never the same after that. He dived into a bottle. Did drugs. They kicked him off the force. He loved being a cop, same way your father did, Darby. And that day when I came to his house and found him sitting on the bedroom floor with a gun in his mouth, I begged him not to do it. But he went ahead with it anyway – that's how much the guilt and shame ate him. These people tortured him at every corner; all because he wanted to do the right thing, to tell the truth. Good people get killed and punished all the time, and people like Briggs and Murphy just go on with their lives. But not any more. Now everyone knows.'

'They don't,' Darby said.

'Of course they do. It was all over TV.'

'You weren't on TV. The whole thing was staged.'

Laura Levine recoiled, her chains rattling.

'But I saw it,' she began.

'They fed the TV into the camera,' Darby said. 'Staged it.'

The woman looked like she had been told her child had been killed.

'I'm sorry,' Darby said. 'I didn't know.'

'I should have figured as much. But the reporter was there. He'll have to tell the truth.'

'At some point, yes.'

'But they'll try to prevent it.'

'Yes.'

'Did the TV cameras outside capture his death? Briggs?'

Darby nodded.

'Good,' Laura Levine said. 'So now the world knows I did it – that I was the one who took action. And the truth will get out, Darby. There will be a trial and I'll get to tell my story and everyone will have to listen to me this time. To me and Grace.'

Then Laura Levine closed her eyes and smiled dreamily, content and at peace, maybe, for her world had been balanced, the essential order of things properly restored.

Acknowledgements

Thanks to my agents, Josh Getzler and Caspian Dennis; Donna Bagdasarian; Mark Glick and Stephen Breimer; my editor, Emad Akhtar, Rowland White and the sales staff at Penguin. A special thanks to 'Tim', who walked me through all the bomb stuff. I took liberties with bomb and police matters, and with certain locations in and around Boston, because this is fiction, which means I made everything up.

UNCOVER THE DARBY

1

'A scary, breakneck ride with thrills that never let up'

Tess Gerritsen

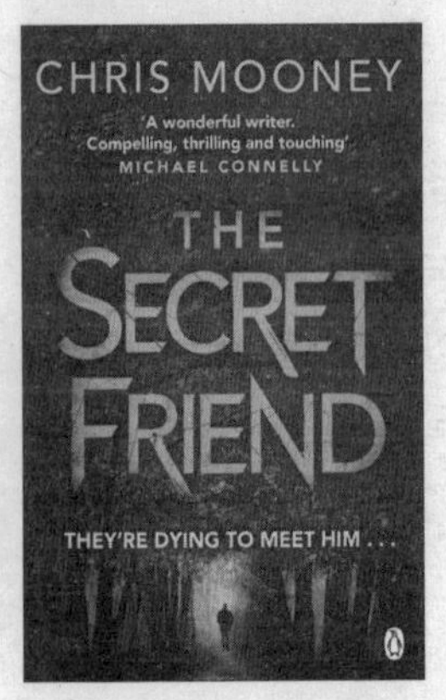

2

'Chris Mooney is a wonderful writer. Compelling, thrilling and touching'

Michael Connelly

3

'This will keep you up past your bedtime'

Karin Slaughter

You Tube